THE POISONING IN THE PUB

A FETHERING MYSTERY

THE POISONING
IN THE PUB

SIMON BRETT

FIVE STAR
A part of Gale, Cengage Learning

GALE
CENGAGE Learning

Detroit • New York • San Francisco • New Haven, Conn • Waterville, Maine • London

Copyright © 2009 by Simon Brett.

Five Star Publishing, a part of Gale, Cengage Learning.

Set in 11 pt. Plantin.

Printed on permanent paper.

LIBRARY OF CONGRESS CATALOGING-IN-PUBLICATION DATA

Brett, Simon.
    The poisoning in the pub : a Fethering mystery / Simon Brett.
— 1st ed.
    p. cm.
    ISBN-13: 978-1-59414-890-3 (alk. paper)
    ISBN-10: 1-59414-890-2 (alk. paper)
    1. Seddon, Carole (Fictitious character)—Fiction. 2. Jude
(Fictitious character : Brett)—Fiction. 3. Women detectives—
England—Fiction. I. Title.
PR6052.R4296P65 2009
823'.914—dc22   2009014850

First Edition. First Printing: November 2009.

Published in 2009 in conjunction with Tekno Books and Ed Gorman.

To George and Marianne,
remembering many convivial drinks
and excellent meals
and
to Sally Monks,
whose husband David won
an eBay auction in aid of Oxfam
to have her name included in this book

CHAPTER ONE

One of the most inauspicious events for any restaurant is to have a customer vomiting on the premises. However distant the cause may be from the establishment's kitchens, whatever rare gastric bug may have triggered the attack, such a happening is never good for business. There is always an assumption on the part of the general public that blame must lie with the food served in the restaurant.

Ted Crisp, landlord of the Crown and Anchor near the sea at Fethering in West Sussex, found that out to his cost one Monday lunchtime in July. His dish of the day was pan-fried scallops with spinach and oriental noodles, and unfortunately it was a choice for which a large number of his customers opted.

Amongst those customers were two women in their fifties. The one whom most people, particularly men, would notice first was called Jude. She had an abundance of blonde hair twisted into an untidy knot on top of her head and a body wobbling between the voluptuous and the plump. She wore a bright cotton skirt and blouse, draped over with a tangle of multi-coloured scarves.

Her companion, by contrast, looked as though she wanted to melt into anonymity. Women are said to become invisible when they get into their fifties, and Carole Seddon's appearance suggested that was a tendency of which she strongly approved. She had on a grey Marks & Spencer jumper, beige trousers and shoes so sensible they could have given lectures in civic responsibility. Grey hair was cut into the shape of a helmet; rimless glasses fronted surprisingly shrewd pale blue eyes.

The two were discussing Carole's granddaughter Lily. 'It's down to you,' Jude was saying. 'If you don't feel you're seeing enough of her, then say something to Stephen and Gaby.'

'It's not that I don't feel I'm seeing enough of her,' said Carole. 'It's just I feel I should see more of her if . . .' She petered out.

'If what?'

'Well, if . . .' Carole Seddon was clearly having difficulties with what came next, but Jude's look of innocent quizzicality did eventually begin to elicit an explanation. 'The fact is, Stephen and Gaby have spoken of going away for a long weekend . . . you know, him taking the Friday off and . . .'

'How nice for them.'

'Yes, but . . .' Jude waited patiently. She had the feeling the problem would not be an enormous one. Or at least only enormous to Carole. Her friend and neighbour had a great capacity for getting upset over trifles or, as some of Jude's more New Age friends might put it, 'sweating the small stuff'.

'The thing is,' said Carole in a rush, 'they want to leave Lily with me.'

'Over this long weekend they were talking about?'

'Yes.'

'Well, that'd be lovely for you, wouldn't it?'

'Ye-es.' The length of the vowel betrayed the extent of Carole's anxiety. 'The fact is, Jude, it's years since I've looked after a baby . . . well, since Stephen was born, actually. And I wasn't very good at it then. I don't really think I have much in the way of maternal instinct.'

'Nonsense, you'll be fine. And it's not as if you'll be on your own.'

'How do you mean?'

'I'll be next door at Woodside Cottage. If you have a crisis, you can call on me.'

'Oh, Jude, would you really help?' There was an almost pathetic appeal in the pale blue eyes.

'Of course I would.'

'Thank goodness. Now, please, promise me you'll let me know which weekends you're going to be away, so that I can make sure Stephen and Gaby choose one when you're around.'

'Yes, of course,' said Jude easily. She was continually amazed and slightly puzzled by how seriously her neighbour took things. For Carole Seddon life was a minefield; every step in every direction—particularly a new direction—was full of potential hazards. Jude had always had a more relaxed attitude. There were things which she took seriously, but she really didn't sweat the small stuff. And in this particular instance she couldn't help being amused by the comfort Carole took in her potential as an assistant baby-minder. Jude, despite a varied and exciting love life, had never had any children. The right man for such a commitment had never appeared at the right time.

But Carole Seddon, despite her dauntingly efficient exterior, and despite the fact that she had held down a responsible job at the Home Office with icy control, was totally lacking in confidence when it came to her private life. She had felt even less certainty in such areas since she had divorced Stephen's father David, but she had never really felt at home at home. Her neuroses had made her create a wall of privacy around herself, and Jude was one of the few people who was occasionally let inside that wall.

Carole, embarrassed to have strayed onto such an emotional subject as her granddaughter, looked round the pub for a new topic of conversation, and her eye was caught by one of many identical posters stuck on any available space. DAN POKE COMEDY NIGHT, read the legend. FOR ONE NIGHT

ONLY. TV STAR REVEALS ALL HIS NAUGHTY BITS—
FANCY A POKE . . . ? The date was the following Sunday
evening and the venue—surprisingly to Carole at least—was the
Crown and Anchor.

'Know anything about that?' she asked.

Jude shrugged. 'Well, I know about Dan Poke. Was quite a
big name on television a few years back.'

'Really? I've never heard of him.'

'One of the first round of alternative comedians.'

The intonation of Carole's 'Oh' suggested that that was
hardly the kind of thing she might be expected to know about.
Except for her secret vice of a particular afternoon chatshow,
she didn't watch much 'entertainment' television. Carole still
had a rather Reithian view of the medium as a purveyor of
education and generally watched only news and documentaries.
Watching the first was easy—news proliferated from every
outlet—but decent documentaries had become an endangered
species. Drama, generally speaking, Carole eschewed, though
she would watch classic book adaptations featuring Empire-line
dresses or crinolines. And, of course, anything with Judi Dench
in it.

'Are there people in Fethering who would want to watch
someone like that?' she asked Jude, in a tone that very definitely
expected the answer no.

'Presumably. Otherwise why would Ted be putting it on?'

Carole's only response was a 'Hm' that was very nearly a
'Hmph' of disapproval. There was a silence while they ate,
before she observed, 'These scallops are good.'

'Yes. Ted's new chef is really doing wonders.' Jude looked
round the pub. The weather was very hot, so the outside tables
were full, and there was very little space in the interior. All the
pub's doors and windows were open, but only the slightest
breeze drifted lazily in from the sea.

Fethering would always be predominantly a retirement community, so the average age of the clientele was high. The tourists the area attracted tended to be quite mature too. Small children were few, and those that were there were with grandparents rather than parents. Otherwise, a lot of well-heeled people in their sixties and seventies, representatives of the last generation whose pension provisions would be adequate to their needs, sat on the outside benches or in the alcoves of the Crown and Anchor, eating and drinking. As they did most lunchtimes in various pubs along the South Coast. And good luck to them.

'Word of mouth is spreading,' Jude observed. 'Do you remember how gloomy Ted was about the effect he reckoned the smoking ban would have on his business? Looks like he got it wrong. For a Monday lunchtime, the place is heaving.'

Her choice of word was perhaps unfortunate, because at that moment, a pensioner in one of the alcoves rose in panic. Long before he could make it across to the safety of the toilets, his semi-digested lunch spewed in a yellow arc across the floor of the pub.

It is an instinct among the British people to try to pretend unpleasant things have just not happened, but this one was hard to ignore. The Polish bar manager, Zosia, was quick to fetch a bucket and mop from the kitchen behind the bar and Ted Crisp himself followed her out. The landlord was a large man with ragged hair and beard, dressed in his permanent livery of faded T-shirt and equally faded jeans. He gestured for Zosia to get a move on.

But before the clean-up operation could begin, there was another casualty. An impossibly thin little old lady with rigidly permed white hair had risen from her seat in another alcove and tottered forward. She was sick too, though not as profusely as the man had been. Something like mucus spilled from the corner of her wrinkled mouth as she slipped slowly to the floor.

11

And lay ominously still.

Though Jude had no medical qualifications, her work as a healer meant that she knew a lot about the human body and its frailties. So she was quickly crouching beside the stricken pensioner, feeling for a pulse. Ted Crisp looked on in horror as a silence descended on the Crown and Anchor.

A little old man, surely the woman's husband, had tottered out of the alcove after her and was looking down at Jude, his rheumy eyes beseeching her not to bring bad news.

'It's all right,' said Jude. 'Her pulse is weak, but it's definitely there.'

'Thank God,' said the little old man.

'Maybe she just fainted because of the hot weather . . . ?' Ted suggested hopefully.

The husband didn't buy that explanation. 'She was right as rain this morning.'

'What did she have for lunch?' asked Carole.

'The scallops. She insisted on having the scallops.' He was unaware of the communal intake of breath from other customers who had ordered the same. 'Bettina always liked seafood. I could never take it myself. Got one of them allergies to all that stuff.'

Carole and Jude exchanged a look and knew they were both thinking the same. Scallops could all too easily go off in the kind of weather they were having.

The old man's eyes once again appealed to Jude. 'Is Bettina going to be all right?'

'I'm sure she is,' came the brisk reply, 'but I think it might be as well to call an ambulance and get her looked at at the hospital.'

'I'll ring them,' said Ted, relieved to have something positive to do. After the recent excitements, the pub settled back into some kind of normality. Zosia made quick work of cleaning the floor. The man who had vomited first was helped to the Gents to clean himself up, and soon taken home by his friends. Bettina, whose surname Jude discovered from her husband Eric was Smiley, was picked up and settled into a chair. She hadn't fully regained consciousness, but mumbled softly to herself. Eric took her thin liver-spotted hand in his. His grip was so tight that he seemed to fear she might slip away from him.

Gradually, but quite quickly, the Crown and Anchor emptied. Customers who'd ordered other dishes finished them up quickly. Most who had ordered the pan-fried scallops with spinach and oriental noodles just stopped eating. Zosia and her waitresses showed no emotion as they repeatedly asked, 'May I clear that?' In every case the answer was yes.

Carole Seddon had finished her plateful before the vomiting began, and she felt extremely uncomfortable. Her stomach churned. She knew the sensation was probably just psychosomatic, but she still wasn't enjoying it. Carole had always had a terror of disgracing herself in a public place.

The ambulance arrived and its practised crew got Bettina Smiley wrapped in blankets and onto a stretcher. They had virtually to prise away her husband's hand, then gently led him out to accompany her to the hospital.

An anxious-looking Ted Crisp emerged again from the kitchen just in time to see their departure. Carole and Jude were about the only customers left. Carole looked on edge; Jude's brown eyes beamed sympathy to the troubled landlord.

'Maybe it wasn't the scallops,' she suggested hopefully.

'Bloody shouldn't be. I've used the same supplier for my seafood ever since I've had this place. Never had any trouble before.'

'And everything in the kitchen's OK . . . you know, from the Health and Safety point of view?'

'Yes, it bloody is! Only had our annual inspection last week.

Passed with flying colours. They couldn't find a single thing to criticize . . . which always makes them bloody cross. They like to find some little detail to pick you up on.'

'Will you have to report this?'

'Perhaps not, but I'm going to do everything by the book. Since the old girl's gone to hospital, I should report it under RIDDOR.'

'RIDDOR?' Jude looked puzzled. Carole looked increasingly uncomfortable.

' "The Reporting of Injuries, Diseases and Dangerous Oc-currences Regulations 1995," ' Ted parroted. 'And I've just called them. Done everything by the bloody book, like I said. Rang through to their Incident Contact Centre.' He looked even more troubled. 'But when I did, there was something odd . . .'

'Excuse me,' Carole announced suddenly, 'I must go to the ladies' room!' And she rushed off.

Jude passed no comment on her friend's disappearance, but gave the landlord a sympathetic grin. It didn't seem to raise his spirits. 'You said there was something odd . . . ?'

'Yes. When I got through to the Incident Contact Centre . . .'

'Hm?'

'They knew about what'd happened. Someone had rung them only minutes before. Less than twenty minutes after the old girl got sick and the authorities had already heard about it.'

Ted Crisp might have said more, but he was interrupted by the ringing of the phone behind the bar. 'Crown and Anchor, Fethering,' he answered automatically. Under the beard his mouth contorted with anger as he responded, 'No, I bloody haven't got anything to say to you!'

He slammed down the phone and looked at Jude. His face showed a mixture of puzzlement and fury as he said, '*Fethering Observer.* Wanted to know if I had any comment to make about the outbreak of food poisoning in my pub.'

'Good heavens.'

'How did they know?' asked Ted Crisp, almost to himself. 'How did they know so quickly?'

CHAPTER TWO

Jude had hoped she might escape the effects of the scallops, but it was not to be. She had escorted a very wan-looking Carole back to her house, High Tor, and returned to the adjacent Woodside Cottage. Her plan to clear her mind with some yoga exercises was thwarted by the sudden metallic taste of nausea in her throat. Fortunately she just managed to make it to the loo before losing her lunch down the bowl.

She was sick twice more before deciding that the day was a write-off and going to bed. Once there, she fell instantly into a deep sleep, from which she woke about eight thirty, feeling distinctly more human. She had a hot bath, drank a lot of water and went downstairs. It was still light and the day's heat stayed in the air. There was not enough breeze to stir the windchimes that hung by her open windows.

Jude thought about the attack of food poisoning at the Crown and Anchor and reckoned she had got off lightly. The two people who'd actually been sick in the pub had been pretty frail, which was probably why they were affected so quickly. She wondered how many other customers had spent the afternoon laid up like her. She rang Carole.

'The scallops got me too,' she said. 'I was just wondering if you were feeling any better?'

'No,' replied the strained voice from next door.

'Have you been sick?'

'No!' Carole's voice shuddered with horror at the very idea.

'You'll feel better if you are.'

'That I doubt.' From childhood onwards, Carole Seddon had been terrified by the very idea of vomiting. She hated losing control in any area of her life, and throwing up seemed to her the ultimate loss of control. She would do anything to avoid it happening, tensing her body with iron—and painful—willpower.

'Have you slept?'

'No. It's daytime. I'm not in the habit of going to sleep in the daytime.'

'It's different when you're ill.'

'I'm not ill. Just a touch of food poisoning.'

'Is there anything I can do for you?' Jude knew the answer to the question before she posed it. There were times when she got frustrated by her neighbour's unwillingness ever to be beholden to anyone else, but she rarely voiced her reaction. Like most people, Jude reasoned, Carole Seddon was a complex bundle of illogicalities, which anyone who wanted to be her friend must just take on board.

'Well, ring me if you do need anything.'

'I can't imagine there will be anything I need, thank you.'

'I'll call in the morning to see how you are.'

'I will be fine in the morning,' said Carole icily, daring her body to do anything other than mend itself overnight.

To her surprise, when she had come off the phone Jude almost felt hungry. Her ready vomiting must have thoroughly cleared all the poison out of her system. Maybe she fancied a little soup? Or even something more substantial? But just the mental image of food prompted another wave of queasiness.

She decided she'd better check how things were with Ted Crisp and was surprised by how long it took for the Crown and Anchor phone to be answered. Perhaps just busy in the bar, she thought, about to hang up.

But then she heard Ted's voice. And there was no background

17

noise of a busy bar.

'Sorry it took me so long. I was upstairs in the flat.'

'I thought you were just busy.'

He let out a hollow laugh. 'Can't be busy when the pub's closed, can you?'

'What?'

'Someone made a complaint . . . you know, after what happened at lunchtime. I've been closed down by Health and Safety until they do an inspection.'

'And when are they going to do that?'

'Hopefully tomorrow. They may not be able to do it for a few days though. God, and I've got this Dan Poke gig set up for Sunday. It's the bloody limit! The longer a place like the Crown and Anchor's closed, the longer it'll take to build up my trade again. And this is my busiest period. What I take this time of year offsets those endless winter nights when I've just got three old farts nursing one half of bitter all evening.'

Ted Crisp sounded so gloomy that Jude couldn't resist inviting him round for a drink. An offer that he took up with considerable alacrity.

He refused her offer of soup or anything else to eat. The fact that he asked for Scotch to drink and the despatch with which he downed it were measures of how upset he was. Ted had never succumbed to the temptation that has ruined the health of so many publicans. He didn't normally sample his wares during the day, contenting himself with a single pint at closing time.

Jude had never seen him quite so desolate. She tried desperately to think of anything that might cheer him up. She sipped her water—her stomach didn't yet feel up to anything stronger—and asked, 'Are you worried what the Health and Safety inspectors will find?'

'No, they were only there last week. And I've never had any

trouble with them before. Place is as clean as a whistle. Standards are higher then ever since I've had Zosia keeping an eye on things.'

'She's worked out well.'

'Yeah.' He was always slightly grudging in any praise he gave to his bar manager. 'Even though she is Polish.'

'Presumably the Health and Safety people will be checking your seafood supplier as well?'

He nodded and scratched his scruffy beard. 'Which isn't exactly going to make me popular with them.'

'Scallops are notorious . . . you know, if they're slightly off . . .'

'I'm sure it's not from the supplier. They're a big company, and they've always had the most exacting hygiene standards.'

'Then how come you got a dodgy delivery from them?'

'I can't work it out,' Ted Crisp replied wearily. 'I've been through all the possibilities and . . .' he sighed '. . . I don't know what to think.'

'It's incredibly bad luck.'

'You can say that again. And I just don't know how much more bad luck the Crown and Anchor can take.'

'How do you mean?'

He let out another deep sigh. 'Licensed Victuallers' trade's always been an up-and-down business. Every week you hear of more pubs closing—or being bought up by the big boys, the chains. Gets increasingly difficult to make a profit—particularly if you borrowed as much as I did to get the Crown and Anchor in the first place. And there are constantly new problems. Another government clampdown on drink-driving and your trade drops off. Then the smoking ban didn't help. Been a long time since you could make a living just by pulling pints, so you have to organize other attractions to get people through the doors. Darts, quiz nights, wall-to-wall football—though I don't want to go down that route myself. Just like I don't want to have that CCTV so many pubs have these days—looks like you don't trust your customers. Then of course I used sometimes to get the punters in with live music, though that's got hideously more expensive with the new entertainment licences the government saw fit to bring in a few years back. I tell you, Jude, it's a bloody nightmare.'

'I'm sure it is.' She was good at supplying sympathy. 'And you've got this Dan Poke comedy night coming up. That should bring them in, shouldn't it?'

'Yes, assuming I'm open by then. But that's a one-off. Dan's just doing it as a favour, only charging expenses, because he's a mate from the days when I was on the stand-up circuit. Yeah, I'm sure—if I'm allowed to open by then—Sunday'll be fine. Dan says I'll be able to judge from how it goes whether it's worth having a regular comedy night, but that's going to cost. No other comedians are going to do it for free, are they?'

'So what you come back to is the food. You got to do food that's better than the local competition. Which means you need a good chef . . . and they're like gold dust round here. And you have to pay them as much as if they were bloody gold dust.'

'But I thought your new chef was very good. Word of mouth about the Crown and Anchor's food has been great.'

'Yes,' Ted Crisp agreed gloomily. 'I thought I'd turned the corner with him. And I had until those bloody scallops came in.'

'Who is the chef? I haven't met him.'

'Boy called Ed Pollack. Trained at catering college in Chichester. Used to moonlight here a bit while he was finishing his course.'

Jude vaguely remembered Ted mentioning the young chef before, while she and Carole had been enquiring into an unexplained death at Hopwicke Country House Hotel. 'But he's fully trained now?'

'You bet. Been working in a very snazzy restaurant up in Soho, but his mum's got ill, so he wanted some work down here to keep an eye on her. Sounds to me like the old girl's on the way out, so I doubt if I'll keep him long.' He sighed. At that moment every trouble in his life seemed insuperable. 'Which means I'll have to start looking for another chef . . . God, and what a nightmare that can be.'

'You don't think Ed Pollack could have had anything to do with the dodgy scallops?'

'No, that generation are really picky about hygiene stuff.'

'How often do you have seafood deliveries?'

'Every day. Has to be every day, if you say you've got "fresh seafood" on the menu.'

'And do you check in the deliveries yourself, Ted?'

'Depends what I'm doing. They deliver round the back. If I'm in the kitchen when they come, I'll sign for the stuff. If someone else is there, they'll do it. Not a big deal, happens so often.'

'And did you sign for the delivery this morning?'

'No, and obviously I've checked out who did. It was Ed. Van arrived just after ten. I was out front fixing a duff light switch in the bar.'

'And Ed didn't notice anything odd about the scallops?'

Ted Crisp shook his head wearily. 'If he'd thought there was anything odd with them, he wouldn't have cooked them. Like I said, he knows his hygiene regulations inside out.'

'And the scallops would be delivered frozen?'

'No, Jude,' he replied patiently. ' "Fresh seafood" means "fresh seafood". They're chilled for transportation, but not frozen.'

'So what did Ed do with them after they'd been delivered?'

'Put them in the fridge in a tray with a light lemon-juice-and-soy-sauce marinade. That's what he always does for that recipe.'

'And was there anyone else around the kitchen that morning?'

'Well, Zosia would have been there . . .' Jude looked at Ted quizzically. She knew he had been less than welcoming when the Polish girl had started working for him. The landlord had a rather unappealing thread of xenophobia in his make-up. But now he could find nothing in his bar manager to criticize. 'Mind you, she's about the most trustworthy staff member I've ever had.' He still couldn't quite make the compliment sound whole-hearted.

'No waitresses around at the time of the delivery?'

'No, they don't come on duty till twelve.'

'And Ed does all the cooking?'

'Yes. Zosia and one of the girls might help him plating up if he's really pushed, but he does virtually everything himself. Bloody genius, he is. That's why it's going to be such a bugger when he goes back up to London.'

'So would Ed have stayed in the kitchen all morning?'

'Most of it. But he would nip out every hour or so.'

'Oh?'

'Boy's a smoker. Knew he couldn't smoke in his kitchen, even before the ban came in. So he nips out to the car park or round the back for a drag every now and then.'

'For how long?'

Ted Crisp shrugged. 'How long does it take to smoke a cigarette? Such a long time since I've touched one of the things, I've forgotten.'

'And is there anyone else who might have been in the kitchen that morning?'

'No.' Ted seemed uncertain, then said, 'Well . . .'

'There was someone else?'

'Only Ray,' Ted replied reluctantly. Jude raised an interrogative eyebrow. 'Ray. You may have seen him around. Short bloke in his forties, looks a bit vacant, walks a bit funny.'

'Oh, I think I've seen him, yes. Does he work for you?'

'Well, not on an official basis. But I give him the odd fiver for sweeping the place out, doing the odd bit of washing up, you know. Ray's, you know . . . he's . . . don't know what the politically correct acceptable phrase is these days? "Simple"? "Differently abled"? You know what I mean, anyway.'

'Sure. So you give him odd jobs to help him out?'

The landlord looked uncomfortable at this exposure of his philanthropy. 'Well, yes, a bit. He is quite useful round the place, though,' he added defensively. 'Moving heavy stuff, you know . . .'

'And Ray's entirely trustworthy, is he?'

Again Ted looked embarrassed. 'Yeah. Not bright enough to do anything crooked.'

'Was he likely to have touched the scallops?'

'No, no chance,' came the brusque reply. 'Thing with Ray is he'll do anything you tell him to, but nothing off his own initiative. He wouldn't have touched the scallops unless someone had told him to.' The landlord looked anxiously at his watch. 'I wonder what's happening with that old girl at the hospital . . . ?'

'Bettina Smiley.'

'Right. If she pegs out . . . God, that'll be all I need.'

'She looked terribly frail. If she does peg out, I'm sure it won't be simply because of the scallops.'

'No, but it doesn't look good, does it? Local paper with a headline reading: "Old lady dies after eating meal in the Crown and Anchor." Not exactly the sort of headline I've been looking for all my life.'

Jude was silent for a moment, then asked, 'Ted, do you think the scallops were tampered with?'

'I don't know. That's the only explanation I can find that fits the facts. Though how it happened or who . . .' His words petered out in incomprehension.

'Have you got any enemies?'

He reached for the whisky bottle and recharged his glass. 'Where do you want me to start?'

CHAPTER THREE

Jude woke feeling better the next morning and, after a breakfast of toast and honey, thought normal life might be once again a possibility. It was another beautiful day, the July sun already high in a cloudless sky. Her instinct was to go round and knock on the door of High Tor, but then, thinking that Carole might still be bedridden, she used the phone.

'I just wondered if you were feeling any better?'

'No,' Carole's strained voice replied.

'Have you been sick?'

This received another appalled 'No!'

'Well, if there's anything I can get you from the shops . . .'

'No, thank you. I don't feel like eating.'

'Any medicines you need?'

'I don't need any. I'll just drink water to flush it out of my system.'

'Oh. And you're sure you don't feel any better?'

'No.'

'Ah.' There was one test Jude knew she could use to find out if her neighbour really was as ill as she claimed. 'Ted came round for a drink last night . . .'

'Really?' Carole was instantly alert. Rather surprisingly, she had once had a brief affair with the landlord of the Crown and Anchor. It had long ago fizzled down into friendship, and they could meet without awkwardness in the public territory of the pub. But the idea of Ted Crisp paying a social visit to Woodside

Cottage . . . well, that did challenge Carole Seddon's proprietorial instincts.

'He was very miserable. He's been closed down pending a Health and Safety inspection.'

'Well, he can't complain,' said Carole rather prissily. 'If his kitchen is careless enough to serve dodgy shellfish . . .'

'I agree. If that was what happened. But from what Ted said, it was more than just carelessness.'

'What do you mean?' The alertness with which Carole picked up the hint suggested that her health might possibly be on the mend.

'He thinks someone might have arranged what happened, deliberately, to sabotage his business.'

'Did he suggest who might have done that? Did you ask whether he had any enemies?' Carole's questions were now positively eager.

'I did. He replied at great length, but I'm afraid didn't say much that was very coherent.'

'Oh?'

'He had drunk rather a lot of whisky.'

'That's unlike him.'

'I agree. He's in quite a bad state. That's why he was drinking so much.'

'But didn't he say what was wrong?'

'His basic problems seem to be financial. From what he said, he's only just managing to keep the Crown and Anchor open.'

'Would he make anything much if he sold the place?'

'Yes, I think he'd probably do all right. But the one fact that came through very clearly was that he doesn't want to sell up. In spite of his less than enthusiastic manner, Ted really loves running the Crown and Anchor. He'd be shattered if he had to leave the place.'

'I know. He talks about the pub a bit like people talk about their children. He can criticize it as much as he likes, but once someone else starts, he gets very defensive.'

'Yes.'

'But are you saying, Jude, that Ted thinks what happened with the scallops . . . assuming it was sabotage . . . was an attempt by someone to force him to sell up?'

'He implied that, without putting it in so many words.'

'And when you asked him about having any enemies, did he mention any names?'

'No. All he said was that his "bloody ex-wife" had come back into his life.'

'Oh, really?' said Carole Seddon.

Stuck on the main doors of the Crown and Anchor was an A4 sheet on which had been printed in a large font: CLOSED UNTIL FURTHER NOTICE. Under this someone had scrawled in red felt pen: 'Dew to customers being poissoned'. Jude felt pretty sure Ted Crisp hadn't yet seen the addition; he wouldn't have let it stay there for long. So when, at about twelve o'clock, Zosia opened the locked door to her, Jude pointed it out. The girl immediately tore down the notice and said she'd print up a new one.

Jude had met Zosia when she had come over from Warsaw following the murder of her brother Tadeusz, and the two had bonded immediately, in spite of their age difference. The girl's full name was Zofia Jankowska, but everyone called her Zosia. When she had first arrived in England her English had been limited, but she had applied herself and now spoke with only a trace of an accent. She had enrolled in a journalism course at the University of Clincham, and managed to fit her commitments at the Crown and Anchor around her studies. She always wore her blonded hair in pigtails, and her hazel eyes sparkled with energy.

'Ted will not be pleased with that,' she said, indicating the graffiti on the notice.

'I got the impression he wasn't very pleased with much at the moment. He came round for a drink to my place last night. Seemed to be in a bad way. That's really why I dropped round this morning—just to see that he's OK.'

'When the pub's closed, he is like a . . . what do you say— "bear with a headache"?'

' "Bear with a sore head".'

'Yes, that is right. Though he doesn't look like one, he is a real workaholic. He cannot be doing nothing.'

They were now inside the empty bar. 'Ted's out the back,' Zosia went on. 'I'll take you to—'

'Just a minute.' Jude held the girl back with a touch on her arm. 'Before I see him, I just wondered if you had any ideas about what might have happened yesterday.'

'With the scallops? I'm sorry, Jude, I'd forgotten. You were one of the people who ate them, weren't you?'

'Yes, but I'm fine now, don't worry.'

'And Carole?'

'Not so good, I'm afraid. But I'm sure she'll soon be better. Incidentally, have you heard anything from the hospital? About the woman who was taken there? Bettina Smiley?'

Zosia's pigtails swayed as she firmly shook her head. 'We have heard nothing. Ted is worrying about that too. Mind you, there's no reason why the hospital should tell us, is there?'

'Probably not. Maybe I could make an enquiry . . .'

Zosia made as if to lead her friend through to the kitchen, but Jude again resisted. 'Just a quick word before I see Ted. Have you any idea what went wrong with the scallops yesterday?'

Another decided shake of the head. 'I suppose it must have been the suppliers.'

'Ted said they were normally very reliable.'

'They are. And they don't like what is being said about them. Ted had a furious managing director on the phone for a good half hour this morning.'

'You haven't had your Health and Safety inspection yet?'

'No. They rang first thing, and said they'd try to fit it in this afternoon. But they didn't sound optimistic. Ted'll go mad if he has to keep closed for another day.'

'Last night he said . . . well, he was rambling a bit, but he said he thought someone might have tampered with the scallops, that it might have been sabotage.'

'That is the obvious thing to think, when there is no other explanation. Except I don't see how it could have been done. Either Ed or I was in the kitchen all the time.'

'Did you see Ed take the delivery?'

'Yes, I did. I was in and out to the bar all the time, but I was actually in the kitchen when the seafood delivery came. Ed checked it, signed for the stuff, it was no different from usual.'

'Ted mentioned someone called Ray who helps out.'

'Yes, poor old Ray. He is not . . .' Zosia made a circling movement with a finger by her temple '. . . not right in the head, you know.'

'Is he in today?'

'No. He rather comes and goes when he feels like it. That's why Ted can't really employ him on an official basis. Ray's not good at following a regular schedule. And he seemed very upset by what happened yesterday. We might not see him for a while now. He takes things very much to heart.'

'Do you know where he lives?'

'One of these projects where people with the same sort of disabilities share flats. You know, they are independent, but they are quite carefully supervised. Where it is exactly I don't know. In Fethering, though, I think. I'm sure Ted would have an address for him.'

'And you don't think Ray could have had anything to do with sabotaging the scallops?'

Zosia's brow wrinkled as she dismissed the idea. 'Even if he had the intelligence to work out something like that—which I'm sure he hasn't—Ray would never knowingly do anything that might hurt another person. Ray is *too* good, *too* prepared to believe the best of everyone.'

'But is he—?'

Jude's question was interrupted by the ringing of the phone behind the bar. Zosia moved towards it, but Ted Crisp, emerging suddenly from the kitchen, got there first. 'Crown and Anchor. Yes, that's me. Oh, right, we spoke earlier. What? Oh, are you sure you can't? Very well. Expect you tomorrow. When you like. I'm not going anywhere. Goodbye.'

He slammed the handset down and let out the burst of expletives which he had been restraining while being polite on the phone.

'Was it them?' asked Zosia when he was quiet.

'Yes. Can't come till bloody tomorrow now.'

'Your Health and Safety inspection?'

Ted Crisp nodded savagely, too preoccupied by his anger to welcome Jude. He banged his fist down on the counter. 'Another whole bloody day! Another day without business, right in the middle of the tourist season. Another day for the rumour mill to go into overdrive. Another day for the gossips of Fethering to inflate a small outbreak of food poisoning into the bloody Black Death!'

'It'll be fine,' said Jude soothingly. 'You said last night that you'd pass any inspection.'

'That's not the point. The worst thing that can happen to any pub's business is to be closed. And the longer it stays closed, the harder it is to get the punters back. Anyway, knowing the way my luck's going at the moment, Health and Safety probably will find something wrong.'

'But surely—?'

This attempt at reassurance was cut short by the sound of the pub door opening. Zosia had omitted to relock it after letting Jude in. The man who entered was a kind of dapper hippy. He wore jeans, a flowered shirt and cowboy boots, but they were designer jeans, the shirt was too well cut to be cheap, and the cowboy boots had been buffed to a high gloss. Their substantial heels made some compensation for his shortness. There was a neat square of grey beard on his chin and his long grey hair was gathered in a ponytail. From some context Jude could not immediately place, he looked very familiar.

The newcomer took in the empty pub and his lip curled into a cynical smile. 'I thought you said the place was doing good business, Ted.'

CHAPTER FOUR

He moved forward and flashed the whitened teeth of a professional charmer at Jude and Zosia. 'Hello, ladies. Dan Poke's my name. You probably recognize me from the television.'

Jude now knew exactly who he was. Zosia, who didn't even possess a television because she had no time between her studies and work at the Crown and Anchor, gave a polite grin that implied she did too.

'So, Ted, how's tricks—which is the one thing you mustn't say at a convention of conjurors!' The lip-curled smile reappeared as he enveloped the landlord in a bear hug which somehow didn't seem as spontaneous as it was meant to look.

Ted appeared ill at ease; his participation in the display of bonhomie was forced. But he grinned stiffly as he replied, 'Dan, I'm as fit as a flea . . . on a dog that's just been covered with flea powder.'

The fact that Ted had gone so instantly into a comedy routine reminded Jude of his background as a stand-up comedian. And seeing Dan Poke in the flesh gave her a context in which to place him. One of the first surge of Thatcher-bashing stand-up comedians, he had been on television quite a bit in the 1990s, doing his 'right-on' act, guesting on chat shows, then hosting panel games. Jude couldn't recall having seen much of Dan Poke in recent years, but, then again, he didn't appear on the kind of programmes she watched. For all she knew, his career might still be thriving.

'Blimey, Ted, this place is a silent as an audience during one of your gigs.'

'Ha, bloody ha. Look, sorry, Dan mate, I completely forgot we'd got a date for today.'

'Forgot?' Dan Poke's face took on an expression of outraged femininity. 'After everything we once meant to each other?'

'I been a bit preoccupied the last twenty-four hours.'

'Huh. And I wonder what you've been preoccupied with?' The comedian's camp routine continued. 'You haven't got another feller, have you—you Jezebel? I bet you have. You men are all the same.'

But Ted Crisp had had enough of the comedy routine for the time being. He looked embarrassed and said, 'Come on, let's go out, Dan. Get a drink and a bite to eat, eh?'

'I thought you'd invited me to have a drink and a bite to eat here.'

'Yeah, maybe, but we're not open today.'

'Oh?' asked Dan Poke, suddenly alert.

The landlord's eyes beamed instructions to the two women not to contradict him as he said, 'Maintenance problems.'

'I see.' The comedian spoke as if it was a subject he might return to later. 'But I thought we were going to look at the set-up here for Sunday's gig.'

'Yes, sure. After we've had something to eat. Just got to get my wallet.' Ted hurried out of the door behind the bar.

Dan Poke eyed up the two women. 'Well, how very nice,' he observed. 'Two very attractive ladies. As I say, I'm Dan Poke. Poke by name, and Poke by . . .' He chuckled salaciously and produced two cards from his pocket. 'Should either of you ladies wish to take our acquaintance further, you have only to call this number . . .'

His manner was ironical, as though what he was saying could be taken as an expression of post-modernist sexism, a witty commentary on the whole notion of sexism. If that's what he was trying to do, it didn't wash with Jude. So far as she was concerned his behaviour was plain old-fashioned sexism. But both she and Zosia took the cards.

Ted was back now with his wallet. 'Come on.' He hustled his friend to the door, as if he wanted him off the premises as quickly as possible. Just before they went out, he turned to Zosia. 'You be here for a bit, you know, in case the phone goes?'

The girl understood him immediately. 'Yes, I have to work through the bar orders for next week.'

'Great. See you.' And the two men were out of the door.

Jude watched as Zosia tore up the card she had been given and dropped the pieces into a waste bin. Catching her eye, the bar manager explained, 'Happens a lot in my line of work. Men thrust their phone numbers at you. Particularly later on in the evening. You know, it's good for a girl's self-esteem working behind a bar.'

'Oh?'

'The later the evening gets, the more pretty you become.'

Jude grinned, but she tucked her card into a pocket. 'Did you know him?' she asked.

The Polish girl shrugged. 'Never seen him before. I didn't understand what he was saying about television.'

'He's a comedian.'

'Ah.' Zosia seemed grateful to have an explanation for the man's presence. 'That explains it. Ted had said he was meeting someone about the possibility of starting a comedy club in the pub.'

'Well, it's Dan who's doing this gig on Sunday . . .'

'Ah.'

'. . . but I didn't know Ted was thinking of setting up a permanent comedy club.'

'He's talked about it.'

'Really?'

Something in Jude's intonation made Zosia ask, 'Why? Wouldn't you like the idea of a comedy club?'

'*I'd* like the idea quite a lot. But I'm not sure that Fethering would.'

When she returned to Woodside Cottage, Jude rang through to next door with some trepidation, remembering how ghastly her friend had been feeling earlier in the day. But, to her surprise, Carole sounded completely recovered. And characteristically, now she was better, she didn't want to admit even that her illness had existed. Fulsomely overassertive in her recovered health, she announced that she was really hungry. 'Could quite fancy a pub lunch.'

'Well, you're out of luck. The Crown and Anchor's closed till further notice.'

'I wasn't thinking of the Crown and Anchor—not after what happened on Monday. Let's go somewhere up on the Downs. Might be more breeze up there than there is down here. And Gulliver could do with a walk.'

Carole, in efficient no-of-course-I-haven't-been-ill mode, said the ideal pub to go to would be the Hare and Hounds at Weldisham, and Jude, amused by the sudden change in her friend, did not argue with the proposal.

Gulliver was stowed on the back seat of the Renault and the two neighbours drove up into the Downs.

Though they hadn't been there since their involvement in an investigation in the village, both had a very clear recollection of the Hare and Hounds in Weldisham. They remembered the decor, themed round some designer's idea of a comfortable country house. Old tennis rackets in wooden presses, croquet mallets pinned to the walls, faded nineteen-thirties novels on shelves too high for them ever to be reached, gratuitous farm implements and saddlery hung from the beams.

But as soon as the Renault was parked opposite the main entrance, they could see that things had changed. No longer was the pub sign an eighteenth-century hunting scene. It was now a mulberry-coloured board with 'Hare and Hounds' written in grey calligraphy.

Inside again mulberry and grey dominated the decor. The bar, tables and chairs were again chunky pine. Carole and Jude remembered an interior of small rooms and snugs, but all the partitions had been removed, and the bar was just one large unbroken space.

'New owners, do you reckon?' asked Jude.

'Or maybe rebranding by the old owners. I seem to remember that this place was owned by a chain.'

'Which chain?'

'Look, I don't have instant recall of everything,' said Carole, rather pettishly.

At the bar they bought two glasses of Maipo Valley Chardonnay from a girl dressed in mulberry and grey livery, and ordered salads. (It was noticeable that neither went for the seafood option.) Fortunately they managed to get a table outside the pub, sheltered from the sun by a big umbrella. As Carole had hoped, here some way above sea level, they could feel the gentlest of breezes. Gulliver, after a big slurp from the dogs' water bowl by the front door of the pub, settled down comfortably to lie in the shade of their table.

The setting was stunning. Weldisham nestled into a fold of the Downs, an archetype of the kind of serenity which was expected from an English country village. Of course, as Carole and Jude had cause to know, the image of serenity could be deceptive. Seething passions lurked beneath that harmless exterior.

The thought prompted Jude to say, 'Difficult to be here

without remembering the murder we solved, isn't it?'

'Yes. What was the name of that slimy specimen who managed the pub then?'

'Will something, wasn't it?'

'Will Maples,' Carole pronounced with satisfaction at having remembered. 'Thin, shifty character, wasn't he? I wonder where he went.'

'As far away from here as he could get. When his bosses found he'd been peddling drugs at the Hare and Hounds they can't have been best pleased. And what was the name of that girl with M.E. whose parents lived up here?'

'Can't remember. Anyway, never mind that.' Carole was much more interested in the current investigation than in nostalgia for an old case. 'Tell me what happened this morning at the Crown and Anchor.'

Jude gave a quick summary, and got the sniffy response that if Ted Crisp had been poisoning the people of Fethering then his pub deserved to be closed down.

'But it's not his fault. He and I are both convinced he's been the victim of sabotage.'

'Oh really, Jude. I think you're being a little melodramatic. Ted has broken the law and he must face the consequences. It must have been a foul-up in his kitchen. Some past-their-sell-by scallops must've been served up by mistake.'

'That seems very unlikely. He's used the same supplier for years—their stuff's always been perfect. And his staff are very reliable.'

This was treated to a sceptical—'Huh. So the place gets inspected tomorrow?'

'Yes. Unless the Health and Safety people delay it yet again.'

'And if something is found to be wrong, what kind of penalties might he be liable for?'

'I don't know in detail, but Ted talked about a hefty fine. In the worst-case scenario he could be closed down for good.'

'And what would make it a worst-case scenario?'

'I'm not sure. If somebody died from the food poisoning, perhaps?'

'But nobody has, have they?'

'Well, we know you and I haven't, but the old lady who was carted off to hospital . . . I've no idea what's happened to her.'

'Bettina Smiley,' said Carole.

Jude looked curiously at her neighbour. 'You speak as if you know her.'

'I do. Well, know her in the sense that I know who she is. The way one does know people in Fethering. You nod politely if you see them, but you don't actually socialize.'

'But I didn't see you nod politely when you saw her in the Crown and Anchor yesterday.'

'Oh, I did. You didn't notice because you were up at the bar getting drinks. Yes, I've spent quite a few bring-and-buy coffee mornings with Bettina and Alec Smiley . . . even one in their house.' In response to her friend's interrogative expression, Carole went on, 'For the Canine Trust. You know I'm a member of that.' She looked down at Gulliver snuffling contentedly under the table. 'We dog-owners all know each other. We're a kind of local Mafia.'

'Oh.' Then Jude said, 'But you didn't say anything when Bettina collapsed.'

Carole's pale cheeks reddened. 'At that moment I was in no condition to say anything.'

'No. Well, do you reckon you know Eric Smiley well enough to ring up and ask how his wife is?'

'Certainly. And since I was there when it happened, it would only be polite for me to make such an enquiry.'

'Do you want to use my mobile?'

'No, thank you,' said Carole primly. 'I have my own.' And she

38

took out the fairly recent acquisition.

But the call had to be deferred. There was no signal up in Weldisham. So they settled down to enjoy the beautiful setting and their salads. Afterwards they strolled over the Downs, which for Gulliver was a nirvana of unfamiliar and intriguing smells.

When they returned to High Tor, Carole called the Smileys' number from her landline. (She never used her mobile at home—the monthly bills were already expensive enough.) Jude pieced together most of what was said from the half of the conversation she could hear, but at the end Carole confirmed it. Bettina Smiley had been kept in hospital the previous night for observation, but she was now safely back at home in Fethering, a bit frail, but seeming to have suffered no lasting damage.

So the poisoning in the pub had not caused any deaths. Yet.

CHAPTER FIVE

The Health and Safety inspection did happen on the Wednesday, and it brought good news for Ted Crisp. Nothing was found wrong with the standards of food hygiene in the kitchen of the Crown and Anchor. The remains of some of the Monday's pan-fried scallops with spinach and oriental noodles, which had been punctiliously preserved according to instructions, were taken away for laboratory analysis (which might take some weeks). But the Health and Safety officials could find no reason why the Crown and Anchor should not reopen for business on the Thursday.

This good news, however, was counterbalanced the following day, when the *Fethering Observer* was published. The main headline read: CROWN AND ANCHOR SHUT DOWN IN POISONED SCALLOPS SCARE. The ensuing article contained all the righteous indignation of a local cub reporter with delusions of being a crusading journalist. It concluded: 'Following complaints from customers, the Crown and Anchor will be closed until further notice.'

Carole had picked up a *Fethering Observer* from the local newsagent on her way back from Gulliver's morning walk on the beach. (She did not believe in the indulgence of having papers delivered.) The headline couldn't be missed; a paraphrase of it also appeared on the felt-tipped display boards for the *Fethering Observer* all around the town.

After she had towelled off Gulliver's sandy paws and made

herself a cup of coffee, she sat down at the kitchen table and read the whole item. It was another scorching day. The door to the garden was open, but the air didn't seem to move at all.

Once she'd finished reading Carole phoned next door, but there was no reply from Woodside Cottage. Then she remembered that Jude had said something about going off to 'a day's conference on alternative therapies in Brighton on Thursday'. Probably the reason why Carole had forgotten that was the instinct her brain had to switch off whenever she heard the words 'alternative therapy'.

She was surprised at how much the *Fethering Observer* report had upset her. In spite of the 'serve him right' attitude she had expressed earlier in the week, she felt terribly sorry for Ted Crisp. Though their brief affair had ended long before, she didn't like to think of him suffering. So she rang through to the Crown and Anchor to commiserate.

The landlord was in a predictable state of fury. 'I get the all-clear from Health and Safety yesterday. They say I can open up today, and then what bloody happens? The *Fethering Observer* only tells everyone from here to Fedborough that the Crown and Anchor's "closed until further notice"! I think I can be excused for feeling paranoid. It's not my imagination. Everybody bloody *is* picking on me!'

'I'm sure it'll soon blow over,' said Carole. Though, knowing how the gossip machine of Fethering worked, she rather doubted the accuracy of her prediction.

'Well, I've had it up to here.' Ted groaned. 'Anyway, how was the *Fethering Observer* onto it so quickly? Somebody must've snitched to them. Somebody round here's trying to do a number on me.'

He certainly did sound paranoid, but Carole couldn't help feeling some sympathy for him.

'And now I don't know whether I should be pulling the plugs

on this Dan Poke gig on Sunday.'

'Have you sold many tickets?'

'Yes, a bundle. And news about it is up on Dan's website. He reckons we'll get a lot more on the door. There's even an interview with him in the *Fethering Observer* entertainment section. Plugging the gig in the same paper that says the Crown and Anchor's closed "till further notice". Talk about the right hand not knowing what the left hand's doing. I don't know— should I call Dan? I mean, if people think the pub's closed . . . He's doing me a favour. Doing the gig for just expenses. But then say I can't get an audience for him . . .'

'If people have bought tickets,' Carole reasoned, 'they'll come. Or they'll at least ring you to check whether the pub will be open on Sunday.'

'Yeah, maybe. I don't know, it makes me bloody want to spit . . .' He took a deep breath. 'Anyway, look,' he went on, controlling his anger and trying to speak in a more conciliatory tone, 'what I'd like to do is invite you and Jude down here for lunch today. On the house. By way of compensation for what happened on Monday. What do you say?'

'Well,' Carole replied cautiously, 'Jude's away for the day at some conference.'

'Then you just come on your own. I want to have someone in the bloody bar at lunchtime. With the publicity I've been getting recently, you're likely to be the only one.'

It wasn't quite that bad, but lunchtime business at the Crown and Anchor was very slow. The contrast with the bustling energy of three days before could not have been more marked. There was a Dutch family of four sitting outside, presumably tourists unaware of any adverse publicity. At the bar lounged a couple of the regular lunchtime drinkers, returning for reasons of habit and geographical convenience. And there was Carole.

The menu offered a couple of seafood dishes, but she steered clear of them and, as her compensatory lunch, ordered sausage and mash. She determined that, since she was going to have such a substantial midday meal, she wouldn't eat anything that evening. And she restricted herself to one small glass of Chilean Chardonnay.

The advantage of the slackness of business was that Carole did get a chance to talk to Ted Crisp. He looked more haggard than she had ever seen him. Above the beard line his cheeks were hollow and his eyes were sunk into dark circles. Leaving Zosia in charge behind the bar (not that she had any customers to deal with), he came to sit at Carole's table. He nursed a glass of mineral water. The fringes of his hair were spiked from earlier sweating.

She felt she wanted to reach out to hug him, to make it all better. That's what Jude would have done. But of course, being Carole Seddon and not Jude, Carole didn't.

'Trade'll pick up,' she said.

'Huh.'

'At least you've got a clean bill of health from the Health and Safety.'

'Yes, but it's still going to take a while to get the punters back. And this is the time of year I should be coining it.'

Ed Pollack had come out into the bar. Even without much cooking to do, the kitchen was an uncomfortably hot place to be on that kind of day. A tall, thin boy, he looked younger than his twenty-five years. He was wearing stylish glasses, those very thin ones with dark frames that make people look like aliens from cheap sci-fi movies. Dressed in rubber clogs, black and white checked trousers, a white button-across top and a tight black cap, he was just untying a white scarf from around his neck to mop his brow. In his hands he held a packet of cigarettes and a lighter. Clearly about to go out to the car park for one of his fag breaks.

But when he saw Carole, the boy changed his destination. Crossing to the table, he offered his sincere apologies for the effect his scallops had had on her. Ed Pollack had a surprisingly upper-class accent for Carole's preconception of how a chef should talk. 'I feel terrible about it. Worst nightmare you can have in my profession.'

'Don't worry about it,' said Carole, unwilling to increase Ted Crisp's self-recrimination. 'These things happen, Ed.'

'Yes, but I pride myself on the way I keep my kitchen. Come and have a look.'

Carole looked across at Ted Crisp, who shrugged permission. If that's what the boy wanted to do to make himself feel better, then fine. So Carole was given a quick tour of the kitchen. Every surface was spotless. There was no trace of black on the hobs or grills. The white-handled knives and other utensils gleamed, as did the magnetic strip to which they were attached. Ed Pollack even opened the fridges for his visitor. He turned and appealed to her. 'All perfectly clean, isn't it?'

'Better than most hospital intensive care units,' said Carole, in an attempt to lift the woebegone expression from his face. She led the way back into the bar and, showing more social grace than she could usually command, asked, 'Can I get you a drink, Ed, to show there are no hard feelings?'

'On the house,' said Ted. 'Coke, isn't it?'

'Please,' said the boy as he sat down languidly at their table. 'God, I'm drinking so much at the moment. Not booze, just water and stuff. I seem to have a permanent thirst.'

'An occupational hazard, I would imagine,' said Carole. 'Spending all your time in a hot kitchen.'

'Maybe.'

There was a silence, as she tried to think what to ask next. Carole realized that she was being given a perfect opportunity to continue her investigation into the poisoning at the Crown and Anchor. She owed it to Jude not to mess up the chance. Besides, she relished the idea of taking her neighbour back some new titbit of carefully elicited knowledge.

'I suppose, Ed, you have no more idea than Ted what might have caused the dodgy scallops to get through?'

The chef shook his head. 'I just can't see how it happened. And obviously I'm furious, because it's a black mark against my professionalism. I mean, one thing they din into you at catering college: you always have to be careful with shellfish, particularly in weather like this. So I've been double-checking everything.'

'How long would chilled scallops last normally?'

'Couple of days tops. If you've had them any longer than that, even in the fridge, you should chuck them. Which is what I always do. But that lot on Monday came in fresh from the suppliers. I signed for the delivery myself, put them straight in the marinade and into the fridge. Before I did that, I cleared out some that'd been delivered on Saturday. Now if it had been that lot the customers had been served with, I wouldn't have been at all surprised at what happened.'

Ted Crisp joined them silently at the table and slid a glass of Coca-Cola across to the chef, as Carole asked, 'If the new scallops had been substituted by old ones, would you be able to tell?'

'I certainly would before they were in the marinade. They'd smell "off". Once they'd been marinaded, I'm not so sure. Soy sauce can be pretty pungent, it might mask the bad smell. So I suppose under those circumstances it would be possible to make a mistake.'

'Except,' Ted asserted peevishly, 'that couldn't be what happened on Monday, because you took the fresh delivery yourself.'

'I was just asking hypothetically,' said Carole. 'I mean, in the event that someone had actually switched the tray of fresh scallops in the fridge for a tray of past-their-sell-by ones, it would have been possible that you'd have cooked them, Ed, without noticing anything was wrong?'

'It is just possible, yes.'

'But it could never have happened,' Ted repeated.

'As I say, I'm just working out possible scenarios. And, Ed, you didn't leave the kitchen for any length of time on Monday morning after the scallops had been delivered?'

'I nipped out for the odd fag. Just as I'm going to do now.'

He looked down at his cigarette packet, as if about to leave for the car park, but Carole pressed on, 'But there wasn't a longer time when you left the kitchen unattended?'

'Zosia and I were in and out, anyway,' said Ted, and continued as if he wanted to forestall any further argument, 'The kitchen wasn't left unattended for any length of time after the scallops had been delivered.'

Carole caught the quick look exchanged between Ed Pollack and Zosia at the bar. There was something that hadn't been told. She wondered how she was going to be able to winkle it out, but fortunately the chef saved her the trouble.

'Ted, we might as well tell her.'

The landlord looked truculent. 'I don't see any reason why we need to.'

'Well, I need to. As a professional chef, I want some explanation for what might have happened.'

Ted Crisp looked away towards the bar, as if hoping for support. But Zosia's expression of defiance showed that he wasn't going to get any from her. 'All right,' he mumbled.

Ed Pollack took up his cue. 'There was another delivery on Monday morning. Beer. The delivery man sends the barrels down to the cellar from a chute outside. On Monday a couple of the barrels rolled on the floor and got jammed against a table down there. Ted couldn't shift them, so he asked Zosia and me to give him a hand.'

'We weren't down there that long,' the landlord argued.

'Twenty minutes at least,' said Ed implacably. 'I know, because I'd had time to put the scallops in their marinade before we started, and when we finished there was still time for me to have a fag in the car park before we opened up at eleven.'

'So the kitchen was unattended for twenty minutes?' Receiving a nod from the chef, Carole turned the full beam of her pale blue eyes onto Ted Crisp. 'Did you tell that to the Health and Safety inspectors?'

He shook his shaggy head.

'Why not?'

'I don't know.'

'Yes, you do,' said Zosia's voice from the bar. The regulars had left; she had no anxiety about speaking out loud. 'You do it because you don't want there to be any trouble for Ray. That's why you don't tell the inspectors he was here Monday morning.'

Carole's pale blue eyes focused back on the wretched landlord. 'Is that true, Ted?'

He sighed. 'Look, poor bloke, he hasn't exactly been dealt the best hand in life, has he? Ray never made it at school, he's never been able to hold down a proper job. Everywhere he's gone, people've made fun of him, all because of a disability he was born with. Made fun of him or bullied him. It's not his fault he's like he is. And there's no way he could have done anything to the scallops, anyway.'

'If that's so, why didn't you tell the Health and Safety people he could have been in the kitchen?'

'Because they'd have given him hassle, and he can't stand it when people try to get at him. I wanted to spare him that.'

'But you also want to keep your business going, and lying to the Health and Safety inspectors is not the best way of—'

'Listen, Carole!' said Ted, suddenly angry. 'Ray trusts me,

and I pay him for doing odd jobs.'

'Which is, I'm sure, very charitable of you, but when your livelihood—'

'I said "Listen!" If I tell the Health and Safety people about him, they're going to ask questions about his terms of employment here. They're going to ask about contracts, minimum wage, whether he's registered with the tax authorities, all kinds of stuff. Then they'll no doubt report their findings to some other bloody bureaucrats and a directive will come down from on high to say that I can't continue to use Ray's services. And the poor bugger will lose the one thing that gives him any sense of self-esteem—not to mention a little bit of pocket money— and I'll feel even more bloody useless than I usually do!'

Even during their brief relationship, Carole had never heard such an impassioned speech from Ted Crisp. There was a shocked silence after he'd finished. Then she said, 'Look, that's very admirable, Ted, but you must see that it's going against your own interests. You've been in trouble with the Health and Safety authorities. Lying to them can only get you into more trouble with them.'

'That would only be true, Carole, if there was any chance Ray had had any hand in what happened. He couldn't have. He has the mental age of . . . I don't know . . . a five-year-old, maybe. He certainly hasn't got the intellectual capacity to plot the poisoning of my customers.'

'But he could have made a mistake . . . put the old scallops in the fridge in place of the others.'

'That, Carole, would assume that there were any old scallops around.'

She turned gleefully to Ed Pollack. 'You said you'd just cleared out the old scallops from the weekend.'

'Yes, but I put them in a plastic bag which I sealed before putting it in the bin. And the bag was still sealed when the

Health and Safety people checked it out yesterday.'

'Ah.' Carole was crestfallen to have her moment of triumph taken away. 'So we're still no nearer finding an explanation for what happened on Monday.'

'No,' agreed Ted, with something like finality.

'I don't suppose . . .' said Carole tentatively, 'that you'd tell me Ray's address?'

'You don't suppose correctly.'

'But I would like to talk to him about—'

Ted Crisp was about to bawl her out again, but was distracted by the opening of the pub door and the entrance of a sharp-featured woman in a skimpy red top and white jeans.

'Oh God,' he groaned. 'More trouble. Talk about hitting a man when he's down.'

49

CHAPTER SIX

Introductions were made. The woman, as Carole rather suspected she might be, was identified as Ted Crisp's ex-wife, Sylvia. Her presence made him look more hangdog than ever. For Carole it was a novel sensation. Being in the same room as an ex-lover and another woman he'd slept with was not something that had happened to her before, neither in her private or professional life. Though such situations were probably very common in the Home Office, it hadn't been a part of her experience there. She couldn't deny, though, that, amidst her mixed emotions, there was a certain amount of excitement at the idea.

Also a natural feminine interest in what the woman looked like. Early forties probably, thin, but with the beginnings of a roll of fat at her midriff. Brown hair a bit too chestnutty to be entirely natural, worn swept off her face and shoulder length, fixed rigid with spray. A sharp nose, wide thin-lipped mouth over prominent front teeth. Hazel eyes, attractive but without depth, like an animal's.

But Ted's ex-wife was undeniably sexy. One of those women who made Carole Seddon feel very conscious of her own dowdiness.

Ed Pollack and Zosia had perhaps encountered Sylvia before. They both certainly took their first opportunity to melt back into the kitchen. And, despite the pleading look in Ted's eyes, Carole too soon made her excuses and left. In the stifling heat

of the July afternoon, there was a feeling of a storm about to break.

Just as she was approaching the door, Carole said, 'Oh, I haven't settled up, have I, Ted?'

'You're forgetting. Nothing to pay. I said today was on the house.'

As she went out of the pub Carole heard Sylvia's hard nasal voice behind her saying, 'That's no way to run a business. No wonder you say you haven't got any money. Do you pick up the tab for all your lady friends, Ted?'

Through the open windows of her sitting room Carole saw Jude arriving back from her conference in Brighton. Many people would have called out a greeting there and then but, being Carole, she waited till her neighbour had had ten minutes to settle in before telephoning her. She was relieved to hear that Jude was very definitely up for a glass of wine.

They sat in the High Tor garden, which maintained the same impersonal neatness as the house's interior. Neither Carole Seddon nor her husband David—they had still been married when they made the purchase of it as a weekend cottage—had wanted a garden that would need much maintenance. So the small rectangular plot was mostly paved over, with a two-foot frame of flowerbeds running up to the well-maintained fences. No weeds were ever allowed to attain maturity in the beds; they were removed with the same alacrity that Carole would wipe a stain off her kitchen work surface. A path led from the paved rectangle to the back gate, which opened on to an area of rough ground, where Carole would take Gulliver out to do his business when the weather was too bad for a proper walk.

She and Jude sat on green metal chairs at a green metal table with a bottle of Chilean Chardonnay in a cooler between them. A statutory enquiry was made about the day in Brighton, to which Jude, knowing the level of Carole's interest in alternative therapies, replied with commendable brevity.

Social niceties observed, Carole was quickly into an account of her lunchtime visit to the Crown and Anchor. In particular, she wanted to know whether Jude knew any more than she did about Ted Crisp's ex-wife.

'I don't think I do really. He's made enough jokes about her over the years, but most of them sounded as if they were just out of his old stand-up routine. But you've heard those as much as I have. He tells them all the time in the Crown and Anchor for the benefit of anyone who happens to be listening.'

'I thought you might have heard more about Sylvia when Ted poured his heart out to you on Monday evening.'

'All he said was that his "ex-wife had come back into his life"—or to be more accurate, that his "bloody ex-wife had come back into his life". Which I told you.'

'Yes, you did. Nothing more, though?'

Jude shook her head. 'But Ted didn't say anything to you, did he . . . ?' For a rare moment she almost felt the approach of coyness as she asked, 'I mean, when you and he . . . when you were together?'

'What do you mean?' Carole reddened, thrown by the question. 'Why should he have done?'

'Well, it's just . . . men and women, in an intimate situation . . .' Jude, tired of her own pussy-footing. 'In bed. People often talk about their former lovers when they're in bed with someone new.'

Carole Seddon looked deeply shocked. 'Ted and I didn't talk about anything like that,' she said primly.

'Right. Just a thought.'

Deliberately changing the tack of the conversation, Carole said firmly, 'I wish I could remember what he actually had said about Sylvia in the pub. There might have been some truth hidden away in all the jokes.'

'Well, I remember one that he told. He said that, fairly soon into their marriage—only three months or so—his wife had run off with a double-glazing salesman.'

'Had she really?'

'That I don't know. It could just have been a set-up for his next line.'

'Which was?'

'As I recall: "I can't see what she sees in him. He's so transparent." '

Carole winced. 'Oh dear.'

'But it might have been true. Who knows?'

'Hmm. Jude, has Ted ever said to you that he's actually divorced?'

'I can't remember. I'm pretty sure he has. I mean, I've always assumed he was. Why?'

'Oh, I was just thinking that a divorced ex-spouse can cause problems . . .' Carole coloured again '. . . as I know with David, but those problems are nothing to those that can be caused by someone to whom you're still married.'

Jude nodded. 'You're right. And Ted does seem to be over-reacting to Sylvia's reappearance. Yes, be worth finding out whether their separation ever was legalized.'

'But how do we do that?' asked Carole.

'Next time we're in the Crown and Anchor,' said Jude with a grin, 'we ask him.'

'Oh.' Carole's expression showed that she regarded this as far too frontal an approach. Once again she was glad to move the conversation along. Particularly glad to be moving it on to the one important gobbet of news she had been hoarding till it would have its fullest dramatic impact. 'I did actually find out something else at the pub at lunchtime . . .'

'Oh?'

And Carole told Jude about Ray having been unmonitored in the kitchen while Ted, Ed and Zosia had shifted the beer barrels in the Crown and Anchor's cellar.

'You say Ted didn't mention that to the Health and Safety people?'

'No. He suddenly got all protective about Ray. Almost crusading about how society treats people like that. I must say, it was a side of Ted I had never seen before.'

'Not even when you and he—?'

'Never,' said Carole, firmly stopping that train of thought in its tracks.

'Well, it sounds like we ought to speak to this Ray.'

'If we can find him. Ted wouldn't give me his address.'

'No, but we know he lives in a flat in a block for other people with special needs. And there can't be many of those in Fethering.'

'So you think you could track him down, Jude?'

'I'm sure I could. Fortunately I have very good contacts in the local social services. If I could just use your phone, I'll try—'

But that line of enquiry was at least temporarily postponed by the sound of High Tor's front doorbell.

Both women recognized the man whom Carole ushered through into the back garden, though neither of them had ever met him socially. It was impossible to live in Fethering for any length of time without knowing who he was. He was present at every public event, and more weeks than not there was a photograph of him in the *Fethering Observer*. The place was not big enough to have a mayor, but it did have a village committee, and the chair of that was Greville Tilbrook.

Like Carole Seddon, he was a retired civil servant, though she knew from contacts within the organization that he'd never reached even as high up the system as she had. But he was one of those men whose entire life seemed to have been waiting for the blossoming that would attend retirement. For some years while still employed he had been a Methodist lay preacher, but when he gave up the day job he was soon climbing other local hierarchies. He was a leading light of the Conservative Association, on the committees of Fethering Yacht Club, the Fethering Historical Society and the local Probus Club (for retired *profes*sional and *bus*iness people).

He was a living warning, an embodiment of the truth that a colleague had told Carole before she moved permanently to Fethering: 'If you live in the country, never volunteer for anything, or you'll end up doing everything.' It was advice she had stuck by, and it had served her well.

But of course Greville Tilbrook's personality was very different from hers. He positively *loved* civic responsibility. In retirement he was having the time of his life.

He was dressed that evening in his uniform of pale-grey . . . well, they could only really be called 'slacks' . . . and soft brown loafers. As a gesture to informality and the July weather, he had removed his blue-striped seersucker jacket and swung it roguishly over his shoulder in distant recollection of some photograph he'd seen of Frank Sinatra. This revealed a short-sleeved pale-blue shirt, round whose neck was a neatly knotted tie bearing the insignia of one of the many organizations he belonged to. Under his jacket-carrying arm he nursed a leather document case.

Though coming from very different backgrounds and values, Carole and Jude had both, before meeting Greville Tilbrook, thought he would turn out to be a right pain. And so it proved.

In all his various committees, Greville Tilbrook dealt with a lot of mature women, whom he treated with a gallantry that bordered on the flirtatious. Though there was a Mrs Tilbrook somewhere locked away in a secure marriage and pension, her husband did see himself as a bit of a non-practising ladies' man. And he set out to exercise his self-defined fatal charm on the two women in the garden of High Tor. (The two women in question, it should be mentioned, found themselves strangely impervious to that charm.)

'I'm so sorry to disturb you ladies,' he said after he had been introduced to Jude and refused the offer of a glass of wine, 'on an evening of such exceptional beauty—not to mention two ladies of such exceptional beauty—but I'm sure you, like me, as residents of this delightful village of Fethering are as committed as I am—well, possibly less committed than I myself am, due to the nature of the official positions which, for my sins, I represent within this community—but still committed to the maintenance of the loveliness of the region—to call it "God's own acre" might be by some thought to be excessively poetic, and yet why not be poetic when one has the good fortune to live within the environs of such a delightful area . . .'

God, both women thought as he droned on, does he actually *know* how to finish a sentence?

And then suddenly they were both aware of silence. Greville Tilbrook was looking at them quizzically. He must finally have got to the end of his sentence and asked a question.

'I'm sorry? What did you say?' asked Carole and Jude together.

'I said: "Is that what you want to happen to Fethering?" '

After a unison 'Umm . . .' Carole had the presence of mind to ask, 'But do you think it's likely to?'

'I think it could be the beginning of the, as it were, thin end of a very slippery slope, and I feel it's my civic responsibility, with my Fethering-Village-Committee hat on, to alert my fellow residents to this menace.'

Short of admitting they hadn't been listening, neither woman could think of an appropriate supplementary question, but fortunately Greville Tilbrook was not the kind of man who needed prompting to continue his monologue. 'And I'm not speaking now with my Methodist-lay-preacher hat on—though I could be—but I'm sure there are some residents of this delightful village who would have objections on religious grounds, because the Sabbath, even in these benighted times, is, I am glad to say, still respected by some as a special day—and do we really want that special day to be tarnished by blasphemy and filthy language?'

Carole and Jude, still clueless as to what he was talking about, agreed that they didn't want the Sabbath tarnished by blasphemy and filthy language. But Greville Tilbrook's next words did make the purpose of his visit absolutely clear. 'It's not the first time that there has been cause to complain about goings on at the Crown and Anchor, because although I am in no way a killjoy—I enjoy the benefits of fellowship just as much as a pub-goer does, though my personal preference is to conduct such conversations over a cup of tea or coffee rather than anything stronger, the fact remains that the unbridled consumption of alcohol can lead to a certain amount of rowdiness—I'm sure you've read in the papers about the modern curse of "binge-drinking", particularly amongst the young, and that kind of thing can easily spread in the, as it were, environs of a public house . . . and there have been complaints from residents about the noise at closing time, drunken shouting, the slamming of car doors and so on . . .'

He was incautious enough at that point to take a breath, which gave Jude the opportunity to object, 'But the Crown and Anchor isn't near to any houses.'

'Maybe not,' said Greville Tilbrook smugly, 'but that is just a measure of how loud the departing customers must be in their cups . . . and anyway if it were just the drinking that's a problem with the Crown and Anchor, perhaps that might be regretted but tolerated. However, there are other complaints against the place, of which the most recent is of course the attack of food poisoning caused by the appalling standards of hygiene obtaining in the kitchen of the Crown and Anchor and—'

Jude wasn't going to stand for that. 'Ted Crisp has very high standards. He had the Health and Safety people in there yesterday, they checked everything and couldn't find a single breach of hygiene regulations.'

'Ted Crisp, eh?' Greville Tilbrook repeated the name sourly. 'I didn't realize that he was a friend of yours, because, to be quite honest and not to beat about the bush, I hadn't put you two ladies down as "pub people".'

It cost Carole a lot not to break in there and assure him that she had never been a 'pub person', but she managed to curb her tongue.

'Well, even if you are friends of Mr Crisp, you must—'

'Have you ever met him, Mr Tilbrook?' asked Jude.

'No, I have not had that pleasure, but I know him by reputation . . . and not everything I've heard of that reputation is entirely, as it were, favourable.' He was now getting quite aerated, spluttering in his condemnation. 'While not going quite as far as some residents who feel that Fethering should not have a pub at all, I do think it's regrettable that the one we do have should be run by a foul-mouthed, scruffy individual who—'

This finally was too much for Carole. 'Mr Tilbrook, I'm sorry, but you're talking about someone who is a friend of ours. And I think you should form your own estimation of people by meeting them rather than listening to scurrilous gossip.'

Greville Tilbrook was about to repeat her last two words, but he only got as far as 'scurrilous' before Carole said, 'And I think, if you have no other purpose in being here than to slander our friends, I must ask you to leave.'

'But I do have another purpose,' he spluttered.

'Oh?'

He withdrew some stapled A4 sheets from his leather document case. 'I came here to ask you whether you would add your, as it were, signatures, to this petition.'

'And what's the petition for?' asked Carole implacably.

'It is to stop the appearance of the vulgar and blasphemous comedian Dan Poke in the Crown and Anchor public house this coming Lord's Day.'

'Right,' said Carole. 'Glad we've finally got to the point. Well, no, thank you, Mr Tilbrook. I have no wish to add my "as it were, signature" to your petition.'

'Nor do I,' said Jude. 'We strongly support Ted Crisp's initiative to use the Crown and Anchor for such purposes, and in fact we have both bought tickets to see Dan Poke's appearance on Sunday.'

A discomfited Greville Tilbrook realized he wasn't going to get anywhere with this particular visit and beat a wordy retreat. When Carole came back from seeing him out of the front door, she asked Jude, 'Have you really booked tickets for the show?'

'No. But I think we should.'

Carole recharged their wine glasses and the two women looked at each other. 'You can see why Ted's paranoid, though,' Jude observed. 'He seems to be being attacked on all sides, doesn't he?'

CHAPTER SEVEN

On the Friday morning Jude rang one of her friends in the social services, a woman called Sally Monks, who owed her a favour. Jude had once used her healing skills to help out a couple of Sally's more difficult teenage clients, and so the social worker was more than happy to return the favour. She readily supplied an address for the Ray who sometimes worked at the Crown and Anchor. 'But I happen to know that he's not there today,' said Sally.

'Oh?'

'He tends to go back to his mother's from time to time. She's quite old and infirm, so she can't look after him full-time, but she can manage for a few days.'

'You don't know where she lives, do you?'

'Yes. Worthing. Do you want me to give you her address? I will if it's something really important, but Ray's mother's an old lady and . . .'

Sally Monks sounded reluctant, and Jude was forced to ask herself how important her quest actually was. Yes, she wanted to help Ted Crisp, but not to presume too far on the social worker's goodwill. Anyway, Ted himself had tried to cover up Ray's involvement in what had happened in the Crown and Anchor. He might not welcome her investigating.

As it happened, what Sally Monks said next simplified things.

'If you really do want to contact Ray, I know he'll be at the flat tomorrow.'

'Oh?'

'Saturday. Football. He loves his football. His mother doesn't have Sky, but they have it in the communal sitting room at the flats.'

'Oh, thank you for telling me. Maybe I'll try and contact him tomorrow.'

'That'd be better.' The social worker sounded relieved. 'I don't want to put any more pressure on his mother.'

'More pressure? What do you mean?'

'Well, it's just that Ray only goes to see her when he's upset. She has quite a problem calming him down sometimes.'

'You've no idea why he might be upset at the moment, do you?' asked Jude, keen to advance her investigation.

'Jude,' said Sally patiently, 'I haven't seen Ray for months. I've no idea what's upset him this time. It's could be anything. He gets hurt very easily, always worries that people are against him. He's one of those people who seems to have been born with too few layers of skin.'

As she thanked Sally and rang off, Jude realized that any approach she made to Ray would require all of her considerable tact and gentleness.

Because it was so hot that Friday, Carole delayed taking Gulliver for his afternoon walk until the evening. She felt sorry for him. A Labrador's coat wasn't designed for this kind of weather. He was still full of enthusiasm to tackle the invisible monsters of the beach, but he tired quickly and his long tongue lolled from panting mouth.

He looked so hot and pitiful in the fading light that she thought she would find him a drink before they got back to High Tor. There was always a dog bowl of water outside the

Crown and Anchor, so she walked back from the beach that way. The route would also give her a chance to see whether Ted's trade had picked up at all since his enforced closure.

The noise as she approached the pub answered her question. A lot of customers—and not just the smokers—were drinking outside, and all the windows and doors were open. The crowd seemed much bigger than it would have been for an ordinary Friday night; the atmosphere was positively rowdy. Her destination, the dogs' water bowl, was just outside the main doors, but the density of the crowd deterred her. Also the nature of the crowd. Despite the evening heat, there were a lot of black leather jackets with gratuitous chains attached. Carole decided Gulliver could wait for his drink till they got back to High Tor.

As she walked through the car park back to the High Street, she noticed a surprising number of motorbikes. She also saw someone who looked vaguely familiar leaving the pub and approaching a sleek pale blue metallic BMW.

He was a tall man, probably in his early forties. The immaculate cut of his suit could not completely hide the fact that he was spreading to fat. Though his face was chubby, its features were small, thin lips, slightly beaky nose. He wore glasses with thick black rims. His hair, longish and swept back, was too black to be natural.

Carole felt sure she had seen him somewhere before, but the context wouldn't come. She racked her brains as she walked back home, but her memory didn't oblige. Finally, with a mental shrug, she gave up trying to place the man. He probably just looked like someone she had once met.

After eleven, as Carole Seddon prepared for bed, she heard the screeching, whining and revving up of motorbikes departing. Rather than following the coast road, where there was little residential property, they had chosen to drive up Fethering High Street. Through the open windows of the bedroom of

High Tor, the noise was very loud.

If that kind of thing continued, Carole Seddon reckoned that Greville Tilbrook might find his petition filling up rather quickly.

CHAPTER EIGHT

Jude's relationship with Carole was easy, but it required effort on Jude's part to keep it that way. She had to avoid many areas of spikiness in Carole's personality. Most of these were predictable, but there was always the danger of inadvertently touching on some new, unpredictable one. So Jude anticipated a potential problem in their approach to Ted Crisp's occasional helper, Ray.

Basically, she knew it was the kind of interview that would work better if she did it on her own. From all accounts, Ray was a highly strung individual, and Jude's work as a therapist had given her plentiful experience of dealing with such people. But she knew how sensitive Carole could be about the idea of being excluded from any part of an investigation.

On this occasion, however, her neighbour seemed to recognize her own limitations. After Jude's call to Sally Monks, they had agreed that an attempt should be made to see Ray the next day. But when Jude called at High Tor on the Saturday morning, Carole seemed preoccupied. She said she needed to do a big shop, and would Jude mind visiting Ray on her own?

Jude recognized the excuse for what it was. Carole was very organized about her shopping, paying a monthly visit to Sainsbury's for non-perishable essentials. And always mid-week. She would never willingly expose herself to the bigger crowds of weekend shoppers.

But the talk of a 'big shop' was her graceful way of backing off. Carole too knew in her heart of hearts that Jude would be better with someone like Ray than she would. She just couldn't bring herself to say that in so many words.

Jude was grateful for her friend's uncharacteristic moment of self-knowledge, and immediately set off for the address that Sally Monks had given her.

Everything in Fethering was within walking distance, but because the village sprawled almost enough to be called a town, some destinations involved a longer walk than others. So it was with Copsedown Hall, the sheltered accommodation where Ray lived, set on the northern fringe furthest from the sea in the less salubrious part of Fethering known as Downside.

The cars that lined the roads were older and shabbier than those in the smarter parts of the village. Front gardens were ill-maintained, many of them serving as repositories for defunct kitchen equipment. Shreds of plastic bags lay in the gutters. They would have fluttered about had there been any wind, but the hot air lay heavy on the July day.

Copsedown Hall, however, looked smarter than the old council housing that surrounded it. The small block of flats had probably been built in the thirties, but recently modernized. Paint still gleamed on door and window frames. Except for a disabled ramp over-riding the front steps, there was nothing to suggest anything unusual about the residents.

The double glass doors were locked when Jude pushed against them. On the wall was an intercom. She was beginning to wish she had got more information about the place from Sally Monks. Presumably there would be some kind of warden monitoring the activities of the house. It might have helped if she had a name to ask for. Still, too late. She'd have to trust to her instincts and natural charm.

She pressed the intercom button. After a longish pause, a crackly young female voice answered, 'Yes?'

'It's Jude.' She couldn't think of anything else to say.

But the voice at the other end didn't seem to require more. 'I'll come and let you in,' it said. 'The buzzer button's broken.'

Again there was a pause. Then, through the glass, Jude saw someone coming down the stairs. A short chubby girl with a slight limp moved slowly towards her. Dealing with the latch seemed to require a lot of concentration, but when the door was flung open the girl beamed with satisfaction at her achievement.

She had the flattened face characteristic of Down's Syndrome. Her hair was reddish-brown. Through her thick glasses blue eyes were set in distinctive rounded lids. She transferred her beam to the visitor and announced, 'I'm Kelly-Marie.' Her speech was a little hesitant and childlike. It was hard to assess her precise age, though Jude, who had encountered other people with the same condition, would have said late twenties.

'As I say, I'm Jude.'

There was a comfortable silence as they both beamed at each other. Then the girl said, 'Ken's not here. He's never here at weekends.'

Jude assumed she was referring to the social worker who was responsible for keeping an eye on Copsedown Hall. 'It's not Ken I've come to see. I'm looking for Ray.'

'Oh, Ray.' The girl's smile grew bigger. She certainly recognized the name, but she didn't volunteer any other information.

'Is Ray here?' Jude prompted.

'Yes. He came back.'

'Could I see him?'

Kelly-Marie hesitated. 'He's in his flat.'

'Could you show me where it is?'

The girl was silent for a moment. Then she said slowly, 'Ray doesn't like . . . people in his flat.'

'Ah.' Jude tried another big smile. Kelly-Marie smiled back.

But she didn't move. She was still inside the door, and Jude outside.

'Do you think Ray might see me in one of the communal rooms?'

Kelly-Marie considered the proposition. At length she conceded that he might.

'Well, would you mind asking him if he'd come down to see me?' Jude was assuming that all the flats were up the stairs down which Kelly-Marie had come.

After further deliberation, the decision was made. 'Yes.' She drew back to let Jude into the hall and turned towards the stairs.

'Where shall I go?'

This answer again required thought. 'Do you want to see Ray on his own?'

'It would be better, yes.'

'Well, there'll be people in the television room.' Kelly-Marie giggled and said in a child's version of a woman-of-the-world manner, 'Men and their sport.' She limped across to open a door. 'Be better in the kitchen.'

As Jude walked past her, the girl giggled again and asked, rather daringly, 'Are you Ray's girlfriend?'

'Just a friend.' It was a lie, but a fairly white one.

'I'll see if he'll come down.' And Kelly-Marie crossed slowly towards the stairs.

The kitchen in which Jude found herself was large. The size of the range, the number of fridges and the extent of the cupboard space suggested that this was where all the cooking in Copsedown Hall was done. The residents did not have their own kitchens in their flats. Whether this was because they could not be trusted to cook unsupervised Jude did not know, but she suspected that it might be the case.

Stuck on the fridge doors were handwritten names on green

fluorescent labels. Four fridges, two names on each, suggesting that Copsedown Hall contained eight residents, presumably each in a different self-contained flat. Kelly-Marie shared her fridge with another girl. Ray shared his with someone called 'Viggo'.

Whoever did the cooking, there was clearly a strict tidiness regime enforced. The draining boards were bare, and every surface gleamed. There were two large bins, sternly marked FOR RECYCLING and NOT FOR RECYCLING. The functional, institutional space gave Jude the feeling of an army kitchen. Not that she'd ever seen an army kitchen except on film or television.

The table at which she sat was surrounded by eight chairs, suggesting that at least sometimes the residents ate communally. She waited nearly five minutes before Ray appeared in the doorway.

CHAPTER NINE

He was slight and very short, not much more than five foot. He couldn't have been much use at the Crown and Anchor when it came to heavy lifting, but then Jude had already decided that Ted Crisp's support for the man was pure—if embarrassed— philanthropy. It was difficult to estimate Ray's age. There was a boyishness about his reddish hair, but the pale skin of his face was etched with a tracery of deep lines. And his eyes looked older than the rest of his body. Older and slightly disengaged. It was from the eyes that one might deduce that he had mental problems.

He wore grubby black jeans and a thin green cotton blouson, over a T-shirt for a tour of some female singer Jude didn't recognize. His expression was cautious, but not unwelcoming.

'Hello, I'm Jude.'

'That's what Kelly-Marie said you was.' He lingered in the doorway, not yet certain about entering the kitchen. 'She also said,' he went on, 'that you was my girlfriend. But I know that's not true. Because if I had a girlfriend, I'd have seen her before, and I don't think I've ever seen you before.'

He spoke this long speech cautiously, as though he were speaking in a language that was unfamiliar to him.

'You might have seen me in the street,' Jude suggested. 'I do live in Fethering.'

Ray considered this proposition for a moment, then advanced a little way into the room. 'Kelly-Marie didn't really think you was my girlfriend. She was joking. She makes lots of jokes at me.' But he spoke without rancour. And a broad smile spread across his face, completely transforming his appearance. Smiling seemed to come naturally to him. It was expressing other moods that he found difficult.

He seemed by now to have made the decision that Jude did not represent a threat, so he moved right into the room and put his hand on the back of the chair next to hers. 'Would you like tea or coffee? I can make tea or coffee,' he added with a vestige of pride in his voice. He moved towards the fridge he shared with Viggo.

'Are you having some?'

Her question prompted another moment of deliberation before Ray decided that he wasn't.

'Then I won't bother. Do please sit down.'

He did as he was told, seeming almost relieved that someone was making a decision for him. He sat quietly, not looking at Jude, just straight ahead, the smile still playing around the corners of his lips. The silence, the lack of explanation for Jude's appearance, did not seem to worry him.

She wondered whether his response would be equally calm when she mentioned the poisoning at the Crown and Anchor. Still, that was why she had come to see him. No point in beating around the bush. 'Ray,' she began, 'I'm a friend of Ted Crisp's.'

'He's a nice man.' Ray nodded vigorously to emphasize the point. 'A nice man.' His smile grew broader.

'Yes. And I gather you sometimes help him at the pub . . .'

Another enthusiastic nod. 'He lets me. People think I can't do things. Ted Crisp thinks I can.'

'And you were helping at the Crown and Anchor on Monday?'

Only after he had keenly agreed to this did a slight caution come into his vague eyes. 'Yes, on Monday,' he agreed with a little less confidence.

'But you haven't been back there since?'

'No.'

'Are you going to go back?'

'Well, I don't know . . .' Then, unexpectedly, the wide smile returned. 'I'll have to be there on Sunday.'

'Why?'

'They've got this man from the telly there on Sunday.'

'Dan Poke.'

'Yes, I'll have to see him. I've only seen two people from off the telly before. One was Lyra Mackenzie.'

He spoke the name with such reverence that Jude tried to avoid showing it meant nothing to her. But she must have failed, because Ray felt he had to explain. He pulled back the sides of his blouson to reveal the picture on his T-shirt. Jude still didn't recognize the singer. 'You know, from *The X Factor.*'

'Ah. Right.' She knew her pretence at familiarity was pretty unconvincing, but Ray didn't seem to notice. 'She did a concert at the Pavilion Theatre in Worthing. I waited round the back afterwards to get her autograph.'

'And did you get it?'

'Yes. She signed my programme.' Enthusiastically he rose from his seat. 'It's up in my room. Would you like to see it?'

Jude managed to assure him that, impressed though she was by his trophy, she didn't actually need visual proof of its existence. He sank back into his chair, only momentarily disconsolate. 'I must get Dan Poke's autograph on Sunday. He'll be the third person I've seen off the telly.' The thought reassured him.

'So who was the second one?' asked Jude. 'You know, after Lyra . . . um . . . ?' She couldn't remember the surname.

'He was a footballer.' His voice dropped to a level of suitable awe. 'I once saw Gary Lineker at Brighton Station. I didn't say anything to him. He didn't see me. But it was him. From off

71

the telly.' He looked at his watch.

'Are you worried about your football this afternoon?' asked Jude.

'Yes, I like to see everything from twelve o'clock. Soccer Saturday starts on Sky at twelve o'clock.'

'Don't worry. You've got plenty of time. I'll be gone long before then.'

'Yes.' He seemed reassured, but perhaps a little less relaxed than he had been. The smile was not quite as broad.

Jude pressed on. 'But you haven't been back to the Crown and Anchor since Monday?' He shook his head. 'Why?'

Ray seemed at a loss to explain this fact, but then a thought came to him. 'My mother. I've been to see my mum.'

'How is she?' asked Jude gently.

'She's old, very old.' He seemed to find the idea funny. 'She can hardly move now. She's very old.' He smiled again.

'Do you see her often?'

Ray shrugged. 'Sometimes.'

'Do you see her when you're happy or when you're unhappy?'

Jude's voice was now very soft, soft and warm, the voice of a therapist. And it worked, soothing the troubled man into security.

'I see my mum when I'm unhappy.'

'And she makes you feel better?'

The question seemed genuinely to puzzle him. 'I don't know. When I see her there aren't other people there. Just me and her. Not other people wanting things.'

'What kind of things?'

'Wanting me to say things. Asking me things. Telling me off for things.'

'Does Ted Crisp ever tell you off for things?'

'He did on Monday.'

'What did he tell you off about?'

'He was in a bad mood.'

'Was this in the morning or the afternoon?'

'In the afternoon.'

'Ray, you know what happened at lunchtime on Monday, don't you?'

'People were sick,' he said quietly.

'Yes. And it was after that that Ted was cross with you?' He nodded. 'Can you remember what he said?' The nod turned to a shake of the head. 'He just shouted.' The memory was painful.

'Did he shout at you? Or at everyone?'

'At everyone. But then he shouted at me.'

'And you really can't remember what he said?'

This time the headshake was very firm. 'When people shout at me, often I get confused. I don't want to hear what they're saying. I want to shut my ears. I just want them to go away!'

He was reliving the kind of painful experience he described. His hands had risen involuntarily to cover his ears. Jude knew he was near to panic, the kind of panic which sent him back to his mother's. She would need all of her therapeutic skill to keep him in the kitchen with her.

Very gently, she asked, 'Has Ted Crisp ever shouted at you before?'

The headshake was small, but definite. Into Jude's mind came the thought that perhaps Ted's action had been deliberate. In the aftermath of Monday's poisoning, the landlord would undoubtedly have been furious, but given the way he had nurtured and helped Ray, he would have been unlikely to vent his anger on him. So perhaps Ted had shouted because he knew such behaviour would send Ray scurrying off to his mother. And keep him off the scene for any ensuing Health and Safety inspection. Ted Crisp's uncharacteristic shouting could have been an act of protection. Which, if it were the case, could well mean that he suspected Ray did have some involvement in the sabotage at the Crown and Anchor.

Now Jude had to be doubly careful. 'You know it was the scallops that caused the food poisoning last Monday, don't you?'

'Yes. It couldn't be prevented.'

This seemed a very odd response to her question. 'What exactly do you mean, Ray?'

'Well, scallops are seafood . . .'

'Yes.'

'. . . and seafood shouldn't be left out in the hot weather.' He sounded as though he were parroting something he had been told.

'No, I agree. It can go off very quickly.'

'Which the scallops must have done. They must have gone off. Got poisoned by flies landing on them or . . .' he ran out of steam '. . . something like that.'

'Except,' Jude reasoned, 'that the scallops last Monday had only been delivered that morning. Ed Pollack took the delivery and signed for them.'

'But they were the bad ones.'

'They can't have been. They'd come directly from the supplier. In a refrigerated delivery van.'

'They were the bad ones,' Ray insisted.

'I don't understand what you're saying.'

For the first time in their conversation Ray became furtive. He looked uneasily through the kitchen door towards the hall, as though he expected someone might be eavesdropping. Then, lowering his voice, he said, 'Someone was trying to poison the people in the Crown and Anchor.'

'Yes, that's rather what I was thinking.'

'But I should have stopped that happening.'

'*You* should have stopped that happening?'

'Yes. By taking away the bad scallops and putting the good ones in the fridge.'

Jude didn't let the excitement she was feeling show in her voice, as she asked, 'Are you saying that you took out the tray of scallops that Ed had put in the fridge and replaced them with another tray?'

'Yes.' The bewilderment grew in Ray's face, as he mumbled, 'It shouldn't have happened. What I did should have stopped the poisoning. But it didn't.' He looked almost tearful. 'And Ted shouted at me.'

'Ray . . .' said Jude very softly, 'who told you to change the trays of scallops around?'

Alarmed, he looked directly into her eyes for the first time. 'It wasn't Ted!' His voice was suddenly loud.

'I never thought it was Ted.'

'No. Ted didn't know about the people going to be poisoned.'

'But someone else did?'

He nodded. 'And they told me I could stop it happening by changing the trays round. I could save Ted from getting into trouble.'

'Who told you that, Ray?'

He opened his mouth to speak, but was distracted by the sound of another door opening in the hall. He turned, and Jude looked up to see the kitchen doorway filled by the frame of a large man in jeans and a Black Sabbath T-shirt. In spite of the heat he also wore a black leather jacket, rubbed grey at the seams. He had a dark beard and hair combed greasily back; in his nose there was a silver stud. His eyes were as black as two olives.

'Football's on, Ray,' he announced. The words sounded too big for his mouth.

Ray had risen to his feet the moment he saw the man. His expression showed respect with a strong undercurrent of fear.

'But the football doesn't start till twelve,' said Jude desperately.

'There's other stuff on earlier.'

The man made no pretence to be addressing her, and Ray responded to his cue. 'Yes, Viggo.' And without a word or a look back to Jude, he scuttled across the hall to the open door of the television room.

Viggo didn't say anything more. Ignoring Jude's questions and entreaties, he watched her rise from the table and cross to the front door. Immediately she had passed through, he slammed it shut behind her, and followed his friend to watch the football build-up.

Jude's excitement at getting so close to the truth was replaced by total frustration. And also, from her short encounter with Viggo, a sense of menace.

CHAPTER TEN

On the Saturday night the Crown and Anchor again did good business. Though again it probably wasn't the kind of business Ted Crisp was looking for. Carole and Jude didn't go to the pub, but from their bedrooms they both heard the late-night roaring procession of bikes up Fethering High Street. Greville Tilbrook's task of signature-gathering must have been getting easier by the minute.

And still the Sabbath-breaking Dan Poke evening lay ahead.

The event was billed to start at eight o'clock, but when Carole and Jude arrived just before seven-thirty, the Crown and Anchor already seemed full to the gunwales. A large heavy-drinking crowd had spilled out into the garden area and car park. If all of them were planning to watch the show, the pub threatened to burst at the seams.

Judging from the people standing outside, the presence of Dan Poke had certainly brought out a mixed clientele. A few aged pub regulars had been drawn by curiosity to witness their local's new venture. There were also a surprising number of couples in their forties, whom Carole and Jude recognized from the streets of Fethering, but whom they'd never seen before in the Crown and Anchor. A lot of really young people were there too, talking loudly and swigging from beer bottles. They were dressed as for a night's clubbing, the girls revealing acres of firm brown flesh, the boys in voluminous shorts and sleeveless T-shirts.

The bikers, who had shattered the evening calm of Fethering for the last two nights, were also present in numbers. In spite of their chain-bedecked leather uniforms, close to they looked pretty harmless, but still incongruous in a place like the Crown and Anchor.

There was one surprise component in the Sunday evening crowd. At the entrance to the car park, some distance from the rest, stood Greville Tilbrook and three of his lady acolytes. In spite of the warmth of the evening they were all wearing suits, rather old-fashioned Sunday best. What was more, they carried banners. KEEP THE LORD'S DAY FOR THE LORD, NO FILTH IN FETHERING, BATTLE AGAINST BLASPHEMY and, rather incongruously, KEEP OUR STREETS CLEAN.

As he saw Carole and Jude approaching, Greville Tilbrook favoured them with a thin smile. 'Good evening, ladies,' he said. 'It's still not too late to change your minds.'

'About what?' asked Jude, deliberately obtuse.

'About attending the blasphemous performance in the Crown and Anchor tonight.'

'How do you know it's blasphemous?'

At that moment a girl walked past them. On the black T-shirt across her ample bosom was printed one of Dan Poke's catchphrases: FANCY A POKE?

Furious, almost losing control of himself, Greville Tilbrook spluttered and pointed to the slogan. 'Look, does that answer your question? What could be more blasphemous than wearing that slogan on the day that is dedicated to the Lord? People who behave in such an offensive way are insulting Almighty God!'

'It seems to me,' Jude responded mildly, 'that you have a very idiosyncratic definition of "blasphemy". In what way do the words "Fancy a Poke?" have anything to do with God?'

'This is the Lord's day and the Lord should be afforded the respect that is his due! T-shirts of that kind are an abomination and those who wear them should be cast into the outer darkness! Along with this evil man who calls himself a comedian!'

He was almost manic now in his denunciation. His group of geriatric cheerleaders looked very excited. They clearly loved seeing their idol in passionate mode.

'Excuse me, Mr Tilbrook,' said Carole, 'but have you ever seen Dan Poke perform, either live or on television?'

He seemed shocked by the suggestion. 'No, of course I haven't.'

'Don't you think your argument might have more validity if you had actually seen the performance you are protesting against?'

Now it was the turn of his female acolytes to look shocked. Also distressed that their crusading hero should be taken to task in this way. One, the youngest of the three, a fluttery woman in her early sixties dressed in Black Watch tartan, looked positively mortified.

But they needn't have worried. Greville Tilbrook could be relied on to come up with the argument wielded by opponents of free speech down many centuries. 'I don't have to immerse myself in filth to know that it's filth!'

'Possibly not immerse yourself,' suggested Jude, 'but maybe just dip a toe in. At least then you would have some knowledge of the subject you're talking about.'

'I will not watch a so-called entertainment whose only purpose is to deprave and corrupt!' The eyelashes of his female acolytes fluttered. They loved it when he talked like that. He was magnificent. The eyes of the one in Black Watch tartan narrowed in ecstasy.

'You must be very insecure about the strength of your own

personality,' observed Carole Seddon, 'if you're worried that watching a stand-up comedian is going to corrupt and deprave you.'

And she and Jude moved magisterially towards the door of the Crown and Anchor.

Inside, the pub already seemed almost full to capacity. Some customers were crowded round a table selling Dan Poke merchandise, T-shirts, DVDs, books and so on. But most were gathered at the bar. The crowd through which Jude elbowed her way was four-deep. Ted, Zosia and three extra girls brought in for the evening were rushed off their feet. Catching Jude's eye, Zosia quickly produced two large Chilean Chardonnays and mimed, 'Pay later.'

'Oy, come on, darling! Get your Polish ass over here! I want some service!' The speaker, pressed close against Jude, was a tall man whom she had noticed at the centre of the bikers' group. But he wasn't wearing their leather livery. He had on khaki combat trousers, heavy Caterpillar boots and a camouflage-pattern sleeveless T-shirt. He was surrounded in the strong, animal scent of a hot day's sweat. The man's hair was shaved almost to baldness, one side of his face was heavily scarred, and the hand with which he rapped the counter had two and a half fingers missing. As Jude moved away from the bar, he turned suddenly towards her. His hazel eyes were already glazed with alcohol, or maybe drugs. 'Weren't queue-jumping, were you, *darling?*' His tone bleached all warmth out of the word.

'No, no, just getting a drink.' The man gave her an evil look for a moment, then turned back to continue shouting at Zosia for service.

Jude found Carole still marooned in the middle of the room, looking round for a place to sit. All of the dining alcoves appeared to be full, at least all of the alcoves that would get a view of the entertainment. A small black-painted stage had been set up at the far end of the bar. Hired spotlights, currently switched off, but focused on the area, left no one in any doubt that that was where Dan Poke would be doing his act.

Fortunately, just as they were looking for a seat, a short man appeared from the kitchen, weaving his way through the crowd with a pile of chairs held up in front of him. Only when he put them down could Jude see his face and recognize Ray. He was wearing a black T-shirt, so new its packing creases were still visible. On its front was printed the inevitable catch-phrase: FANCY A POKE? Clearly, as with Lyra Mackenzie, he liked buying merchandise connected with his idols.

'Ray, can we grab a couple of those?' asked Jude, lifting two of the chairs off the pile.

She desperately wanted to talk further to him, but Ray looked busy and harassed. 'Got to get some more chairs,' he said, on his way to the kitchen. Then he turned back. 'Could you save a seat for me, and all? I want to have a good view of Dan Poke.' His voice dropped as he confided to Jude, 'He's off the telly. I'm going round the back to get his autograph after.'

Jude appropriated a third chair before they were all snatched up. She and Carole sat down and placed Carole's handbag firmly on the empty one. Jude grinned. 'That's a bit of luck, getting him sitting next to us.'

'You going to pick up where you left off with him yesterday?'

'Do my best. Have to choose my moment, though. I think this could be rather a rowdy occasion for intimate interrogation.'

She was right. The noise level was by now very high. There was a buzz in the Crown and Anchor of something about to happen. The customers from outside were pressing in, squeezing up against each other. The room was steamy with odours of sweat and beer. Thank God, both women thought, smoking was no longer allowed in pubs.

Thank God, too, that they'd been lucky enough to get seats. It was a real problem hanging on to the one they'd saved for Ray. People kept coming up and asking if it was taken. One man unceremoniously removed Carole's handbag and was only just prevented from plonking down his large backside. Eventually Jude just raised her legs and laid them across the chair.

Carole looked around, still surprised to see so many faces in the Crown and Anchor that she didn't recognize. There were a couple, though, that she had seen before. One was the tall man she'd recently observed getting into his BMW in the pub car park. Black hair was still swept back from his chubby face, and he had thick-rimmed glasses like the young Michael Caine. Maybe as a concession to the weekend, he wore no jacket, but he still contrived to look as though he was wearing a suit. He sat at a table with a group of equally well-tailored young men. They were all drinking Belgian beers from the bottle. The atmosphere amongst them was raucous, but the tall man seemed removed from the action, observing, not missing anything that was going on.

Again, he looked very familiar, but again, frustratingly, Carole couldn't recall the context in which they had previously met.

The other person Carole recognized was over by the bar. Ted Crisp's ex-wife Sylvia had taken up position on a tall stool near the stage area. She was dressed in tight jeans and a skimpy white blouse, showing a deep cleavage and distinct signs of intoxication. The way she draped herself over the tall man on an adjacent stool looked proprietorial, but whether he was a long-term partner or that evening's pick-up Carole could not guess. He wore black leather jeans and had a black leather jacket slung over his T-shirted shoulder, so maybe he was one of the bikers.

Ray scuttled out of the kitchen and claimed his seat next to Jude. He was sweating heavily and jittery with excitement. 'They're going to start,' he said, 'any minute. I actually saw Dan

Poke back in the kitchen there. He's on the telly. I'm going round to get his autograph later.'

He looked up as a huge figure in black leather elbowed his way through the crowd to stand behind him. Jude recognized Viggo from Copsedown Hall. Though the man moved with a swagger, his pose didn't look quite convincing. He lacked the raucous ease of the other bikers. None of them took any notice of him. He was not part of their gang. But his presence could still impress—or possibly frighten—Ray, who stopped talking and kept looking up towards his housemate, as if searching for approval.

Viggo, like most of the men in the pub, had a pint in his hand. He raised it in a toasting gesture towards the scarred man, who was now in the centre of the group of bikers, but he received no acknowledgement. Viggo looked momentarily hurt by the lack of reaction.

Carole could see Zosia worming her way through the churning crowd—and a barrage of sexist banter—towards the light controls. Though the spotlights were on a dimmer, the pub's ordinary lighting could only be snapped off. But when Zosia pulled the switches, the blackout was far from complete. It was one of those July evenings that never got properly dark. The crowd, aware of the lighting change, shouted and barracked as they tried to nestle themselves into slightly more comfortable watching positions, craning towards the stage area.

Slowly Zosia faded up the spotlights to reveal Ted Crisp.

CHAPTER ELEVEN

The landlord of the Crown and Anchor was sweating heavily, no surprise perhaps in a crammed-full pub on a July evening, but to Carole the sheen on his forehead looked more like nerves. And when he spoke, it was with nothing like his usual fluency. He seemed inhibited by the presence of his more successful former colleague. Or maybe of his ex-wife and the man she was nuzzling?

'Good evening,' Ted began, 'and welcome, all of you, to the Crown and Anchor, Fethering, for a very special evening. Yes, tonight is the very first Crown and Anchor Comedy Night!'

'It's not the first! Bloody place has always been a joke!' shouted a heckler whom Ted couldn't identify because of the lights in his eyes. His bearded jaw set firm as he continued, 'And I'm very lucky to have here, to entertain us this evening, someone I used to work with back in my days as a stand-up comic. Back then they used to say about me that I was . . .' He spoke the words as a set-up to a joke, but then seemed to lose his nerve and trickled away into confusion. 'Er, that is to say . . . anyway, the bloke I'm going to introduce has come a long way from those early days when . . . he, um, he's done a lot of television, he's—'

'Oh, get on with it, for God's sake!' a voice called out from the darkness somewhere behind the bar. 'We haven't got all bloody night!'

The audience roared their appreciative recognition of Dan

Poke's distinctive tones. Ted Crisp looked even more wretchedly uncomfortable. Carole felt an uncharacteristic urge to rush across the room and give him a big hug.

'Yeah, anyway,' Ted stuttered on, 'he's now a big star on the television, he gets paid for single gigs more than most of us earn in a year, but he's agreed to be here tonight, just for the price of his travel expenses.'

'Don't forget the merchandising!' Dan Poke's voice bellowed again, to the audience's delight.

'Ah, no, sorry,' Ted Crisp floundered. 'You can buy lots of Dan Poke merchandise, if you want to. Badges, T-shirts, CDs, DVDs . . . so if any of you—'

'Don't forget the book!' came the prompt from its author.

'Yes, of course. Not forgetting Dan's book. I don't know if you call it an autobiography, but it had massive sales a few Christmases back. And the book's called—inevitably—*A Poke in the Eye!* So, as I say, you'll be able to buy all that stuff at the table over there. And in fact, halfway through Dan's set there'll be a break to give you an opportunity to charge up your glasses—and also buy some of the merchandise. So . . .' Ted Crisp looked off into the murk. 'Anything else I've forgotten, Dan?'

'No just introduce me and get off the bloody stage!'

The audience was rendered ecstatic by this charming shaft of wit, and the humiliated landlord continued, 'Right . . . Ladies and gentlemen, will you give a big hand for one of the original naughty boys of stand-up comedy—Mr . . . Dan . . . Poke!'

Ted Crisp scuttled back into the darkness like a rabbit relieved to escape the headlights, and Dan Poke slowly moved into the glare. His lip curled into his trademark sneer, and the audience erupted into screams of ecstatic recognition. At the back of the crowd, caught up in the communal excitement, Zosia had her mobile phone to her eye in photographic mode. She may not have known who Dan Poke was before that evening, but she wasn't going to miss getting a shot of him. Round the room other mobiles flashed.

Jude looked at Ray and saw the gleam of fanatical devotion in his eyes. He grinned at her and said in awed tones, 'Dan Poke. Dan Poke from off the telly.'

The comedian swept his hands slowly apart as if smoothing down a duvet and the crowd was obediently silent. 'Don't waste it, don't waste it. I don't want you lot to peak too early. It's a bad thing, peaking too early . . . as many of my girlfriends have told me. Quite a common bloke's problem, actually. We think about it so much of the time, that when we actually get to the point we're more than ready. Tend to jump the gun. Women complain men don't do foreplay—it's only because we've already done it in our heads so many times before we even meet the girl.' He grinned, so that no one should miss any of the innuendos.

'Anyway, enough about masculine inadequacy. And, talking of masculine inadequacy, you may have gathered from that crap introduction I was given by Ted Crisp that I am Dan Poke. Poke by name . . .' he leered '. . . and if any of you fit young chicks'd like to put it to the test by coming round the back afterwards you'll find out I'm also Poke by nature. So anyone . . .' he timed the pause expertly ' ". . . Fancy a Poke"?'

The catchphrase brought in its predictable harvest of delirious recognition. Jude, as the recipient of one of his come-on cards, wondered whether he did actually get many offers of sex backstage after gigs. Comedy had been described as 'the new rock 'n' roll', so maybe it had its groupies too.

As the laughter and applause began to die, the comedian went on, 'It's no fun, you know, being born with a name that's a four-letter word.' His face took on an expression of piety. 'Now I hope nobody out here is offended by four-letter words . . .'

Then looked round at his audience in dismay and said, 'Oh, fuck!' The younger and more drunken contingent gave an automatic laugh at the word. The older Crown and Anchor regulars were silent.

Carole and Jude exchanged looks. Carole was trying not to look shocked, but she couldn't help herself looking disapproving. Jude, who wasn't particularly bothered by the language, found herself musing on the development of comedy, and how endlessly it could regenerate itself. The 'alternative' comedians of the nineteen seventies, though seeming revolutionary with their political stances, their four-letter words and their opening-up of taboo subject matter, were in a direct line of descent from the music-hall comics they so derided. When young, many of that new wave had studiously removed the traditional element of charm from their acts, but with age most of them softened into lovable quiz-show hosts. Someone like Dan Poke traded on his reputation as an *enfant terrible,* in just the same way that Max Miller had done for an earlier generation. Any affront that he caused was now a very safe kind of affront.

Jude recognized exactly the kind of man Dan Poke was, brash on the exterior, a mass of anxieties and paranoia inside. She had once had a long relationship with a comedian. It had been the most dispiriting part of what had been generally speaking an upbeat life.

'Actually,' the comedian went on, 'I was talking to my old mate Ted Crisp about this gig earlier this evening, and he asked me if I could moderate my language for the fine folk of Fethering. He said, "Dan, Dan, cut out all the four-letter words." I said to him, "Ted, if I cut out all the four-letter words, I won't have any fucking act left!" ' Another knee-jerk laugh from the young.

'You all know Ted Crisp, don't you? He's the guy who gave

me that crap introduction—you know, looks like a brush that's been down the toilet a few times too often. Last time I saw something that furry round the edges, it was bit of cheese I'd left in the fridge for a month.

'I've known Ted since we were on the stand-up circuit together. He saw the light, mind you, and gave it up—good thing too. God, you think my act's crap—you should have heard Ted's. There've been funnier lines than his queuing up in chapels of rest.

'So Ted became a publican—here in the Crown and Anchor, in Fethering—the Jewel of the Costa Geriatrica. Do you know, there's only one day of the week when you can tell if a resident of Fethering is alive. Thursday—yeah, some of them move then. And if one doesn't go and collect his pension, then you know he's snuffed it.

'Still, Ted's done wonders with this pub. He's made it one of the premier tourist destinations on the south coast—' Dan Poke paused and grinned wickedly—'. . . for people who want to get food poisoning . . .'

Carole and Jude glanced nervously across to the landlord. He looked as if he'd been slapped in the face.

'Actually,' Dan Poke continued, 'I haven't had food poisoning for a long time—not since I last had a meal cooked by Ted Crisp, as it happens. Ooh, how embarrassing that was. 'Cause I got lucky that night and I got this girl in bed with me . . . like I said, ladies, Poke by name and . . . Anyway, I was at it with this chick and suddenly . . . the food poisoning hit me! Honestly, I didn't know whether I was coming or going!

'Tell you, it's hard to maintain the old romantic atmosphere when you've got this great spout of shit coming out your arse. Also it was in her bed. Dead embarrassing. I always like to feel I've left my mark on a woman, but not like that. I met the same girl again at a club quite recently. I said, "Do you remember me?" She said, "Oh yes. I may not be any good with names, but I never forget faeces!" '

This joke was a bit too subtle for the younger audience. The older ones, who got it, didn't laugh. But that didn't slow down the irrepressible Dan Poke. He was into his riff about the poisoned scallops, and nothing was going to deflect him from it. 'Nasty business, food poisoning, though, isn't it? Like a seriously unfunny version of a woman-in-bed-with-two-men sandwich—getting it both ends. The shits and the vomiting. You have to be a bloody contortionist to sit on the lav and bend over it at the same time!

'Ooh—bit of advice about vomiting. Serious bit—"author's message".' He paused and took on an expression of mockseriousness. ' "Never throw up into the wind . . ." though, mind you, it *is* a way of getting your own back!

'Anyway, enough about food poisoning . . .' Thank God, thought Carole and Jude. But, of course, he couldn't leave it there. 'Food poisoning—which is of course the Crown and Anchor's signature dish—followed of course by a signature dash to the loo!' Under his beard Ted Crisp's face was contorted with fury.

Dan Poke looked around at his audience as if for the first time. 'So who've we got in tonight? Well, I know we've got some people from Fethering, I can recognize them by that look on their faces—it's called *rigor mortis*. You know how you can tell the corpse from the guests at a Fethering funeral? The answer is: you can't.

'And I know we've got some people from Portsmouth in tonight.' His words were greeted by a raucous roar from the leather-clad brigade. 'Bloody Middy crowd. I used to drink there. Used to be very rough—tell you, the tarts were so dirty they didn't carry condoms for their punters—just masks. And God knows what the landlord did to the beer, but you'd get waterlogged there before you got drunk.'

The bikers continued to guffaw as the comedian went on. 'Ah. Portsmouth. Happy times. You know, I lost my virginity in Portsmouth . . . Well, I say "lost it"—I think, being Portsmouth, it got nicked. Of course, Portsmouth is a *naval* town. Funny word, isn't it? When you hear it, you think of belly buttons. Mind you, I've never heard Portsmouth described as the *navel* of the world . . . though I have heard it described as the *arsehole* of the world!' Those members of the audience for whom rude words didn't need to have jokes attached roared their appreciation. 'Actually, that's not my view, it was said to me by some git I met at a gig in Portsmouth. He said, "Portsmouth is the arsehole of the world." I said to him, "Oh yes, and are you just passing through?" '

It took some of the crowd a moment or two to get that one, but when they did, they screamed and burst into applause. Jude, who'd heard the line many times before, reflected again on comedy as the perfect examplar of recycling. No joke was too old to be pressed into service. Dusted down, freshened up with a topical reference, given extra punch by a four-letter word, and there was still going to be someone out there who hadn't heard it before. Anyway, for fans of comedy, originality is often less important than familiarity. Many school playgrounds have echoed to bad impersonations and lines from *The Goon Show, Monty Python, Blackadder, The Office* or whatever the hit of the moment happened to be. And the people who buy all those comedy CDs and DVDs clearly have a taste for endlessly re-watching their favourites.

So Jude wasn't at all surprised when at one point in his set, Dan Poke did a riff on dogs that could have been delivered by any comedian of the past fifty years—and probably longer. 'I had a dog once,' he began. 'Not a complete dog, you understand. No, he'd been neutered. Oh, come on, I believe in calling a spayed a spayed. And I took my dog for a walk in the woods—stopped between four trees. He was so confused he didn't have a leg to stand on. But my dog liked walks—nothing he enjoyed better than going for a tramp in the woods. Made all the tramps bloody furious, though.'

And so Dan Poke's gig at the Crown and Anchor, Fethering, continued.

CHAPTER TWELVE

'Any time I can help out an old mate,' said Dan Poke unctu-
ously, thrusting out his hand to Ted through the back window
of the limousine, 'you know I'm more than happy to.'

'Help out?' thought Carole, who was standing defensively
close behind the landlord in the milling crowd. 'Stitch up',
more like. She looked around for Jude, but they'd got separated
in the mass of sweating bodies.

Ted looked very uncomfortable as he took the proffered hand.
'No, it's been great, Dan. Can't thank you enough. We'll meet
up again soon for a relaxed beer, eh?'

The comedian detached his hand with a dismissive, 'Sure,
sure.'

'Hard to get at you through all your panting fans.' The new
voice belonged to the tall man who was so infuriatingly familiar
to Carole.

Dan Poke grinned. 'Saw you in the audience, William, but
didn't get a chance to say anything.' At least she now had a first
name for him.

The man called William chuckled. 'Having heard what you
said about other people, I think I got off lightly.' The line seemed
so obviously a reference to Ted that the landlord looked even
more wretched.

'Anyway, great show, as ever,' the tall man continued, oozing
automatic bonhomie. 'I must be on my way, but we'll be in
touch. Eh?' And he melted away towards his pale blue BMW.

92

'I'd better get moving too.' Dan Poke leaned forward and tapped his driver on the shoulder. 'Let's get out of this shithole. And be careful you don't run over any screaming fans on the way out. That really would be bad publicity.' He grinned his crooked grin back at Ted. 'Almost as bad as everyone getting food poisoning.' And the limousine's electric window moved upwards as the car glided gently away from the Crown and Anchor.

Ted Crisp couldn't hold in his feelings any longer. 'Bastard!' he whispered on a long breath of pain. 'Bastard!'

'I agree,' said Jude, who had caught up with them through the milling throng, 'but look on the bright side.' She indicated the huge crowd, who still seemed unwilling to make their way home. None of the motorbikes in the car park had moved. It was as if their owners were biding their time until the moment of maximum annoyance for the residents of Fethering. 'At least you'll have made some money, Ted, from all this lot.'

'Oh yes?' he asked cynically. 'I don't think there'll be much left when I've paid off Dan.'

'But I thought he was doing the show for nothing,' Carole objected.

'Oh yes, the *show*. No, the generous-hearted Dan Poke, television's Mr Lovable, didn't ask for any fee. Just expenses . . .'

Jude caught on to the implication of this before Carole did. 'You mean, the limousine?'

Ted Crisp nodded savagely and turned towards her. Jude got a blast of Famous Grouse into her face. Oh no, had he tried to anaesthetize his humiliation with whisky? 'Yes' said Ted. 'Mind you, the limousine's only taking him to Brighton, where he's booked in overnight at the Hotel Du Vin—apparently he's got some woman set up there—and then the limousine will take him tomorrow morning back up to his pad in London. All that on expenses.'

'But how much is it all going to cost?' asked Carole, appalled.

'Certainly more than I'll get for all the pints I've pulled this evening. And, of course, he's cleaned up on selling all his books and DVDs and other tat. No, our Mr Poke is a very smooth operator.'

It was not Carole Seddon's custom to use strong language, but she couldn't help herself from echoing Ted's 'Bastard!'

They might have got further into the perfidious economics of charity work, but they were interrupted by the sound of a beer bottle smashing. Before they had had time to react, there was another smash and a great welling of feral shouting from the crowd. A fight had started. The bikers were pushing to get as near as possible to the action, and the Fethering residents as far away. They bumped into each other and more drunken blows were thrown. The steamy heaviness of the July day had erupted into full-scale violence.

'God, this is all I bloody need!' said Ted Crisp, before throwing himself into the mêlée. His intention was to separate the combatants, but the tensions of the day—not to mention the large amounts of Famous Grouse he had ingested—meant that he swung his fists as ferociously as any of them.

'No,' murmured Carole. 'If Ted gets himself arrested for being in a fight, he's finished.'

It was almost impossible to see what was going on. The outside coach lamps of the Crown and Anchor had been smashed as soon as the violence started, and into the strips of light thrown out by the open doors heaving masses of bodies swayed and rushed to and fro, arms, beer bottles and chairlegs flying. Windows had been smashed, window-boxes ripped from their fittings and hurled about. Shouting, grunting filled the air. Shafts of light revealed splashes of blood on summer T-shirts. Knives had been drawn.

Jude looked around, wondering whether the scarred man or Viggo had initiated the violence, but she could see no sign of either of them in the struggling mêlée. Like all fights, this one was ugly and incompetent, but that didn't stop people from getting hurt.

Even before the whine of a police siren was heard, Jude had pulled her neighbour by the hand and whispered urgently, 'Come on. Let's get the hell out of here!'

'But Ted . . .' Carole murmured pitifully. 'Ted . . .'

Jude dragged her away. By now the police Panda was in the car park, blue lights strobing across the chaos. 'Round the back way,' hissed Jude. As they moved, they heard the first roar of a motorbike engine starting. The leather-clad brigade weren't planning to stay to be interviewed by the police. Other engines roared and throbbed in the night air.

It was a momentary shock to realize that the motorbikes were coming in their direction. Rather than risking being stopped at the entrance to the Crown and Anchor car park, the bikers were going to make good their getaway across the dunes. Carole and Jude shrank against the back of the pub as the cavalcade thundered past. Incongruously, in their midst, also making its off-road escape, was a silver Smart car. Its tiny bubble of a body bounced dangerously on the uneven surface as it surged towards the freedom of the coast road.

From somewhere on the seaward side of the pub came the sound of running footsteps departing across the shingle at the top of the beach.

The door to the kitchen was open, letting out a very white rectangle of light on to the rough dune grass. Approaching, Carole and Jude saw there was someone standing in the doorway. As he turned to rush inside, they saw the anguish on Ed Pollack's face. And the blood spattered down the front of his white chef's jacket.

Unblocked by his shadow, the shaft of light was stronger still. It illuminated a small body lying on its back.

The T-shirt retained its newly purchased creases, but some of the white letters of 'Fancy a Poke?' were now red. From Ray's still chest protruded the white handle of a kitchen knife.

CHAPTER THIRTEEN

Carole Seddon was faced with an ethical dilemma which challenged everything she had accepted as gospel when she worked in the Home Office. She and Jude had discovered Ray's body. They were possibly the first people to discover Ray's body. And as such, they had a duty to tell the police what they had seen.

On the other hand, part of her—a part encouraged into unethical behaviour by Jude, who didn't suffer from such niceties of conscience—didn't want to tell the police anything. This part of her produced the very convincing, but casuistic, argument that the police had got quite enough on their plates with their investigation into Ray's death. They didn't need the interference of two middle-aged women. If someone who'd seen them at the Crown and Anchor had suggested the police should interview them, then that would be different. In those circumstances they would of course cooperate. But she and Jude didn't want to be responsible for adding to the workload of the investigating officers.

Carole felt considerably relieved—and rather virtuous—when she had reached this conclusion.

When she and Jude discussed what they had witnessed that evening, they found that at every turn they faced unanswered questions.

Where had the bikers come from? Where did they go back to after their getaway across the dunes of Fethering Beach? Come to that, who was in the Smart car that escaped by the same route?

But the most important question of all was: who had killed Ray?

From circumstantial evidence, the obvious conclusion was that Ed Pollack was the perpetrator. The knife was from his kitchen. They had seen him covered in blood. The easy solution would appear to be that Ed Pollack had done it. But surely that couldn't be true? For a start, what motive did the chef have?

Carole and Jude both had the feeling that the murder was part of a bigger campaign, a campaign that was being waged against the landlord of the Crown and Anchor.

Ted Crisp looked out of place in the Seaview Café. In fact, it struck Carole for the first time, he looked out of place everywhere except behind the counter of his pub. That, she suddenly realized, had been one of the problems with their brief relationship. Ted felt awkward going to restaurants for meals, he'd always rather be at his home base, but sitting at the bar of the Crown and Anchor had never been Carole Seddon's idea of an evening out. Which was one of the many reasons why the affair was doomed to failure.

He just didn't look right, though, sitting in a Fethering Beach café whose frontage opened on to the shingle and where hordes of holidaymakers queued up for tea, burgers and ice cream. Amid all the tanned and sunburnt skin on display, Ted Crisp had a prisoner's pallor. But then he never did go outside the pub much. Whether entirely true or not, it was his proud boast that he'd never before set foot on Fethering Beach. And it was only twenty yards from the front of the Crown and Anchor.

But Ted Crisp couldn't be at his home base now. The whole of the pub, including his flat upstairs, the area for the outside tables and the car park, was now a crime scene.

It was the Tuesday, and the police showed no signs of moving on their collection of white cars and vans around the Crown and Anchor. The area behind the kitchen where Ray's body had been found was still shrouded by a white tent-like structure, and there was police tape everywhere. Fethering opinion was that the forensic team had had plenty of time to search every nook and cranny of the place, and that their continued presence meant that they had found 'something very suspicious'. Old prejudices surfaced in conversations outside the High Street shops. The people who weren't 'pub people' shared the views of Greville Tilbrook. They had never really taken to Ted Crisp. He was scruffy and was automatically assigned the role of an alcoholic. Publicans drank, everyone knew that. Then again, his manners were a bit rough. And, though he was welcoming enough—in his own way—to visitors to the pub, he never did anything to help the wider community of Fethering. He wasn't 'part of the village'.

Add to all that the fact that his bar manager was an immigrant . . . Polish . . . Some of their pilots were very helpful to us during the war, but . . . well, they were foreign. Someone Polish couldn't be expected to understand the fine nuances of society in a place like Fethering.

Ted Crisp looked as if he'd personally heard and suffered from all of these slights and taunts. Carole had never seen him so down.

It was the first time they'd met since the confused ending of the Sunday night. And she'd had some difficulty tracking him down. The Crown and Anchor telephone had been answered by an anonymous policewoman, whose brief was clearly to give out no information about anything. And Carole had got no reply from Ted's mobile. But then Jude had made contact with Zosia, and it was through the Polish girl they had found out that Ted Crisp was staying at the Travelodge up on the Fedborough bypass, 'with a bottle of Famous Grouse'. Messages left there had either not been passed on to Ted or ignored by him, and eventually on the Tuesday Carole had decided she would drive to the Travelodge and force him to talk to her. Jude was busy that morning with a healing appointment for a woman with a dodgy hip, otherwise she would have gone along too.

Ted Crisp had taken a while to answer the phone call from reception, and only grudgingly agreed to come down and see Carole. He had quickly vetoed her suggestion that she should come up to his room. Maybe too many empty whisky bottles lying around?

He had looked pretty rough when he finally emerged into the dispiriting foyer. He said he didn't want to go out anywhere, but was in such a diminished state that he put up no resistance when Carole virtually frogmarched him out to her neat little Renault. And he raised only token resistance when she said she was going to take him to the Seaview Café.

Once they were settled down with cups of black coffee, Carole's first question was: 'Presumably you've talked to the police?'

'And how. Talked to them into the small hours of Monday morning.'

'At the station?'

'No, in the pub. Then about four in the morning they told me to leave. I asked if I could go up to the flat and get some clothes and stuff, but they said no, the whole place was a crime scene. They wouldn't even let me go up and get my mobile.'

'So where did you go?'

'Well, they asked if I had any friends I could stay with, but I said no and—'

'Ted, you could have stayed with me.' Carole was embarrassed by this possible reference to their short-lived relationship. 'Or Jude.'

'No, I don't want to dump on my friends. This is my mess, and it's down to me to find a way out of it.' Though he didn't sound optimistic about his chances.

'So where did you go?'

'The police booked me into the Travelodge—though with no mention of who was going to pick up the tab.'

'And have they given any indication of when you're likely to be allowed back in the pub?'

Ted Crisp shrugged with weary resignation. 'Not a thing. They came to talk to me at the Travelodge yesterday and I asked them again and again. Nothing. Wouldn't even give me a clue when they're likely to leave, so what with last week's closure and the loss of goodwill from everything that's been happening . . . my whole business is going down the toilet.'

Carole didn't want to get sidetracked by Ted's financial problems. She had more urgent matters on her mind. 'Presumably the police also asked you if you'd seen anything round the back of the pub . . . you know, where Ray's body . . . ?

'Yes.' He was about to continue, but then almost seemed to choke. He converted the sound into a cough, but Carole could tell he had really been affected by the reminder of his protégé's death. Ted cleared his throat and went on with increased aggression to cover up his lapse into sentiment. 'Anyway, if I had seen anything, I'd have told the bloody police, wouldn't I? But I was out the front, dealing with those bastards who were smashing up the place. God knows what all that's going to cost to put right.'

'Aren't you insured?'

'Oh yes, I'm insured. Everyone's insured until the moment they make a claim. Then suddenly, miraculously, there turns out to be something in the bloody small print of your contract that says your coverage sadly doesn't include the one thing you're claiming for.'

'You don't know that for a fact, Ted. I'm certain your insurance will cover the damage.'

'I doubt it . . . given the way my luck's going at the moment. And will the insurance cover damage done during a fight? I'll bet there's some clause in there that says they won't pay up if I've been found to have been keeping a "rowdy house" or . . . Oh, God knows . . .' He spiralled further down into despair.

'And what about Ed?'

'*What* about Ed?'

'Well . . .' Carole had to phrase her words carefully. The last time she and Jude had seen the chef on the Sunday night he had looked extremely guilty. In fact, he had looked like Ray's murderer. But she didn't know how much Ted Crisp already knew about that, and she didn't want to plant potentially slanderous ideas in his head. 'I just wondered if the police had talked to him?'

'Yes. They did take Ed down to the station. Which is where he may still be, for all I know.'

'So he's under suspicion?'

'I think everyone's under bloody suspicion,' Ted replied apathetically.

Now she could risk a direct question. 'Do you think he killed Ray?'

'No!' It was the most animated response she'd had from him all morning. 'No. Look, I've known that boy since he helped me out when he was a student. He's one of the most honest kids I've ever known. He's as harmless as that poor bugger Ray was, hasn't got a violent bone in his body. He's almost *too* much of a gentleman—certainly lives up to his posh accent. And he'd certainly never hurt Ray, of all people. He was very kind with that guy, really patient. You know, Ray was slow on the uptake and could sometimes get in the way when the kitchen was busy, but I never once heard Ed mouth off at him. No, whoever did kill Ray, I'd swear on . . . on anything you like, that it wasn't Ed Pollack.'

'Then why did the police take him down to the station?'

'God knows.'

'Did you see Ed that evening, you know, after the fight?'

'Of course I bloody did.'

'When Jude and I saw him, he had blood all over the front of his jacket. He looked as if he had just been where Ray was and he was moving back into the kitchen.'

'Ed had got blood all over his whites because he'd been punched in the face by one of those sodding bikers. I don't think his nose was actually broken, but there was blood pouring out of it.'

Carole was surprised at the depth of her relief at this news. She too had warmed to Ed Pollack, and the thought that he might have been responsible for Ray's death had clouded her mind for the past couple of days.

'And you say you don't know whether Ed's still with the police or not?'

'No. I haven't been in touch with anyone since I went to that Travelodge place. I said, the police wouldn't let me take my mobile and . . . anyway, I . . . well, I didn't feel like talking to anyone . . .' Carole got an inkling of the depths of his depression. She had a mental image of him just sitting in the anonymous space of his tiny Travelodge room, contemplating the collapse of everything he'd worked for. Not wanting to make any communication—except with a bottle of Famous Grouse.

He seemed to intuit what she was thinking, and made an effort to shift himself out of his mood. 'I must ring Ed. And Zosia. Find out what's happened. This has got to be as tough for them as it is for me.' He groaned. 'And if the Crown and Anchor's closed for any length of time, I'm going to have to lay them off. God, I hate doing that.'

'The police can't be there that much longer.'

'Don't you believe it. They can stay as long as they like. They'll probably start digging into the foundations to see if any bodies were cemented in there when the bloody place was built.'

'Oh, now you're just being paranoid.'

'And do you blame me for being paranoid?' This was spoken with such vehemence that a few nearby tourists looked up from their burgers and ice cream. In a lower, but no less impassioned voice, Ted Crisp went on, 'Look at what's happened to me in the last ten days. First, the food poisoning—closed down by Health and Safety. Damaging headlines in the *Fethering Observer.* Then when I do reopen, the pub's suddenly full of bikers who alienate the whole bloody village—and of course I get blamed for it. Then we have a full-scale riot and, to top it all, a murder. Call it paranoia if you like, but I reckon I'm justified in thinking there's some kind of campaign against me!'

'Yes, yes,' said Carole soothingly. She wanted to reach across to stroke his hand, but that seemed to her too intimate a gesture for a public place. 'Well, Ted, if that is the case—and I can see why you might think so—who do you think's behind it?'

'Someone who wants me to sell up the Crown and Anchor and get the hell out of Fethering.'

'And do you know who that might be?'

'I'm sure there are plenty of candidates.' He sighed and rubbed a bear-like paw across his tired eyes.

'Any names?'

'No,' he replied brusquely.

'Ted, there's a man I've seen a couple of times at the pub . . .'

'Not recently you haven't. The bloody place is closed.'

'A man,' Carole persisted patiently, 'who drives a pale blue BMW. He was watching Dan Poke's act—and he spoke to Dan afterwards. I thought I recognized him. Tall, running to fat, thick-rimmed glasses, black hair that has to be dyed and—'

'I don't know who you're talking about.'

'But he was in the pub and—'

'OK, so he's a guy who was in the pub. People like that are called "customers". They come in, they buy a drink, they drink it, they go out. I don't bloody *know* all of them!'

Carole had a feeling that Ted Crisp was hiding something. He knew the man she was referring to, but he wasn't about to give that information to her. With Ted sarcasm was always the precursor of sheer bloody-mindedness. No point in antagonizing him further. Her tone was more gentle as she said, 'You won't have to sell the Crown and Anchor, you know. Things'll turn round for you.'

'Oh yes?' He let out the sigh of a man at the end of his tether. 'In some ways it'd be a relief just to get shot of the bloody place. The pub business is tough.'

'But you love it.'

'Don't know. Maybe there was a time when I loved it. I'm not so sure I've loved it much during the past few months.'

'Are you saying there've been problems before the last couple of weeks?'

'Yes. Financial problems, certainly. The economics of a place like the Crown and Anchor are always going to be pretty dicey— particularly if you borrowed as much to buy the place as I did. You're always on a knife edge of profit and loss in this business. It doesn't take much to push you down the wrong way. And there are always sharks out there, ready to snap up a business that's on the downward slide. A lot of pubs may be closing, but there's always demand for the ones in prime sites. Like the Crown and Anchor.'

'You mean you have actually had offers?'

'There are always offers. None of them offering anything like what I reckon to be the market value of the place. Like I say, there are plenty of sharks out there. The business is getting tougher every day. No two ways about it, the smoking ban has cut down the number of punters, then you get another hike in interest rates so I'm paying more on the bloody mortgage and . . .' Listlessly, he concluded, 'Yeah, maybe I should just cut my losses and sell up.'

'You don't mean that.'

'At the moment I bloody do!' He tried to sound rough and dismissive, but he just couldn't do it. Beneath the beard his mouth trembled and there was even a gleam of moisture in his eye. 'I just feel so bloody responsible for Ray. I was meant to be helping him. The Crown and Anchor was one of the few places where he felt vaguely secure and . . . look what I let happen to him.'

'It wasn't your fault, Ted.'

'No? At the moment I feel that everything that's wrong in this bloody world is my bloody fault. Ray never knowingly did any harm to anyone in his life, and then I went and shouted at him, and . . .'

Carole had been about to move the conversation on to what Jude had told her about Ray's involvement in the substitution of the dodgy scallops, but Ted's expression of total defeat gave her pause. And the opportunity passed all too quickly. The next thing she heard was a nasal voice saying, 'So this is where you're hiding out, Ted. With your girlfriend.'

It was Sylvia. Her tall boyfriend had his arm protectively resting on her tight-shorted buttocks. He was again wearing black leather trousers, and his biceps bulged out of a sleeveless T-shirt.

Ted Crisp looked up with the expression of a man who didn't think his day could get any worse, and had suddenly found out that it could.

CHAPTER FOURTEEN

In his diminished state Ted Crisp seemed incapable of speech. Carole stood up and said, 'Sylvia, I'm Carole Seddon. We met briefly in the Crown and Anchor last week.'

She felt herself being appraised, then Sylvia said, 'This is a new thing for you, Ted—going for the older woman.'

Carole was so unused to direct insults on that scale that the words took a moment or two to register. Probably just as well. The delay prevented her from coming back with an equally sharp response. Ted Crisp didn't need more grief that morning.

'And this is Matt.' Sylvia flicked her head towards the boyfriend. 'My fiancé.'

Matt acknowledged them with a curt nod. He didn't seem to think words were necessary. His physical bulk made enough of a statement, and clearly Sylvia was articulate enough for the two of them.

'We know each other,' said Ted, without enthusiasm.

So, thought Carole, Sylvia must have introduced them on the Sunday evening before Dan Poke's act. Just to add to Ted's embarrassment. Still, although she didn't warm to either Sylvia or Matt, Carole remembered her manners and indicated two empty chairs. 'If you'd like to sit down . . .'

'Won't be necessary. We're not staying,' snapped Sylvia. She was looking very sexy that morning and knew it. Her arms, legs and cleavage—of which there was plenty on view—were a rich honey colour. Matt also had a high tan, though because of the number of tattoos on his arms, his didn't show so much.

They made an attractive couple (in what Carole couldn't help thinking of as 'a rather downmarket style'). Sylvia must have been quite a bit younger than Ted. Ten years, perhaps . . . though it was difficult to know precisely how old he was. The ragged beard and hair didn't help, but Carole felt certain Ted was younger than she was. She recalled the subject coming up during their brief affair. He must be approaching the fifty mark. In Sylvia's and Matt's body language there was an element of flaunting themselves, rubbing Ted Crisp's face in the fact of their youth and togetherness. But Carole felt sure that wasn't the only reason why they'd accosted him.

So it proved. 'My solicitor's been phoning you and phoning you for the last couple of days,' said Sylvia accusingly. 'You never rung her back.'

'That's because I haven't been in the pub. In case you hadn't realized, the Crown and Anchor's still being treated as a crime scene.'

'Yes, that's not going to do much good for its image, is it?' Sylvia smiled an infuriatingly satisfied smile. 'Anyway, she's left messages on your mobile too. You haven't answered any of them either.'

'That might be because my mobile's still in the flat above the pub. The police wouldn't let me take it.'

'Oh, come on, Ted, you're not going to make me believe that. The cops must've let you pick up some stuff before they took you off the premises.'

Carole had also thought this odd, that the police should not have allowed him even to take his most basic necessities. But Sylvia caught on to the reason quicker than she did. 'Oh, I get it, Ted. You'd put their backs up so much they weren't going to do you any favours. Drunk, were you? Have a bit of a shouting match with the cops when they wanted to question you?'

The way her ex-husband hung his head showed that Sylvia had scored a bull's eye. The satisfaction in her expression grew. 'So you've alienated the local police too, have you? Another triumph for your Crown and Anchor public relations campaign.' Her voice became hard and businesslike as she went on, 'Anyway, ring my solicitor. Or get your solicitor to ring mine. I've had enough of this faffing around. Matt and I want to get married as soon as possible.' She looked up at her fiancé. He grinned like a huge stallion being offered a carrot. 'If you need to contact us, well, you've got my mobile number. And we're not far away. Staying at Matt's place in Worthing. Though we may go away to a hotel next weekend. Yeomansdyke I've heard is nice.' She referred to about the most expensive hotel in the area. 'For a nice bit of a premarital honeymoon . . .' Sylvia concluded, delivering another stab of sexual one-upmanship.

She tugged at Matt's arm, indicating it was time they moved on. 'Right, Ted,' she said. 'I'll leave you with your somewhat gnarled floozy.' And again, before Carole had time to react to such an overt insult, Sylvia went on, 'Don't envy you, love. Dealing with the drinking, apart from anything else. Still, it's not my problem, thank God.' And she led away her massive fiancé like a docile dog.

Ted Crisp seemed to have caught some of Matt's dumbness. He had shrunk into himself. This time Carole didn't curb her instinct to reach across the table and put her hand on his. Ted made no attempt to resist the gesture, but there was no answering pressure from his hand. Carole wanted to wrap her arms around him, just to protect him from any future blows. In a sudden memory of the kind she usually tried to repress, she recalled the surprising softness and vulnerability of his naked flesh.

'That talk of solicitors . . .' she began gently, 'that's about a divorce, is it?' He gave the briefest of nods. 'But, Ted, I thought you were already divorced. You always talked as if you were, even made lots of jokes about what divorce was like for a man.'

'Old rule of stand-up,' he said with a sigh. 'If something really upsets you, put it in the act. Other old rule of stand-up: never let the truth get in the way of a good line.'

'So what happened? That is, if you don't mind telling me . . .'

He shrugged. 'I don't mind. Not much to tell. I dropped out of university to do the stand-up stuff. Met Sylvia at a gig—she was there for a hen night. I was in my late twenties by then. She was about nineteen, working for a building society. We got together. I took her out a few times . . . and the sex, well . . .' He was embarrassed to be discussing the subject with a former lover. 'Anyway, it all seemed to come together. It was quite fun. I was working late so many nights that we didn't see that much of each other, really, which made the times we did see each other feel more important, more precious, I don't know . . .'

He ran his hand through his sweat-damp hair. He wasn't enjoying the effort of recollection. 'Then, after a few months, Sylvia thought she was pregnant . . .'

'You mean she trapped you into marriage?'

'No, no, I wouldn't say that. But it made me kind of think that I should may be show a bit of responsibility, you know, if there was a nipper on the way, so I asked her to marry me. Pretty soon it turned out there wasn't a nipper on the way, but the idea of marriage stuck. And yes, there was a bit of pressure from her parents, but not that much. Don't think they ever really approved of me. But at the time I really thought it was a good idea. Very nomadic life doing the stand-up circuit, I needed to have a base somewhere. And the idea of kids later, I didn't mind the thought of that. No, I wasn't trapped into the marriage.'

'But it didn't work out?'

'It was all right for a couple of years, but then . . . And I have to take some responsibility for things going wrong. You know, you're out late every night, you want to lie in in the mornings, but you've got a wife who's got to check in nine o'clock sharp at the building society. It puts a lot of stress on a relationship.'

'As did your drinking?' asked Carole rather beadily.

'Yes, OK, I'll own up to that. Stand-up, you're always in bars and pubs. And it's scary stuff. You never know what the audience is going to be like, what they're going to throw at you. And I don't mean just heckling—in some of the rougher clubs it was bottles and glasses too. So you have a couple of bevvies to calm your nerves before you go on, and then you have a couple more to wind down after you've finished. And then you have a couple more for the road, and a long drive home. And you're still wide awake when you get back home, but of course your wife's fast asleep and . . . Well, it's not conducive to a great relationship.'

'Did you have affairs?' asked Carole, uncharacteristically direct, given the intimate nature of the question.

He blushed. 'Nothing major, but you know, away from home so much . . . a lot of booze flowing . . . there's bound to be the odd skirmish . . . only human nature.'

'Really?' said Carole coldly.

'So all right, there were faults on both sides. Perhaps more on my side, I don't know. But when things started to go wrong, Sylvia just clammed up on me. Shut me out, wouldn't talk, wouldn't discuss anything. It was never going to go the distance.'

'But when it did end, she was the one who left you?'

'Yes.'

'You once said she went off with a double-glazing salesman, but I never knew whether that was one of your jokes or—'

'Bloody true. My wife went off with a double-glazing salesman. Didn't seem much of a big deal at the time. We'd made a mistake. I wasn't making her happy, she'd found someone who did—fine. We didn't really have any possessions, lived in a rented

111

flat. After a few months I hardly noticed Sylvia had moved out. Not having her around didn't make much difference to ninety per cent of my life. I was still doing as many gigs—though that did begin to drop off after a while—but Sylvia had never gone to my gigs, anyway. She'd heard it all before.'

'One question, Ted?'

'Hm.'

'Had Sylvia met Dan Poke before last Sunday?'

'I'm not sure. As I say, she didn't go to any of my gigs. Though, actually, now I come to think of it, she must've met him. When Dan finished the gig on Sunday, she was all over him, saying how good it was to see him again, introducing him to Neanderthal Man.'

'Neander—?'

'Her fiancé.'

'Matt, the biker.'

'Don't know whether he's a biker or not. I do know that he's a delivery driver.'

'Ah. Sorry, go on. You were talking about your marriage . . .'

'Or the Third World War, as it was affectionately known.'

'But why has Sylvia suddenly reappeared in your life?'

'Money. It always was money with Sylvia. Maybe working in the building society all day made her obsessed with the stuff. That's what a lot of our arguments were about when we were married. She said I was off every night, boozing away anything I made from the bloody gigs—which wasn't a million miles from the truth—and we ought to be saving a deposit for a house and getting a foot on the property ladder . . . Oh, it went on and on . . .'

'But had the double-glazing salesman got money?'

'You betcha. He was a very successful double-glazing salesman—got a big spread out near Chelmsford. Sylvia liked that, liked being the lady of the manor, liked giving up work, liked spending his money. So she wasn't bothered about getting a divorce. I was as poor as a church mouse. She wouldn't get anything out of me, just be a waste of solicitor's fees.'

'So what's changed?'

'Two things have changed. One, Mr Double-Glazing Salesman suddenly took a look at the woman who'd been sharing his bed for the last however many years and decided she was beginning to show signs of wear and tear. And since they weren't married, there was nothing to stop him replacing her with a younger model. Which he did with remarkable alacrity and gave Sylvia the old heave-ho. So she's out in the cold cruel world the wrong side of forty, and she hasn't got anything, not even the tiniest toehold on the bottom rung of the old property ladder.' He spoke almost with satisfaction, and took a sip of the coffee which must have gone cold long before.

'You said two things had changed.'

'Yes, well, the other thing of course is that I'm no longer the old church mouse, am I? I've built up the Crown and Anchor, haven't I? And though the actual finances there are very shaky, to my greedy little ex-wife it looks like I'm coining it. So suddenly divorce becomes a rather more attractive idea.'

In the cause of fairness, Carole felt she should point out that Sylvia also had a new man in her life. 'She does actually want to remarry.'

'Yes, but I reckon marrying Matt is relatively low on her priorities. What she really wants to do is stitch me up.'

'Sure you're not being a bit paranoid?'

'No. This is not a fantasy. Sylvia's out to get me!'

Carole refrained from commenting that she'd never heard anyone sounding more paranoid, instead asking, 'And presumably Matt hasn't got any money?'

'You're bloody joking. Like I said, he's a delivery driver. Very much a step down for our Sylvia.'

'Then how're they going to pay the bill at a place like Yeomansdyke?'

'On her credit card, I imagine—and their prospects of getting half the proceeds when I finally have to sell up at the Crown and Anchor.'

'Oh, Ted, it won't come to that.'

'No? After the couple of weeks I've just had, I wouldn't put money on it.'

'But you've built up that place on your own. Sylvia made no contribution at all. She has no rights on the business.'

'Not what her lawyer says.'

'Really?'

'She's got one of these really sharp feminist solicitors. Real man-hater. All men are rapists—let's squeeze every last penny we can out of them.'

'And what's your solicitor like?'

Ted Crisp shrugged. 'Don't know. I've hardly met the guy. He dealt with the purchase of the Crown and Anchor, that's about it.'

'And was he any good?'

'How can you tell with a lawyer? The paperwork came in. Followed by the bill. Par for the course, isn't it?'

'But does he specialize in divorce?'

'I've no idea.' Ted had become listless now. Cataloguing the history of his marriage had depleted his last resources of energy.

'Don't you think you ought to get someone who does specialize in divorce?'

'I think what I ought to do, Carole,' he said as he rose from the table, 'is to thank you for the coffee—and your concern—but to tell you once again that this is my bloody mess and it's down to me to get out of it.'

He turned and shambled away. His jeans and scruffy T-shirt looked out of place amidst the bright beachwear, and the cheerful shouts of children splashing at the edge of the sea seemed only to accentuate his misery.

'Where are you going?' Carole called across to him.

'Back to the Travelodge.'

And, no doubt, to the bottle of Famous Grouse.

Chapter Fifteen

The healing had worked. The woman with the dodgy hip had left Woodside Cottage walking more easily and in a lot less pain. As always at such moments, Jude felt a mix of satisfaction and sheer exhaustion. Only someone who has done healing can know how much the process and concentration involved drains one's energy.

She was infusing a restorative herbal tea when the phone rang. It was Sally Monks, the social worker who had provided Ray's address for her. Her voice sounded tense. 'I've only just heard the news.'

'About Ray?'

'Yes. Obviously I knew that there had been a death down at the Crown and Anchor, but I've only just heard that it was Ray who died. Wondered if you knew any more about it.'

'A bit. Not a lot.'

'Well, look, I can't talk now. I'm on my way to an appointment and talking in the car—which I know I shouldn't be—but I've got to drive through Fethering later this afternoon. Might you be around then?'

'Sure. What sort of time?'

'I can never be quite sure because my visits can get complicated, but hopefully fourish. That be OK?'

'Fine,' said Jude.

In fact it was after five when a black Golf parked outside Woodside Cottage and Sally Monks came bustling out. She was a tall redhead of striking looks. All Jude knew of her private life was that she didn't wear a wedding ring, but someone who looked like that couldn't lack for masculine attention. Jude had come across a good few social workers in the course of her working life, and found they fitted into three main categories. There were the ones who were simply bossy and always knew better than their clients. There were the ones who got so personally involved with the people they were meant to be looking after that they almost ended up needing social workers themselves. And there were the buck-passers, dedicated to the covering of their own backs, so that wherever responsibility ended up, it wasn't with them.

Sally Monks was an exception who didn't fit into any of the categories. She was the ultimate pragmatist. The moment she encountered a problem, she started thinking of solutions to it. But she didn't impose these solutions, she worked with her clients, so that they felt part of the process of finding a way forward. She was also very direct, she didn't dress up the truth with vague reassurances. This characteristic, as well as an allergy to paperwork, frequently brought her into conflict with her employers. She had been the subject of any number of disciplinary meetings and reprimands, but the social services always stopped short of sacking her. They couldn't afford to lose anyone who was that good at her job.

'Sorry to be late,' she said as she came through the front door (which Jude had left open to get some air moving round the house). 'Client was an old boy who's just moved into a nursing home, and who hates watching television in the communal telly room. I've tracked down his son to get a set into the old guy's bedroom.'

'Are the residents allowed to have their own televisions?'

'No.' Sally Monks grinned. 'But I've fixed that with the

117

managers of the place.'

She put down her leather bag and flopped on to one of Jude's heavily draped sofas, glowing not only with the heat, but also with another small victory over bureaucracy. She wore a black linen shirt and trousers, creased from too long spent in the car, but still looking pretty damned elegant.

'Can I get you a drink?'

'Love one.'

'Virtuously cooling or alcoholic?'

Sally Monks glanced at the watch on her slender wrist. 'Oh, go on, you've twisted my arm. I was full of honourable intentions to write up three weeks' backlog of case notes tonight, but . . . what the hell?'

'White wine be OK?'

'White wine would be perfect. Pinot Grigio for preference.'

'Sorry, don't have that. Can you make do with a Chilean Chardonnay?'

'Oh, yes,' said Sally with a grin. 'I've always been prepared to slum.'

As she got the drinks, Jude reflected how easily she and Sally always slipped back into relaxed banter. They didn't really know each other that well, but there had never been any strain in their relationship. And some things—like their love lives—they just never discussed.

Jude also felt a slight guilt at how much less relaxed the atmosphere might have been had Carole been there. Much as she loved her neighbour, she knew there was always a necessary period of awkwardness when Carole was introduced to someone new. So it had been some relief to hear that that afternoon had been earmarked for one of her neighbour's monthly Sainsbury shops. (Carole had forgotten her fabricated excuse of doing a big shop the previous Saturday.)

The sitting room of Woodside Cottage felt as warm as the

day outside. There was no doubt the weather was getting hotter. Fethering residents mumbled darkly about global warming, with a complacent ignorance and the comfortable feeling that they'd probably be dead before it got really bad.

The two women sipped their wine gratefully. 'So . . .' said Sally, 'anything you can tell me that isn't the usual Fethering inflated gossip?'

'Perhaps a bit. Carole and I were almost the first people to see the body.'

'Almost?'

'The chef at the Crown and Anchor, Ed Pollack, I think he probably saw Ray dead before we did.'

Sally Monks shook her head in pained disbelief. 'I'm still having a problem taking it in. Ray, of all people. I can't think of anyone who's done less harm in his life.'

'That's what everyone seems to say about him. Incidentally, what was his surname? I never heard anyone refer to him as anything other than "Ray".'

'Witchett. Ray Witchett. He was one of the gentlest men I ever knew. I mean he was never going to be playing with a full deck, he'd got serious problems, but they didn't manifest themselves in violence. I suppose he had a mental age of, I don't know, under ten, but so long as he had his football and his television and all his magazines about people from the telly, he was fine. And that independent living scheme up at Copsedown Hall seemed to work very well for him. For all the people there. No, it's a great set-up . . .' her brow darkened '. . . for as long as it lasts.'

'Oh?' asked Jude, picking up the hint.

'Funding threatened there, as well as everywhere else. Central government and local government both trying to close down places like that. Get more people out "into the community" . . . regardless of the fact that most of the people in places like that can't cope "in the community".' The social worker sighed with frustration. 'Oh, don't get me started on that. I'm afraid I very quickly lose my sense of proportion.'

'All right,' said Jude hastily. 'Let's not go there. Tell me, what actually was wrong with Ray? Is there a technical term for what he had?'

'Yes, there are lots of technical terms, lots of "syndromes" describing various aspects of his condition, but basically he suffered the effects of being deprived of oxygen at birth. That's where it all sprang from, his stunted growth, impairment of his motor functions and the mental incapacity.' Sally shook her head again. 'I can't believe he's dead. Still, from all accounts it was total chaos up at the Crown and Anchor on Sunday. In that kind of mêlée anything can happen. I guess poor Ray was just in the wrong place at the wrong time.'

'I'm not so sure . . .'

Sally Monks looked up sharply. 'What do you mean? Are you suggesting it wasn't just a ghastly accident?'

'Well, there are a few odd facts about what happened. For a start, all of the fighting was round the front of the pub, and Ray's body was found round the back. Carole and I looked, but there was no trail of blood. He hadn't been moved. His body was lying where he had been killed. Also the weapon used was one of the knives from the pub's kitchen. Well, all right, in the chaos it's possible that some of the fighters out the front had raided the kitchen for weapons, but I don't think it's likely.'

'So you're saying that Ray was deliberately murdered?'

'It looks that way.'

'But why?' Sally Monks' pretty forehead wrinkled with confusion. 'As I said, he hadn't got an enemy in the world. He wouldn't have knowingly done anything to upset anyone.'

'But he might have known something that somebody wanted kept quiet. I can't imagine that Ray was the most discreet person when it came to keeping secrets.'

'No. He'd blurt out anything to anyone.'

'You seem to know him very well, Sally.'

'Yes, he was part of my caseload while he was still living with his mother. I used to visit them a lot. But she was getting so infirm that the situation couldn't continue. So I arranged for him to go to Copsedown Hall, which, after a few initial hiccups, suited him very well. I thought I'd really got a result there, you know, giving him some independence before the old girl did finally pop her clogs. Copsedown Hall comes under another social worker's remit . . . you wouldn't believe the tangles of bureaucracy in our world . . . so I stopped seeing Ray on a regular basis, but I gather it was really working out for him.' She wiped the back of her hand across her eyes, suddenly teary. 'And now this has happened.' But she quickly halted any potential slide into melancholy. 'Anyway, Jude, you implied Ray might have known something that someone wanted to keep quiet. Am I allowed to know more?'

Briefly Jude filled Sally Monks in on her visit to Copsedown Hall the previous Saturday.

'So he admitted changing the trays of scallops round?'

'Yes. But he thought he was doing good. Whoever persuaded him to make the switch convinced him that he would be saving the Crown and Anchor from an outburst of food poisoning.'

'Whereas in fact he was doing the exact opposite. God, what kind of person would take advantage of someone like Ray in that way? Must have been someone who knew something about his character. The bastard was appealing to one of Ray's most basic instincts. Ray was always trying to help out, trying to make things better. If he had a fault, it was his desire to please everyone. Which is why he hated it so when people lost their tempers with him. That used to upset him terribly.'

'And when he got upset, he went to his mother's?' said Jude,

121

thinking of the effect of Ted Crisp's uncharacteristic outburst against Ray.

'Yes,' said Sally. But she sounded preoccupied as she continued with the chain of logic she had been constructing. 'So Ray was stopped from telling you the name of the person behind the poisoning by the appearance of Viggo?'

'Yes. Do you know Viggo?'

'Come across him a few times. Fantasist, and I'd have thought pretty harmless. But I may be wrong about that. As I recall, he had an obsession with guns, watched lots of violent movies. I think he wanted to go into the army, but they wouldn't have him. Big disappointment for him, I seem to remember. But are you suggesting that he deliberately stopped Ray from spilling the beans to you?'

'No, I think his appearance in the Copsedown Hall kitchen at that moment was just coincidence.'

'But you reckon whoever it was who got Ray to swap the trays of scallops was also the person who killed him to keep him quiet?'

Jude shrugged. 'It's a vaguely plausible theory. Only one I've got, anyway. Mind you, I don't have anything in the way of proof.'

'Don't be picky,' said Sally Monks. Her red hair swung as she shook her head at the enormity of what had happened. 'God, I'd like to get the bastard who did this.'

'So would I.'

'If there's anything I can do to help in any investigation you may be carrying out . . . ?'

'Thank you. I'm sure there'll be other things I want to ask you,' said Jude, ever mindful of the danger of Carole's extremely sensitive nose being put out of joint. 'And one thing I can ask you right now. Do you think Ray's mother would talk to me?'

'I'm sure she would.' Sally Monks produced a Post-it note

and scribbled a phone number down on it. 'Nell will be absolutely devastated by what's happened. I must go and see her too, but I can't for a couple of days. Ray was her world, you know.'

CHAPTER SIXTEEN

Nell Witchett lived in a ground-floor flat near West Worthing station. She had been very pleased to get a phone call from Jude and keen that she should come round as soon as possible. She said that though it was only two days after his death, nobody wanted to talk about Ray, everyone avoided the subject.

The street was rundown, dusty in the July heat, and there was a smell of dustbins that hadn't been emptied recently enough. Nothing happened for so long after Jude pressed the bell-push that she was beginning to wonder whether it was working. But then through the frosted glass of the front door she saw a slight figure slowly approaching.

The appearance of Nell Witchett explained the slowness of her approach. She was stick-thin and edged forward on a Zimmer frame. In spite of the heat, she wore two cardigans over a woollen dress and thick stockings. In their velcro-strapped shoes, her feet looked knobbly and painful.

'Come in quickly, love,' she said. 'I don't like to leave the front door open too long. There are some nasty types around here. They'd burst in and steal your purse before you could say Jack Robinson.'

Jude did as she was told and was ushered along a narrow hall whose floor was littered with junk mail. 'You go ahead of me, love. If you wait for me, you'll be here till the Christmas after next.'

Again Jude followed her instructions and found herself in

what used to be called a 'bed-sitting room' before its dimensions were massaged by estate agents into a 'studio flat'. The doors off the hall indicated that four such units had been carved out of the small ground floor. Nell Witchett's was basically a single room with bathroom and kitchen attached. These were separated by sliding doors; there wouldn't have been room to have ones that opened outwards.

While its owner made her effortful journey back from the hall, Jude had time to take in the room. It was very stuffy. The windows at the front were closed, and didn't look as though they'd been opened for a long time. Whether that was for fear of draughts or of the 'nasty types' around the area, Jude couldn't know. A bit of each perhaps.

And the room was absolutely crammed with furniture which must have come from a larger house, stuff its owner couldn't bear to part with. Just moving across the room was potentially hazardous; there were so many sharp edges of tables and dressers to bang against. Nell's bed was piled high with blankets and eiderdowns; the old lady had probably never slept under a duvet in her life. There was a low sofa that must have been where Ray dossed down when life in the world outside got too tough for him.

And there was a small television on, showing some early-evening quiz programme where contestants vied noisily for cash prizes. It must be on one of the terrestrial channels, of course, because Sally Monks had said that Ray's mother didn't have Sky. Had she had Sky, Jude briefly wondered whether Ray might not have returned to Copsedown Hall the weekend before, and so might not have been at the Crown and Anchor on the Sunday, and so . . . But she curbed such speculations, they were pointless.

Though he was dead, the room was full of Ray. There were photographs on every crammed surface. Faded ones of him as a

125

baby, the outlines becoming more defined as he grew into adulthood. And in every photograph a huge smile. He had clearly loved having his picture taken.

As Nell Witchett inched her way into the room, Jude was struck, not for the first time, by the importance of mobility, and how the approach of death was so often preceded by a gradual but accelerating slow-down. It was nature's way. So long as a human being can move about, he or she can keep up some kind of fitness regime. But as mobility diminishes, with it goes confidence. Confidence in the most basic actions which one has taken for granted for so long. Being able to walk, being able to lift oneself out of a chair, being able to reach down to put on a shoe. Then a lack of confidence can lead to falls, and falls are often the precursor of the end.

Thinking along such morbid lines was unusual for Jude. She didn't fear death, she knew it to be as integral a part of being human as any other experience. And normally her outlook was resolutely positive. But the sight of Nell Witchett, for whom simple locomotion was now such a painful effort, had lowered her spirits. Or maybe that had been caused by the death of Ray, who was so clearly the sole focus of the old woman's life.

And yet, as she talked to Nell, Jude didn't encounter the misery she had anticipated. Although her son was not two days dead, Nell Witchett seemed very much in control of her emotions. Almost serene.

Before Ray's mother finally deposited herself into her chair, she offered Jude tea or coffee, but seemed quite relieved when the invitation wasn't accepted. There was also relief as she sank on to the piled cushions and leaned against the stiff back of her chair. Jude wondered how much of her time was spent sitting there, how much her life had dwindled to this single piece of furniture.

Nell immediately raised the subject of Ray, but still without becoming emotional.

'I met him for the first time last week,' Jude explained. 'At Copsedown Hall. It seemed a nice place,' she added rather vacuously.

'Yes. He's settled there. Most of the time. It's good, the first time he's managed to live independently.'

'How independent was he really?'

The old woman shrugged. 'As independent as someone like Ray ever could be. He's always going to need support.'

'From you?'

'From me or someone else.' Nell was quiet for a moment. 'Usually me, to be honest.'

'What about the social worker who looked after Copsedown Hall? Ken, was that his name?'

'What about him?'

'Was he someone Ray could turn to for support?'

Nell Witchett let out a dismissive grunt. 'He's useless. Lazy bugger. Hardly ever goes there. Not one of the good social workers. Mind you, they're as rare as hen's teeth.' She spoke with a lifetime's experience of the breed.

'But everything was very well looked after at Copsedown Hall. Neat and tidy.'

'No thanks to Ken. It's the residents who keep it like that. Particularly a girl called Kelly-Marie.'

'I met her last Saturday.'

'She's very organized, in her quiet, dogged way. She keeps the men up to scratch.'

'Is she the only female resident?'

'Yes. She may not have all her marbles, but her head's screwed on the right way.'

'And was she a particular friend of Ray's?'

'They get on all right. Nothing more. They talk quite a lot together, I think.' Jude made a mental note to have a further word with Kelly-Marie, as Nell went on, 'Ray spends most of his time with the men at Copsedown Hall.'

'Like Viggo . . . ?' Jude suggested.

The old woman's tight brow wrinkled with disapproval. 'Yes, too much time with Viggo. He's not a good influence.'

'In what way?'

'Viggo's a fantasist.' Jude was struck that Sally Monks had used the very same word. 'He's always full of wild ideas,' Nell Witchett went on. 'Sees himself as various kinds of flashy characters.' Like a biker, thought Jude. 'But it's all in his head. Anyway, I don't think he's good for Ray. Stuffs his head with ambitions the poor boy has no hope of fulfilling.'

'Would you say they were friends?'

The old woman snorted. 'Not my idea of friendship. Ray's afraid of Viggo, always trying to placate him, do what he wants. I wouldn't call it a friendship, where Ray does all the giving, while with Viggo it's just take, take, take.'

Jude couldn't understand the way Nell Witchett was behaving. She was showing no grief at her son's death. And she kept talking about him in the present tense. Jude wondered whether the old woman had actually taken in what had happened. Cautiously, she raised the subject.

'I was desperately sorry to hear about Ray.' Probably not the moment to mention that she and Carole had found his body. Time for that later, perhaps.

'Yes, very sad,' Nell agreed, but with sorrow, rather than anguish.

'You've no idea who might have killed him, have you?'

'No. And I'll be surprised if we ever find out.'

This seemed an unusually incurious response. 'But presumably the police are on the case,' said Jude. 'They'll be investigating.'

'Yes.' But Nell Witchett didn't sound very interested in the

subject. 'Yes. I doubt if they'll find the killer, though.'

'Why do you say that?'

'Because it sounds like there was a riot down at the Crown and Anchor. Lots of people caught up in the fighting. When you get a mob like that, anything can happen. Poor Ray just happened to be in the wrong place at the wrong time. Not for the first time, either,' she added, but still with pity rather than grief.

'Have the police talked to you, Nell?'

'Oh yes. First a couple of them came in the early hours of Monday morning to tell me what had happened. Young they were, a boy and a girl. I felt sorry for them. Must be a dreadful part of the job for kids that age, telling people their relations have died.' All her sympathy was for the police officers, none for herself. 'And then they came again yesterday. Another two. These weren't in uniform, the second lot. Detectives, I think they said they were. They asked me lots of questions about Ray, and I told them what I could. But of course I didn't know anything about what happened Sunday night.'

'Did they seem to have any suspicions about who might have killed him?'

It was a question unlikely to get an answer, and Nell Witchett batted it away pretty quickly. 'If they did, they didn't share them with me.'

'No, I bet they didn't,' said Jude. Throughout her experience as an amateur sleuth she had been constantly disappointed in how unwilling the police were to share details of their investigations.

'And what about you?'

'What about me?' Nell seemed genuinely confused by the question.

'Do you have any thoughts about who might have killed Ray?'

'One of the people in the fight.' The way she spoke, the answer was self-evident.

'You don't think Ray was deliberately targeted?'

'No. That's just how Ray was. I always worried that something like that would happen. He trusted people and I kept trying to tell him that some people were bad, that some people shouldn't be trusted. But he never really took it in.'

Jude thought how he must have trusted the person who told him to switch the trays of scallops, and felt another pang of frustration about how close she'd got to finding the identity of that person.

'So you think Ray just wandered into the fight and that's how he got killed?'

Nell Witchett nodded. 'The police said it must have been very quick. He wouldn't have suffered much. So that was good.'

She spoke with real satisfaction, and Jude could still find no explanation for the old woman's behaviour. Nell had lost the son round whom her whole life had revolved, and yet she seemed to feel no pain. Jude still didn't think it was the moment to reveal that Ray had been found at some distance from the fighting. Instead, she decided to go for a bit more background information.

'Is Ray's father alive?' she asked.

'I've no idea,' the old woman replied without interest. 'I haven't seen him since Ray was tiny. As soon as it was clear the boy wasn't going to be normal, my loving husband upped and slung his hook.'

'Did Ray remember him?'

'Don't think so. There was always just the two of us.'

Then why, Jude desperately wanted to ask, aren't you more upset by his death? But she continued to hold the question back, instead asking, 'And do you know if Ray had any enemies?'

The idea was so incongruous that Nell Witchett laughed out loud. 'How could someone like Ray have enemies? All he wanted to do all his life was to please people. That's why he got so

upset if anyone shouted at him. Ray never knowingly hurt a soul. Oh, maybe there were people who he got the wrong side of, or who took him the wrong way, but that was never his fault.'

'Was he ever bullied?'

'Why do you ask that?'

'Well, people like him, people who are different from the rest of the world . . . sometimes they get victimized.'

The old woman was silent as she thought about this. Jude was aware of the rasping of her breath, and the thinness of her body under the layers of clothes. At last Nell Witchett said, 'Yes, he did get bullied. Does still. I reckon the way Viggo treats him is a kind of bullying. And Ray's suffered that all his life. When they tried him at ordinary school, there was a lot of kids who picked on him, because . . . well, because, like you say, he was different. And the same at some of the special schools he went to. There's always someone out there who's going to take it out on a boy like Ray.' A gleam of anger came into the faded eyes as she said, 'It made me mad. I could protect him when I was with him, but at those schools he was on his own. However much I wanted to be there for him, I couldn't be.'

Jude was now even more confused. Nell had the natural instinct of a mother to protect her child, possibly, because of the circumstances, stronger in her than other mothers, and yet she appeared to show no desire to find out how her precious son had died.

'So,' asked Jude, almost depairing now of getting any useful information out of the old woman, 'you can't think of anyone who would have wanted Ray dead?'

'No. But he is dead. And I've got my memories.' Again there was a note of satisfaction as she looked round the cluttered room, taking in all the photographs of Ray, the insubstantial record of his sad, short life. 'He'll be all right. Now he won't

131

need looking after no more.'

And finally Jude understood. At one level Nell Witchett *was* relieved by her son's death. She no longer had to hold herself together for him. The problem that she had agonized over for decades, of who would care for Ray after she was gone, no longer existed. And that brought her a kind of peace.

CHAPTER SEVENTEEN

Carole and Jude didn't see each other on the Wednesday. At Woodside Cottage there was a full appointment book for clients requiring healing, and at High Tor there was a bit of a panic about Gulliver. The dog had cut his foot on some rusty metal during his morning walk on Fethering Beach. Fortunately the wound was on his shin rather than the soft pads, but it still bled a lot and Carole rushed to the vet's, where she had to wait about an hour to get him patched up and given an antibiotic injection. So great had been her hurry that she'd not put a rug on the back seat and so spent a long time in the afternoon scrubbing canine blood out of the usually immaculate upholstery of her Renault.

Then when she finished that, she had a call from Gaby, who was again talking about her mother-in-law looking after Lily while she and Stephen went away for a weekend. That left Carole both excited and unsettled. All the old doubts about her maternal skills resurfaced.

One good thing did happen that day, though. Jude got a call from Zosia in the evening to say that the police had finished their investigations of the scene of the crime, and the Crown and Anchor would be opening again on the Thursday. Jude rang Carole and they agreed to meet there for lunch. Apart from the opportunity for a bit of snooping, they had to show their support for Ted.

★ ★ ★ ★ ★

As it had done a week before, the pub's reopening coincided with the publication day of the *Fethering Observer*. And, of course, this time they had an even bigger story to splash over the front page: MAN KILLED IN CROWN AND ANCHOR BRAWL. There followed an overexcited article by the same junior reporter, who had read too much about Watergate. And it ended once again with the news that, due to the police murder investigation, the Crown and Anchor would be closed 'until further notice'.

It was inevitable, but it was just the sort of publicity Ted Crisp didn't need.

Not that Carole and Jude heard his views on the subject. When they arrived at the pub round twelve-thirty, he wasn't there. 'Had to go to a meeting at the bank,' Zosia explained. Which sounded rather ominous.

The interior of the Crown and Anchor had been meticulously swept and tidied so that no one would know it had been a scene of violence. But outside the scars were plain to see. Two of the windows were boarded up with MDF, and wires from the broken lights hung from their sockets. Debris of broken chairs, window-boxes and glass had been swept up against the front wall, but there hadn't been time to take it away yet. The place looked rundown and unwelcoming.

That was reflected in the lack of customers. Carole and Jude had anticipated that the pub's new notoriety might have attracted a few local ghouls, but they had misjudged the attitude of village residents to recent events. Greville Tilbrook would now no doubt be able to fill up his petition many times over. Fethering's word for social groups of whom it disapproved was an 'element', and it did not like the idea of having a pub right in its centre which attracted a violent 'element'.

Or then again, the lack of customers might be partly due to

no one knowing that the pub had reopened for business.

It was good news for Carole and Jude, however, because it meant they had the undistracted attention of Zosia. As she poured their Chilean Chardonnays, they asked the Polish girl to bring them up to date with events at the pub since they were last there. Unfortunately, she couldn't be much help, because she hadn't been there either. But, sensing the seriousness of their enquiries, she told them that Ed Pollack was back in his kitchen.

'Do you think he'll mind talking to us?' asked Carole.

Zosia assured them that he wouldn't and, since there were still no other customers, led them out through the door at the back of the bar.

They had forgotten about the chef's injury, so his appearance was quite a shock. His nose looked about twice its normal size and a gauze dressing was held with sticking plaster over the bridge. The bruising had spread to the hollows under his eyes, and he looked like a mournful panda. This image was intensified by a large pair of glasses, less trendy than the ones he'd worn previously, balanced precariously on the tip of his swollen nose.

Carole winced at the sight. 'How is it? Very painful?'

'Not too bad now. So long as nothing touches it.'

'Is it actually broken?'

'No, thank goodness.'

'Do you know who hit you?'

'Couldn't really see in the mêlée out the front. Probably just a swinging elbow. I don't think I was particularly targeted. Just happened to be in the wrong place at the wrong time.'

The same words that Sally Monks and Nell Witchett had used about Ray. But Jude felt pretty sure that in his case the murder victim had been targeted.

They heard the ring of a bell from back in the bar. 'Another customer,' said Zosia. 'Word must be spreading. I'll go and deal with the rush.' And she left the kitchen.

'And how are you feeling?' Jude smiled solicitously at Ed. 'You must still be in shock.'

'Not great,' the chef admitted. 'It was the first time I'd actually seen someone dead and . . . well, seeing Ray, you know, what had happened to him.' His upper-class accent made him sound particularly young and vulnerable.

'Do you mind talking about it?' asked Jude.

'No, be quite glad to, actually. At home my mother has been so studiously avoiding the subject, you know, treading on eggshells, trying not to get me more upset.'

'Did the police give you a rough time?' asked Carole. 'You know, on Sunday night?'

Ed shrugged. 'They were only doing their job. And if they really thought I'd killed Ray—which at first they seemed to— then there was no reason for them to use kid gloves.' His understatement gave both women the impression that his interrogation had been pretty gruelling.

'And why did they think you'd done it?'

'Circumstances were against me, really. I'd got blood all over my front. Ray had been stabbed with one of my kitchen knives. You know, the police come into a situation like that, not knowing anyone, not knowing the background . . . you can hardly blame them for leaping to the obvious conclusion.' He seemed to be bending over backwards to exonerate them from any criticism.

'So how long were they questioning you?' asked Carole.

'They let me go at around four on Monday morning. My mother had been terribly worried about where I was.'

'And what did the police ask you?'

'The same question over and over again, really.' Ed Pollack couldn't prevent a slight shudder at the recollection. 'How well

I knew Ray, what I'd got against him.'

'Why you'd killed him?' Jude suggested.

'Not quite in those words, but that was the gist of it, yes.'

'And what made them finally realize you were innocent?'

'I'm not sure that they do think that yet. I've a nasty feeling I may still be high up their list of suspects.'

'All right then—what persuaded them to let you go?'

'I think it was probably the blood on my shirt. They'd taken a sample of it as soon as I got to the station. I was introduced to a doctor, he must've run some tests on the blood. Anyway, they got the message that the blood was mine, and that it was a different blood group from Ray's. That's when they started to realize they hadn't got anything definite against me.'

'They must have been disappointed. The police like cases that have quick, obvious solutions.' Jude was slightly surprised to hear this from Carole. Given her Home Office background, it was unusual for her to voice even the slightest criticism of the constabulary.

'Well, they were only doing their job,' said Ed generously.

'Do you mind . . .' Jude began, 'do you mind if we actually look at the . . .' She was uncharacteristically embarrassed '. . . look at where Ray died?'

'It's a free country.' Ed Pollack threw open the back door of the kitchen. 'Though I wouldn't think there was much chance of you finding anything after the police have been over the whole area with a fine-tooth comb.'

'I wasn't really expecting to find anything, just get a feeling of the place.'

This prompted a predictably old-fashioned look from Carole. She was more than sceptical of her neighbour's New Age beliefs in auras and synchronicity and healing and similar mumbo-jumbo.

Except for one detail, the scrubby little area behind the

kitchen looked the same as it ever had. It probably had been swept and raked over by police detectives, but the loose sand and rough dune grass had soon blown over to cover any traces of their activity.

The one thing that was different had not been left by the police. It was a jam-jar of flowers. A white label had been stuck on it, with the single word 'RAY' scrawled in a childish hand. The July heat had evaporated much of the water, leaving a greenish scum round the interior of the glass. The flowers drooped, colourless and limp as cooked spaghetti.

'Was that there when you arrived this morning?' asked Carole. When Ed nodded, she observed, 'Looks as if it's been there more than a day to get that dried up.'

'Somebody loved him,' said Jude softly.

'His mother did. We know that.'

'Yes, but these weren't left by his mother, Carole. Having seen the state she's in, I don't think she could have made it this far from her flat.'

'She might have got a taxi.'

'Yes, maybe.'

Jude stood very still in front of the flowers, her eyes almost closed, breathing in deeply.

'Have you got enough of the *aura* yet?' asked Carole, unable to keep the sarcasm out of her voice.

'Just give me a minute more.'

Carole snorted and hung about with bad grace until suddenly she snapped her fingers. 'I've just remembered something.'

'What?'

'When we were here that evening, when we found Ray's body, just before that, we heard footsteps of someone running away over the shingle.'

'That's right,' said Jude. 'I'd completely forgotten.'

Both women turned towards the chef. 'You didn't hear

anything, did you? Or see anyone running away?'

He shook his head. 'There was so much going on. I was still reeling from the blow I'd had in the face, and then seeing Ray's body . . . No, I didn't see anyone.'

'I wonder who it was.'

The two women went back into the kitchen. Ed followed them and looked around with slight unease. 'I wonder if there'll be any lunch orders today.'

'There'll be at least two,' replied Carole. 'From us.'

'Oh, good.' He seemed relieved to be moving the conversation on. 'What would you like?'

But Carole was not to be deflected from her chosen course. 'I'd like, if you don't mind, for you to go through in detail what you actually saw on Sunday night.'

'All right.' He didn't see the point of arguing. 'But there's not much to tell. I've just told you I didn't see anyone running away.'

'Before that, though. Did you actually see Dan Poke's act?' asked Jude.

'Most of it. We weren't serving food that Sunday evening, but it had been busy at lunchtime and people were still eating till round six or so. Ted had got all the girls helping set up the bar for the show, so I was tidying up everything in the kitchen myself. Took me till after Dan Poke started. Then I managed to get to sit on the ledge of one of the front windows . . . I don't know, round eight fifteen probably.'

'Did you like the act?'

He grinned, as though surprised that Jude had needed to ask. 'Yes, of course. He's very good. Very sharp.'

And very cruel, thought Carole. Still, Ed had probably missed most of the rubbishing of Ted Crisp, which had come at the beginning.

'And did you actually see what started the fight afterwards?'

'No. There was such a crush, it could have been anything. One of the bikers got jostled maybe, and then swung a fist at someone. That's how fights usually start.'

'You didn't get the feeling the fight was started deliberately?'

'Hard to tell. It was the sort of crowd that clearly liked a fight—well, the biker lot did, anyway. It's amazing, there are some people who do actually enjoy fighting. You know, feel that an evening down the pub isn't complete until you've drunk yourself paralytic and had a good punch-up.'

Carole shuddered. 'But not at the Crown and Anchor in Fethering.'

'Maybe not.'

'Can you tell us,' asked Jude, 'exactly what happened to you, you know, where you went, when the fight started?'

Ed Pollack smiled weakly. 'Easy. I've had plenty of rehearsal for that answer. One of the things the police kept asking me.'

'Sorry. But if you don't mind . . .'

'No, no, fine. OK, when the fight started, I should have backed off straight away, not got involved. But I saw Ted wading in, and I followed to try and stop him. Struck me he'd got already enough trouble without getting into a fight. But almost immediately I got this elbow or whatever it was in my face. Very hard, smashed my glasses, which fell off and got lost in the general chaos. And, you know, with pain like that you can hardly see for a few moments, and I sort of backed off, trying to keep out of the way of any more flying elbows or fists or beer bottles. So I retreated back to the kitchen to sort of lick my wounds . . . well, to try and wash some of the blood away in the sink.'

'Did you go back to the kitchen through the bar?'

The chef grinned sardonically. 'You're very good, Carole. Asking exactly the same questions as the police did. And I think I know what your next one will be too.'

'Oh?'

'Was the back door to the kitchen closed when I went in there?' he parroted.

Carole looked a little taken aback. 'I was going to ask that, yes.'

'The answer is: it was. And no, I didn't notice whether one of my kitchen knives was missing at that time, but I think it must have been. Certainly no one came into the kitchen while I was there, which means that whoever took the knife must have done so earlier.'

'So when did you open the back door?'

'When I heard the police siren. Self-protection dictated that I should get off the scene as quickly as possible.'

'Exactly what we thought,' said Jude. 'That's why we went round the back, thought it would be simpler to get home that way rather than being questioned by the police.'

Carole couldn't stop herself from saying, 'Not, of course, that we had anything to hide.'

Jude grinned. 'No, of course not. So, Ed, when we saw you, it was just at the moment you'd opened the back door to make your getaway?'

'Yes. Except that I didn't realize it was you two. I'm blind as a bat without my glasses, so I could just see the outline of two people.'

'But you did see what had happened to Ray?'

'Yes. I saw something lying there when I opened the door. I had a close look at him—my eyesight's OK really close.' He swallowed nervously. 'It was a bit of a shock.'

'I'm sure it was. So you could see the knife?'

'Oh yes. And I recognized it as one of mine, but I didn't really have time to take in the full implications of that. I was so shocked I wasn't really thinking straight.'

'I'm not surprised,' said Carole. 'And . . . I think I probably know the answer to this question, but I'm going to ask it,

141

anyway. Did you see anyone else around the back of the kitchen?'

He shook his head. The action must have banged the bridge of his glasses against his nose. He winced before replying, 'No. No one. Well, that is to say, I saw the bikers making their getaway. And that little Smart car.'

'Yes,' Jude mused, 'I wonder who was in that Smart car?'

'Anyway, I didn't see anyone else who was on their feet. Till you two appeared. I was only out there less than a minute.'

'And you're sure Dan Poke didn't go into the kitchen?' asked Carole.

'Not after he'd finished his act, no. He was waiting there before Ted introduced him.'

'While you were still tidying up?'

'Yes, Jude.'

'Did he say anything to you?'

'Not a word.'

'A bit standoffish of him.'

'Well, he was about to do his act. He probably needed a bit of quiet time to, you know, get his concentration together.' Ed Pollack was clearly one of those people who could find excuses for anyone's behaviour.

'And . . . it's hardly worth asking this either, but did you—'

Ed was ahead of Carole. 'No, I did not see Dan Poke take one of my knives while he was here.'

Jude sighed. 'So we aren't really a lot further forward.'

'Further in what?'

'Well . . .' She felt surprisingly embarrassed by the question.

'Further in our investigation,' said Carole firmly. 'Jude and I are determined to find out who killed Ray Witchett. And indeed why.'

Ed Pollack nodded, rather more cautiously this time. 'Good for you,' he said. 'If I remember anything else relevant, I'll let you know. But I think it's unlikely. The police covered all of the ground with me, and you now know as much as I told them.'

'Did you know,' said Jude suddenly, 'that Ray admitted to me that he'd changed round the tray of scallops in the fridge on that Monday?'

The chef looked really amazed by the news. 'But why?'

'Someone told him the ones in the fridge were poisoned. The exact opposite of the truth. Ray thought he was saving the Crown and Anchor from an attack of food poisoning.'

'But who the hell told him that?'

Jude chewed her lip with frustration. 'That's the one thing that I don't know. We were interrupted when Ray was about to tell me.'

'And,' said Carole tartly, 'to stop him telling anyone is quite possibly the reason why he was murdered.'

The door from the bar clattered open and Zosia entered with a small pad from which she tore off a couple of sheets. 'Food orders, Ed. We have actually got a few customers out there.'

'Oh, right, I'd better get on,' he said, taking the orders. Zosia returned to the bar. 'By the way,' Ed asked Carole and Jude, 'what are you two having?'

'What do you recommend?'

'Actually,' he replied hesitantly, 'I do have some very nice scallops. Doing them with crispy bacon and leeks today.'

Jude, on the principle that lightning never struck twice, did go for the scallops. Carole, for whom the very idea revived her terror of being sick, opted for the shepherd's pie. The chef started to busy himself at the stove.

'Ed,' said Jude, 'just going back to the Monday morning when the scallops were switched . . .'

'Right,' he murmured, preoccupied with pouring olive oil into a pan.

'As I recall, you said you and Ted and Zosia were all out of here shifting some beer barrels in the cellar . . .'

'Yes, they'd got jammed down the chute when they were taken off the delivery van.'

'And did the delivery man help you down in the cellar?'

Ed Pollack let out a sardonic laugh. 'No way. The day he does anything helpful, pigs'll fly.'

'Oh, so he's a regular delivery man, is he?'

'Yes. What's more, you two have probably met him.'

Both women looked bemused. 'Have we? Who is he?'

'His name's Matt. He's the one who's knocking around with Ted's ex-wife.'

Carole made eye contact with Jude. 'Is he now?' she said.

CHAPTER EIGHTEEN

Carole and Jude wanted to talk to Ted Crisp, but he wasn't back from his visit to the bank by the time they'd finished their food. A few other customers had arrived in the pub, but they were mostly French or Dutch tourists, who presumably did not know the Crown and Anchor's sensational recent history.

Because business was slack, Carole and Jude managed to talk again to Zosia, but she couldn't add much to their stock of information. Yes, she knew Matt sometimes drove the van that made deliveries from the brewery, but she didn't know much else about him. And she hadn't noticed him doing anything unusual the morning of the food-poisoning debacle.

So the two women left the Crown and Anchor in a state of some frustration. The discovery about Matt might be a breakthrough, but they couldn't quite see how. And they really needed to find out more about Ray, who his contacts had been, how he used to spend his time. Jude wondered whether another visit to Nell Witchett might glean some more information, but she wasn't over-optimistic.

Almost every other potential line of enquiry involved talking to Ted Crisp, and even when they finally found him they weren't sure how cooperative with them he would be.

Mind you, Jude's scallops had been delicious.

When she got back to Woodside Cottage, the light on her answering machine was flashing. There was a brief message

145

from Sally Monks.

That morning Nell Witchett had been found dead in her bed.

CHAPTER NINETEEN

Carole also had a phone message when she returned to High Tor. It was from Sylvia. She just said 'Sylvia' on the phone. Carole hadn't really considered before what the woman's surname might be, but she supposed it was probably still 'Crisp'. Sylvia Crisp. What on earth could she want? Dutifully Carole returned the call.

'Hello,' said the distinctive nasal voice.

'How did you get my phone number?' asked Carole.

'I am capable of using a phone book.'

'Oh.'

'Look, is Ted with you?'

'Is Ted with *me?* Why on earth should he be?'

'I can't raise him at the pub, he's not answering his mobile. I thought he might be hiding out with you.'

'Why would he want to hide out with me?'

'Well, you two are an item, aren't you?'

Carole's instinct was to deny the allegation hotly, but then she stopped to think. Sylvia might be more forthcoming if she believed she was talking to her ex-husband's girlfriend. No harm in letting the deception run for a little while, to see if it did lead to any revelations. So all she said was, 'He's not here.'

'Where do you live?' asked Sylvia brusquely.

'If you're so capable with phone books,' Carole responded frostily, 'I'd have thought you would notice that they contain addresses as well as numbers.'

'Yes, all right, I know your address, but I don't know where it is. I'm not a Fethering resident. Are you near the Crown and Anchor?'

'About a five-minute walk. The High Street leads away from the sea, you know, it's where the parade of shops is.'

'I know it. I think it would save time, Carole, if you and I had a little talk.'

'By all means.'

'I'm in Worthing. I'll be with you in as long as it takes.' And the phone was put down.

Carole Seddon was affronted by the woman's rudeness, but also intrigued. Just when most avenues of investigation seemed to be closing, here was a potential new one opening up. She dialled 1471 and took a note of Sylvia's mobile number. Then she committed it to her memory—she had a photographic memory for phone numbers. You never knew when something like that would come in handy.

They sat in the garden. Even there the air moved very little. Gulliver panted pathetically in the inadequate shade of the green table, and tried unsuccessfully to chew off the bandaging round his leg.

Sylvia was wearing clothes which, though perfectly acceptable for the beach, looked out of place in the austere environment of High Tor. Another pair of microshorts—pale blue this time— and plastic flip-flops. Above the waist nothing but a red bikini top, which did nothing to disguise the ampleness of her charms. Carole was already disposed against Ted Crisp's ex-wife, and the way the woman dressed for her visit did nothing to dilute the strength of that disapproval. Yes, the weather was hot, but standards still had to be maintained. A scarf over the bare shoulders might seem to be a minimum requirement. Carole thought her own ensemble of grey linen trousers and a short-sleeved white blouse went quite as far as casual needed to go.

But clearly, not upsetting her hostess was low among Sylvia Crisp's priorities. As soon as, having turned down offers of tea and coffee, she had been furnished with a glass of mineral water, she launched straight into the purpose of her visit. 'Come on, I want to know where Ted is.'

'So far as I know, he's at the pub. It has reopened. I was there at lunchtime.'

'Did Ted mention I'd been trying to contact him?'

'He wasn't there. He had a meeting at the bank.'

'But you'll be seeing him soon?'

'Possibly.' Then Carole remembered she was trying to maintain the illusion that she and Ted were 'an item'. 'Certainly.'

'Well, when you do see him, will you tell him to answer my bloody phone calls. Not to mention the phone calls from my solicitor.'

'I'll ask him,' said Carole, 'but I can't guarantee that he'll do it. As you must know, when Ted doesn't want to do something, he can be very bloody-minded about not doing it.'

'Look, this is a legal matter. It's not down to what Ted wants or doesn't want to do. I need a divorce, and to get that my solicitor and I have to talk to him.'

'Maybe your solicitor could talk to his solicitor?' suggested Carole.

'Yes, fine. That'd be a start. Except Ted won't give me a name for his solicitor.'

'I will try and find that out for you.'

But her magnanimity didn't get any gratitude from Sylvia. 'Do that. Then I can get things bloody moving.'

'You're so keen to get a divorce because you want to marry Matt?'

'Not *want to*. I am *going to* marry Matt.'

'Congratulations,' said Carole drily.

149

There was an unpleasant light of mischief in Sylvia's eyes as she went on, 'And of course once the divorce has happened, there'll be nothing to stop you and Ted getting married.'

'Thank you. But I don't think that's a very likely scenario.'

'No, I wouldn't have thought so.' The woman looked Carole up and down in a disparaging manner. 'Why should he bother with a piece of paper when he can get what he wants for free?'

It was with great difficulty that her hostess bit back a response to this. Carole had suffered from more in-your-face insults since she'd met Sylvia than she had in all the rest of her nice middle-class life.

She channelled her anger into a polite but direct question. 'Sylvia, do you want Ted to sell the Crown and Anchor?'

'Yes,' she replied, 'unless he's got some other loot stashed away that I don't know about.'

'You want the proceeds of the Crown and Anchor to fund your divorce settlement?'

'Of course. It's quite common when a divorce happens, the assets of the couple are divided up. That's all I'm asking for.'

'But when you and Ted split up, he had no assets.'

'He does now. There's got to be a hell of a lot of money tied up in that pub.'

'It's a business he built up on his own, though. You had noth-ing to do with it. You didn't even meet during all the years he was getting the Crown and Anchor going. You don't have any rights to the money he's made there.'

Sylvia smiled smugly. 'My solicitor says I do.'

'Well, your solicitor is wrong.'

'I would think that my solicitor knows rather more about divorce law than you do, Carole.'

'That's quite possibly true. But Ted's solicitor will no doubt be at least as well informed as yours is.' Even as she said the words, Carole wished she believed them. Ted's casual mention of the man who had 'dealt with the purchase of the Crown and Anchor' did not inspire confidence in the arrival of a new Perry Mason on to his team.

'Maybe, but if Ted won't tell me or my solicitor who his solicitor is, the whole situation becomes rather complicated. My solicitor says that there are legal sanctions that can be brought to bear on people who don't respond to solicitors' letters.' Sylvia was clearly parroting the words of her adviser as she voiced this threat. 'And I'm sure Ted wouldn't want to be in any more trouble with the law than he is already.'

'I'm sure he wouldn't.' Carole took a sip of mineral water before moving into more investigative mode. 'With regard to his being in trouble with the law . . .'

'Hm?' Sylvia didn't look very interested in pursuing the conversation.

'. . . he does seem to have had a sequence of bad luck, doesn't he?'

Sylvia shrugged her tanned shoulders. 'Bad luck or inefficiency.'

'Where would you say he's been inefficient?'

'Well, that food-poisoning outbreak . . . got to be down to slack standards in the kitchen, hasn't it?'

Carole restrained herself from a detailed defence of Ted and Ed Pollack's standards of hygiene, instead suggesting, 'Or down to sabotage?'

Sylvia's puzzled reaction suggested that this was an idea which had genuinely not occurred to her before. And Carole didn't think she was a good enough actress to make such a pretence. Her reactive question also implied she had just been given a new thought. 'But who'd want to sabotage the Crown and Anchor?'

'Someone who wanted to make life tough for Ted. Someone who wanted him to have to sell up.' Carole decided to be bold.

151

'Someone like you.'

The response to this too showed real bewilderment. 'Me?'

'You want Ted to sell up, don't you?'

'I want a proper divorce settlement. If he's got other money stashed away with which he can fund that, well and good. If he hasn't, then my solicitor says he'll have to sell the pub to pay me off.' Every mention of her solicitor seemed to give the woman more confidence.

But Carole's confidence was building too. In authoritative tones she announced, 'The food poisoning was definitely caused by sabotage. Before he died, Ray Witchett admitted that he had changed round a tray of fresh scallops in the kitchen of the Crown and Anchor for some dodgy ones that he had been given.'

'Really?' This was all news to Sylvia.

'What is more, there is a strong suspicion that the dodgy scallops were delivered to the kitchen by your fiancé, Matt.'

'Matt?' came the amazed echo.

'Yes. How long have you known Matt, by the way?'

'Only a few weeks. We met in a pub in Worthing. I'd been staying in a B&B over there since I'd been trying to get some action out of Ted. You know what he's like. He won't answer phone calls or letters. If you want to get something out of him, you have to turn up in person.'

'Are you still in Worthing?'

'Yes.' She grinned with feline satisfaction. 'But in Matt's place now.'

'Right. Well, look, you know he works as a delivery driver for the brewery that supplies the Crown and Anchor . . .'

'Of course I do.'

'On the morning of the Monday when the food-poisoning outbreak occurred, Matt delivered some beer barrels in such a way that Ted and his staff had to go down to the cellar to unjam them. During that time it seems very likely that Matt went round to the kitchen and gave Ray the scallops that caused the sickness.'

'Really?' A change had come over Sylvia. From being bewildered, she now looked almost excited by the news she was getting. 'You think Matt did that?'

'Yes. Did he tell you that was what he was planning to do?'

'No. He didn't tell me anything about it.' She seemed more excited, even ecstatic.

'Are you sure you didn't set him up to do it?'

'No. Why on earth would I?'

'Because,' Carole explained patiently, 'the outbreak of food poisoning caused the pub to be closed down, which put more pressure on Ted, was a threat to his business, and made it more likely that he would be forced to sell the Crown and Anchor and pay you the settlement your solicitor is demanding.'

'Yes,' Sylvia said, as though she were spelling out to herself some wonderful news. 'Yes, now you mention it, I can see that.'

'But are you saying you didn't set Matt up to do it?'

'No. No, he must have worked it all out for himself. Oh, I've underestimated him,' she added fondly.

'What on earth do you mean by that?' it was Carole's turn to be bewildered.

'I mean that I've always been slightly worried with Matt . . . you know, whether he really loves me as much as I love him. I mean, he hasn't got a demonstrative nature. He doesn't really show his feelings much . . . you know, except in bed.' There was no way she was going to miss that out. 'But this shows how much he cares. He knew how upset I was about trying to get the divorce from Ted. He knew how much difference it would make if Ted had to sell the Crown and Anchor . . . and Matt, all on his own, out of his own head, worked out this clever plan to sabotage the scallops.' She hugged herself with glee. 'Ooh, he's such a lovely man.'

God, thought Carole, how stupid can someone be? But she was convinced that, before it was mentioned that afternoon, Sylvia Crisp had known nothing about the sabotage in the Crown and Anchor kitchen.

CHAPTER TWENTY

Jude spoke to Sally Monks on the phone that evening, and caught up with the news that had been travelling along the social workers' grapevine. The police had checked out Nell Witchett's flat, but had not stayed there long. There would be a post-mortem, because she had died so soon after her son, but there seemed to be a general view that there were no suspicious circumstances surrounding the old woman's death.

Sally wasn't surprised by the theory Jude put forward about Nell Witchett being at one level relieved by her son's murder. 'It wouldn't be the first time that had happened, the caring parent feeling that a great burden's been lifted. It's a while since I've had direct contact with Nell, probably seven or eight years back, but even then she was worrying about what would happen to Ray after she'd gone. So, though she may have regretted the circumstances . . .'

'Even the circumstances were perhaps not that bad,' suggested Jude. 'Terrible to have your child murdered, but at least for Ray it must have been very quick. So far as Carole and I could see, there was no sign of a struggle. Whoever stabbed him must have been able to get very close. Which made us think that perhaps it was someone he knew.'

'Could be that,' Sally agreed, 'but then again Ray was so trusting, he'd have let anyone come up close to him, even if they were brandishing a kitchen knife.'

There was a silence, as both women contemplated the sadness of an innocent's death. Then Jude said, 'Sally, I'm determined to find out who killed Ray.'

'Yes, I rather got the impression you were. I also got the impression that your interest was . . . let's say, more than idle curiosity.'

There was a momentary temptation to confess the real extent of Jude and Carole's investigative activities, but she resisted it. 'I want to know for Ray's sake really. It just seems so unfair for something like that to happen to someone like that. And also it's a bit for Ted Crisp's sake, as well.' Which wasn't untrue, though it was a partial truth. 'I wonder if there's some link between Ray's murder and all the other things that have been going wrong at the pub. I want to find out who it is who's got it in for Ted in such a big way.'

'Hm. Well, anything I can do to help . . . We social workers do have quite a lot of insight into what goes on around here.'

'Thanks, Sally. I'll be glad to take you up on that. And, actually, now I remember, there was something I wanted to ask you about.'

'Fire away.'

'That girl Kelly-Marie . . .'

'Up at Copsedown Hall?'

'Yes. Nell Witchett said that she and Ray used to talk a lot together.'

'I can believe it. They're a pair of the gentlest people I've ever met. Would have had a lot in common.'

'I was going to go up to Copsedown Hall and talk to Kelly-Marie.'

'Good idea.'

'I just wondered if there was anything I ought to be aware of. You implied you knew her.'

'Yes. She was my responsibility for a time. Very well organized.'

'That's what Nell said.'

'Knows her limitations. Very aware of the things she can't do. But she doesn't let it get to her. A perpetually sunny disposition. God, I wish more of my charges were like her.'

'Has she got parents still alive?'

'Yes, nice middle-class couple up in Fedborough. And a couple of brothers, I think, who have no disabilities. It was Kelly-Marie herself who announced she wanted to live somewhere like Copsedown Hall, to prove she could be that independent. Which she certainly has proved.'

'How do you think she'll have taken Ray's death?'

'I think she'll be upset, but not totally devastated. Kelly-Marie does understand about death. She does know that her parents won't be there forever.'

'And you don't think my talking to her about Ray would upset her?'

'No. Anyway, Jude, she'll tell you if she thinks it will. She's very direct.'

'No idea what she's doing at the moment, whether she works . . . ?'

'I'm pretty sure she has got a job.'

'I was just wondering when might be the best time to call at Copsedown Hall, you know, when she's likely to be in . . .'

'Oh, don't just go up on the off chance. She's got a mobile. Ring her.'

'And do you, by any chance, have her number?'

Sally Monks did.

The two neighbours met up later for a glass of wine in the garden of Woodside Cottage, which, like its owner, looked lush and abundant. Carole didn't know how Jude did it. There was never any sign of her actually working in the garden, very little evident watering, minimal mowing of the lawn. And there were certainly none of the geometric paths and borders that distinguished the garden of High Tor. But, in spite of this, at the back of Woodside Cottage everything flourished, even in as dry a summer as the one they were currently experiencing. Carole had never liked to ask how this horticultural miracle had been achieved. She was afraid she'd get some more of Jude's New Age mumbo-jumbo. If her neighbour went out and talked to the plants at midnight—which she was quite capable of doing— well, Carole Seddon didn't want to know about it.

Jude quickly brought her up to date with what she'd heard from Sally Monks. 'I'd be very surprised if there turns out to be anything suspicious about Nell Witchett's death.'

'Except that it came so soon after her son's murder.'

'I'm not saying the two are unconnected. I think that Nell had just been holding herself together because she was worried about who would look after Ray when she'd gone. Once he was dead, she relaxed and the death that had been on hold for months, possibly years, caught up with her.'

Carole sniffed. Her logical instincts went against the idea of people choosing the time of their own death, but she couldn't deny that Jude's argument was persuasive.

'Anyway, putting that on one side, you said you were going to speak to Kelly-Marie . . .'

'Yes. I phoned her. Very happy to talk to me, but she can't do anything till Saturday. She's got a job in one of the Fethering retirement homes—just cleaning I think basically—and she's got an eight-hour shift tomorrow.'

'Ah,' said Carole. 'I won't be around on Saturday.'

Though neither said anything, both women were relieved by this news. They both knew Jude would be better on her own with Kelly-Marie.

'Where will you be?'

Carole looked rather embarrassed. 'Fulham. I'm having lunch

with Stephen and Gaby. Then they want to go off and buy a new laptop for Gaby . . .'

'And leave you looking after Lily?'

'Yes. It won't be for long, and she does still have a sleep in the afternoon, but . . .' Carole looked nervous. 'I hope she'll be all right with me.'

'Of course she will,' said Jude in a way that ruled out any negative thinking. 'Anyway, tell me what happened earlier this evening. The lovely Sylvia came to see you?'

'Yes, and what a poisonous woman she is. Deeply stupid too, I reckon. But I think I have got a link between Matt and the dodgy scallops.' Briefly Carole recapped her conversation with Sylvia.

Jude sat back and took a thoughtful sip of her wine. 'That's good. And of course Matt dresses in black leather, doesn't he? Just like the bikers do. Maybe he was behind the sudden influx of bikers into the Crown and Anchor.'

Carole was attracted by the idea. Her pale blue eyes sparkled as a chain of logic began to join up in her mind.

'So it looks,' said Jude, 'like we need to make contact with the monosyllabic Matt.'

'Yes, I thought I'd do that,' said Carole boldly. 'For a start, he knows who I am. Then again, if he and Sylvia are really under the illusion that Ted and I are an *item* . . .' She didn't manage to suppress all of her distaste for the expression '. . . then it might not seem odd if I were to approach him.'

'Makes sense.'

'The question is: where am I going to find him? We don't know his surname, so the basic phone-book approach is out of the question.'

'Ted must have a number for where Sylvia's staying. She keeps on and on about wanting him to ring her back.'

'Yes, but Ted's in such an uncooperative mood at the mo-

ment. I tried ringing him at the Crown and Anchor earlier. Zosia said he wasn't there, but there was a kind of hesitancy in her
voice that made me think he probably *was* there, just not taking
calls.'

'We could go back down to the pub and confront him.'

Carole looked at her watch. 'Nearly closing time. We'd be
lucky to make it before they locked up. Anyway, as I said, I
don't think Ted's very likely to give us much cooperation.'

'Well, he's got to start cooperating. Keeping things to himself
isn't doing any good. If he'd told the police about Ray being in
the kitchen alone that Monday morning when the rest of them
were all down in the beer cellar . . .'

Jude didn't need to finish the sentence. Another silence
ensued. Finally the day was beginning to cool. The slightest of
breezes animated the herbal smells of Jude's garden.

A sudden idea came to Carole. 'I know! The one place I can
guarantee to find Matt is when he makes the next beer delivery
to the Crown and Anchor.'

'Good idea.'

'Mind you, whether Ted will even vouchsafe us that
information . . .'

'Zosia will.' As she spoke, Jude picked up her mobile from
the table and summoned a number from the memory.

The Polish girl answered. There was a very small amount of
subdued mumbling in the background. It didn't sound as
though the Crown and Anchor had yet got its evening trade
back. Still, it had only reopened that day.

When Jude identified herself, Zosia sounded disproportionately pleased to hear her—another indication perhaps that she'd
had a long boring evening without much to do.

Jude thought it worth checking whether she could talk to
Ted, but Zosia said awkwardly, 'No, I'm sorry, he's a bit . . .
tied up at the moment.' Jude had a perfect mental image of the

landlord slouched over a large Famous Grouse miming that he didn't want to take the call.

'Oh well, you could tell me, Zosia. You remember the Monday of the food poisoning?'

'Hardly likely to forget it, am I?'

'No. But I remember you saying that the beer delivery van came that morning. I just wonder, are the deliveries always made on a Monday?'

'That's the regular pattern, yes.' Jude nodded this information to Carole, who looked a little downcast. She'd geared herself up to a confrontation with Matt, and now it looked like she'd have to wait till Monday. Would she still have the confidence then that she had now with a few glasses of Chardonnay inside her?

'But,' Zosia went on, 'everything's all over the place at the moment. We had our first closure, which put the beer takings down, but then we had the Dan Poke evening when we sold infinitely more than we would normally. Then they couldn't deliver Monday, because we were closed down again . . . for reasons which I don't need to spell out to you. So they're making the delivery tomorrow morning.'

'What sort of time?'

'Usually around ten. So we can get everything sorted before we open at eleven.'

Right, ten o'clock tomorrow morning it is, thought Carole when the information had been relayed to her. My confrontation with Matt. And she still had enough Chardonnay inside her to relish the prospect.

CHAPTER TWENTY-ONE

Carole Seddon wasn't quite so confident the following morning at about a quarter to ten as she brought her Renault to a halt in the empty car park of the Crown and Anchor. She felt exposed, and her main anxiety was that Ted Crisp might issue forth from his fortress to ask what the hell she thought she was doing there.

But he didn't appear. There were no signs of life from inside the pub, and from the look of the boarded-up frontage it might have been out of business for some months. Carole settled down to wait. She had brought her customary *Times* crossword, but was too tense even to look at it. She let the paper stay in the capacious handbag, into which, after much indecision before she left High Tor, she had put another item.

Say one thing for Matt, he was good on timing. More or less on the dot of ten his vehicle appeared at the end of the lane that led down to the Crown and Anchor. Carole got out of her car. She hadn't made detailed plans for the forthcoming encounter, but she had decided that the best time to catch Matt would be before he rang or knocked on the pub door. Ted's current unpredictable responses might not make him an ideal witness to the conversation she hoped for.

She was surprised by the vehicle Matt was driving. She had expected one of those long flat-back lorries whose whole back was filled with beer barrels, but instead he was in a white van. A large white van, certainly, but nothing that could be dignified

162

with the title of a 'lorry'. Delivering from that somehow made the inclusion of a tray of scallops in the load look more likely.

Fortunately the driver didn't seem in any hurry to get out of his cab. As Carole approached, she could see him hunched over the steering wheel, checking through some paperwork on a clipboard. Though his van window was open, he didn't see her coming and looked up in surprise as she coughed to gain his attention.

It took him a moment to register where he had seen her before. Politely, she extended her hand and said, 'Carole Seddon. We met at the Seaview Café.'

He did not take her hand. Instead, he sneered and said, 'I remember. You're Ted Crisp's current bit of stuff, aren't you?'

Though deeply offended by the description, Carole decided that this was another occasion where the impression that they were 'an item' might assist the cause of investigation, so she made no objection. All she said was, rather pompously, 'It is not in that capacity that I have come to see you this morning.'

'Oh.'

'I met your fiancée Sylvia yesterday.'

'Really? She didn't say nothing about that.'

'Well, that's her business. The reason I'm here is that I wanted to talk about the delivery you made to the Crown and Anchor the Monday before last.'

'Well, you may want to talk about it—I bloody don't!' He slammed his clipboard down on the passenger seat and got out of the van. Though he had been higher than her in his seat, he hadn't loomed in the way he did now, standing beside her. She was very aware of the intricate tracery of tattoos on his bare forearms. 'I've got a delivery to make. That's what I do—I make deliveries. I don't bloody talk about them.'

Carole decided it was the moment to take a risk. Not a decision that she made terribly often. She reached into her bag and produced the object that had caused her such soul-searching before she left the house. It was her old ID card from work, hopelessly out of date, but it did at least have a recognizable photograph (Carole Seddon hadn't changed her hairstyle since her late teens) and the words 'Home Office' printed on it. She had thought it might prove just sufficient to fool someone of Matt's intelligence.

Her gamble paid off. Looking at the ID with a new caution in his eyes, he asked, 'What's all this then?'

Having set off on her course of duplicity, Carole couldn't backtrack now. 'It's a Health and Safety matter,' she said drily, feeling pretty secure that Matt wouldn't know that Health and Safety came under the Department of Work and Pensions rather than the Home Office.

'Oh yes?' He tried to sound casual, but she had caused him a little anxiety. Health and Safety had become the bugbear of any business, with no one quite sure what new arbitrary prohibition was about to be introduced. Children being stopped from playing conkers, pancake races forbidden, hanging baskets outlawed, all to prevent the unlikely occurrence of someone getting hurt. The papers had pounced on such stories of bureaucratic pettymindedness, so Matt must have heard of them. And no doubt there were as many baffling new regulations for delivery men as there were for anyone else.

'According to our records,' Carole went on, weaving a bit more of her growing fabric of lies, 'you made a delivery here in the morning of the Monday before last.'

Sullenly, he agreed that he had. As Carole went on, she realized that she should really have brought a clipboard or a file of notes. That would have made her enquiries look more official. Still, too late for that now. 'You delivered three barrels of beer . . .'

'Yes, it's a regular order. May change a bit week by week, according to how well the boozer's supply is going. It's not my business what's ordered. I just pick up the dockets with the orders, oversee the loading at the depot, and get off on my rounds.' He was distancing himself ever further from any responsibility for what had happened.

'So the depot . . .' Carole went on, trying to sound as though she were confirming something she already knew rather than seeking new information, '. . . is at the brewery—right?'

'No. The brewery's miles away, Midlands somewhere, I think. The depot's in Worthing. Stocks everything pubs need.'

'Who owns the depot?'

'Snug Pubs. Small chain they are, own a lot of pubs in the West Sussex area.'

'But they don't own the Crown and Anchor, do they?'

'No. But there are quite a lot of local independent pubs that use the service. If the depot's got extra capacity, makes sense to use it.'

'So it's not just beer you deliver. It could be food as well, could it?'

'Look, what is this?' Matt seemed close to losing his patience. Carole, wondering how long the subterfuge could be maintained, flashed her obsolete Home Office ID at him again.

It had the effect of calming him down, at least for a moment. 'Yes, sometimes deliver food,' he said truculently. 'Van's got a refrigerated section in the back. Depends what's on the docket.'

'And what happens to these dockets?'

'Customer keeps one copy, so's they can check the delivery's all there . . . and for their records. Then the top copy, the one they sign, goes back to the office at the depot. I take them all back at the end of each day before I knock off.'

Carole nerved herself. She was about to ask the direct question, whether Matt had actually delivered the tray of dodgy scallops to Ray in the kitchen of the Crown and Anchor. Just before she did, she wondered for the first time whether the police had also questioned Matt about that delivery. Maybe not, if they'd believed Ted Crisp's story about Ray not being in the kitchen that morning. How much trouble the landlord had caused in his attempt to shield his simple-minded helper . . .

She asked the question. 'Did you make any food deliveries here that Monday morning?'

For a moment it looked as though he wouldn't answer. But then something . . . the power of the Home Office ID again, perhaps . . . forced him into a grudging reply. 'There was a tray of stuff that had to come.'

'What was it?'

'I don't know. It was covered with foil. It was on the docket, so I picked it up from the fridge at the depot.'

'I'm surprised you don't know what it was. Surely the contents of the tray were printed out on the docket?'

'No, it'd been written on in pencil.'

'On both copies?'

'Just the top copy, one that went back to the depot.'

So, thought Carole, no incriminating evidence would be left in the Crown and Anchor kitchen. 'And where is the depot?'

'Worthing. I told you.'

'Where exactly?'

'Fleet Lane,' he replied grumpily.

'And what's it called? Snug Pubs?'

'No. They use it, but I don't think it belongs to them. Depot's called KWS. Something Warehouse Services, I suppose.'

'And the K?'

'No bloody idea. Everyone just talks about "KWS".'

'Back to this tray of food you delivered here . . .'

'Look, is this going to take much longer? I do have deliveries to make.'

'Just a couple more questions. Who signed for the tray when

you delivered it to the kitchen?'

'That bloke who's often here. Good few sandwiches short of a picnic.'

'The one who got killed in the fight last Sunday?'

Matt nodded. 'Poor bugger. Wrong place at the wrong time.' This seemed to be becoming a universal view of Ray's death.

'You didn't get involved in that fight, did you? Because I know you and Sylvia were here that evening.'

'No way. We'd gone well before the trouble started.'

'Are you sure about that?'

He looked affronted. 'Of course I'm bloody sure.'

'It's just that the fight appeared to be started by the bikers outside the pub.'

'So?'

'You were wearing black leather that night.'

'Just because you dress in black leather doesn't mean you're a bloody biker!'

'So why were you wearing black leather?'

He looked embarrassed for a moment, then mumbled, 'Because Sylvia likes it. She says it's sexy.'

Having made that admission, there was now a restlessness in his eyes, a look that was verging on suspicion. Carole realized that her interrogation time might be running out. Quickly she asked, 'Going back to the pencil-written instructions on your docket . . . was there anything unusual about them, anything odd you were meant to do?'

He considered his answer, maybe wondering how much information he dared give her. 'I had to pick up another tray from the kitchen and take it back to KWS.'

'Was that an unusual thing to happen?'

'No. Sometimes the publicans—or even more often the chefs—had some complaint about their order . . . or the wrong stuff'd got delivered. So quite often there was stuff to take back.'

'So what happens to that stuff when it gets back to the warehouse?'

'There's a special bay you have to put it in.'

'And then?'

'Dunno. Not my responsibility.' Matt gave Carole the firm impression that he wished everything was not his responsibility.

'Just one last question . . . Were there any other instructions written in pencil on the docket?'

He hesitated for a moment, then said, 'No. Just deliver the scallops, take the other tray back.'

Ah. So he had known the contents of the tray he delivered. Carole was about to press him further, but was stopped in her tracks by the appearance of Ted Crisp in the pub doorway. He looked scruffier than ever, as though he'd slept in his clothes. Which he quite possibly had.

'What the hell's going on?' he barked.

'Come for the delivery,' said Matt.

'Yes, I know why you've come.' He turned to Carole. 'But what the hell are you doing here?'

Ted Crisp stared at her. His look was upsetting. It was entirely without affection. He stood beside Matt, the two of them in some way complicit, united against her.

Awkwardly, making some feeble excuse for her presence, Carole beat a retreat to the Renault. And for the first time she entertained the awful possibility that Ted Crisp himself might have something to do with the series of disasters at the Crown and Anchor.

CHAPTER TWENTY-TWO

She didn't confide that last fear to Jude when she got back to Woodside Cottage, but told her neighbour everything else about her encounter with Matt. Except, of course, for the detail about how she'd used her old Home Office ID.

'So,' said Jude, her brown eyes sparkling, 'we've got a nice paper trail.'

'How do you mean?'

'The docket, invoice, whatever, that had the pencil writing on it. That gave Matt the instructions to get the two trays of scallops swapped round.'

'Yes, and those instructions were obviously suspect, because the original scallops didn't come from the KWS depot. They came from Ted's usual supplier in Brighton.'

Jude unconsciously tapped at her chin as she tried to marshal her thoughts. 'I wonder if the instructions also told Matt to get the beer barrels jammed, so that Ted, Ed and Zosia would have to go down to the cellar to sort them out . . . thus leaving Ray alone in the kitchen?'

'Sounds a lot to write down. I wouldn't be surprised if Matt was given those instructions verbally.'

'By whom?'

'If we knew that,' said Carole tartly, 'then we'd be well on the way to finding our murderer, wouldn't we?'

'Either way,' said Jude, 'it still means that Matt is not an innocent party in all of this. What we need to find out is the level

169

of his involvement. Was he just obeying orders? And if so, who gave him those orders?'

'Having met him,' Carole observed sniffily, 'I can't really imagine him having worked this whole plan out on his own. Even though that's what the lovely Sylvia seems to think he did. I don't think Matt was at the front of the queue when the brains were handed out.'

'No.' Jude rubbed her hands, as if preparing for action. 'Anyway, the first thing we do is track down the invoice with the instructions on it.'

'And how do we set about that?'

'We ring KWS.' Jude picked up her mobile. 'I'll get the number from directory enquiries.'

'Wouldn't it be cheaper to use your landline?' Though she now had a mobile herself, such a frugal thought was a knee-jerk reaction for Carole.

'Mobile's not so easy to trace—unless you happen to be the police,' said Jude as she pressed the keys.

'But even if you do get the number, there's no guarantee that you'll get anyone to talk to you.'

'It depends who they think they're talking to.'

'What do you mean?'

'These days a call from Health and Safety has about the same effect as a knock on the door in the small hours from the Gestapo.'

Carole looked appalled. 'You mean you're planning to impersonate a government official?'

'Certainly am.'

Carole's mouth opened to commence a lecture on morality and civic responsibility, but then swiftly closed, as she remembered the subterfuge she had so recently practised on Matt.

Jude dialled the number that she had been given. 'Oh, hello,' she said, 'could you put me through to whoever keeps your records of orders? Yes, my name is Judith Metarius.' It was what she had once described to Carole as 'one' of her married names, leaving Carole more confused about her neighbour's past than ever. 'From Health and Safety.'

The lie seemed to have worked. Jude grinned at Carole as she was put through. 'Oh, good morning. Judith Metarius from Health and Safety,' she said breezily. 'Just need to check some information about a delivery that was made Monday before last.' She gave the date. 'Delivery to the Crown and Anchor public house in Fethering. Yes, I know you do regular deliveries there. One gone out this morning, is there? Well, well. Yes, if you wouldn't mind . . . Who am I speaking to? Raylene? Well, Raylene . . . Oh, it's just a complaint we've had, probably nothing in it, but we do have to follow up everything. Yes, conkers, I know, and pancake races. Hanging baskets, really? I can assure you, Raylene, this is nothing of that kind. Just a little technical query, no one about to be put out of business. So I'd be obliged if you could check the paperwork for me. Yes, that was the date. And the Crown and Anchor, Fethering, yes. Raylene, all I need is for you to find the signed copy of the delivery form, the one that the driver brought back to the depot at the end of the day. I need to check the details of that order. Thank you, yes, I'll wait.'

Jude put her hand over the receiver and mouthed at Carole. 'Not enough work to do, I'd say. Bit of a chatterbox.' Then she was back into the conversation. 'Are you sure? But what about the other paperwork from that day? Oh, is it? Very strange. Well, Raylene, thank you so much for your help. Oh, getting married, are you? I'd love to hear about the dress, but I'm afraid I do have other calls to make. Thank you again. Goodbye.'

Carole looked eagerly at Jude, as she announced with some satisfaction, 'That delivery note has gone missing. It's not there.

Just that one. All the others for the day are in the file. Now isn't that interesting?'

CHAPTER TWENTY-THREE

The Saturday morning was overcast, but no less hot. In fact the low ceiling of grey cloud seemed to press down on Fethering, making the air stale and stuffy. Kelly-Marie was waiting in the hallway of Copsedown Hall and opened the door before Jude had time to press the buzzer. After saying hello, Jude moved instinctively towards the communal kitchen, but Kelly-Marie gestured and limped towards the stairs. 'My room's a nicer place to talk.'

She was right. The studio flat was high enough for the view from its open windows to miss out the shabby street beneath and go over the roofs of Fethering to the dull silver gleam of the sea. Though the space was small, it had been decorated with intelligence and style. There were bright prints on the wall, mostly of dogs, and on the shelves a collection of canine figurines. Proud photographs in silver frames showed a beaming Kelly-Marie surrounded by what must have been her parents and brothers. One of the shots also featured two large long-haired spaniels. Jude wondered whether Kelly-Marie missed the family dogs now she was living on her own. And there must have been other sacrifices the girl had made to achieve her ambition of independent living.

Next to a radio/CD player on one shelf stood a vase of fresh summer flowers, whose perfume made the air feel less heavy. The sight immediately prompted Jude to ask whether Kelly-Marie had placed the flowers where Ray had died.

'Yes,' she replied simply. 'He was my friend.'

In the corner of the room stood a small television with integral video recorder. Up here Kelly-Marie could escape the wall-to-wall Sky Sport and masculine backchat of the communal room below and watch the kind of programmes she enjoyed. Jude found herself conjecturing what those programmes might be.

Kelly-Marie also had her own kettle, which had just boiled in preparation for her visitor's arrival. Of the options offered, Jude asked for a cup of black coffee.

The girl held up a jar of instant and announced with a big smile, 'Fairtrade.'

'That's good.'

'Yes. We have to look after the planet.' Once again she sounded as though she were parroting words she had been told by someone older. 'Otherwise there will not be a planet to hand on to our children.'

Jude found herself wondering whether the girl was ever likely to have children, but the thought did not seem to worry Kelly-Marie. Her movements, as she prepared the coffee and a cup of tea for herself, were very slow and deliberate, as though she were controlling some tic or tremor in her hand.

Till they'd got their drinks, they kept the conversation bland, continuing to talk about basic ecology and whether the current hot summer was a symptom of global warming. Kelly-Marie appeared to be very keen on Green principles, though her actual knowledge of the subject was limited. She just seemed to know that there was a lot of waste. 'People throw things away all the time. Good things. Things that still work. And people throw them away because they want a new one. Viggo's like that. When he gets new clothes he just throws the others away. I've often rescued stuff of his and taken it down to Oxfam. What a waste. People should always check through the rubbish bins to see that nothing that's still useful has been thrown away.'

'Do you do that?'

'I do it here. At home . . .' She corrected herself. 'At Mummy and Daddy's house Mummy does it.'

As soon as the drinks were ready and the girl was sitting opposite her, Jude launched into the subject that had brought her to Copsedown Hall. 'It was desperately sad about Ray, wasn't it?'

'Yes. Very sad.' But she said it in a matter-of-fact way. There was no sadness in her voice. Maybe she had already done her grieving. Leaving the flowers might have been an act of closure for her. Or perhaps her permanently sunny disposition could process painful events better than more conventional minds.

'You used to talk to him a lot?'

'Yes. But I wasn't his *girlfriend.*' As it had on their previous encounter, the word made her giggle.

'What did you talk about?'

'Everything. I explained things to him. He didn't understand anything about recycling.' Her tone was maternal. She had known that she was more blessed intellectually than Ray and she had done her bit to protect him from the world. Jude found resonating in her mind the old proverb: 'In the kingdom of the blind, the one-eyed man is king.'

'You know how he was killed, don't you, Kelly-Marie?'

'Oh yes. The police came here and told us.'

'Did they ask you lots of questions?'

'Yes.' The blue eyes behind the thick glasses rolled exaggeratedly. 'They do go on, don't they?'

'They certainly do. Did they ask you things like when you'd last seen Ray, whether there were people he was in trouble with, whether he had any enemies?'

'All that stuff.'

Jude was slightly tentative with her next question. Kelly-

Marie would be quite within her rights to refuse to answer it. 'So what did you tell them?'

She needn't have worried. The girl had no inhibitions about spilling the beans. 'I told them I last saw him on the Sunday. Just before he went to the pub.'

'How was he?'

'Very excited. He was going to see Dan Poke, from off the television. Ray got very excited about famous people from off the television. He said he was going round the back afterwards to get Dan Poke's autograph.'

Jude felt another pang for Ray's simple-mindedness. He had thought the Crown and Anchor would become like a theatre, with a stage door. Like the Pavilion in Worthing, where he had gone round to get an autograph from Lyra Mackenzie, his *X Factor* idol. He hadn't realized that, though the evening's star had been in the kitchen prior to making his entrance, Dan Poke was never going to leave the pub by the back way. Ray's misunderstanding was what had led him to wait by the kitchen door, isolated from the warring crowds in front of the pub, a pitifully easy target for his murderer.

'Thank you very much, Kelly-Marie. And the police's next question . . . was Ray in trouble with anyone, so far as you know?'

'He wasn't happy because his boss at the pub shouted at him.'

'Ted Crisp.'

'I don't know what his name was. But Ray was very upset because this man shouted at him, and he'd never shouted at him before. Ray hated it when people shouted at him.'

'Yes, so I'd heard.'

'So he went back to his mother's for a while.'

Jude wondered for a moment whether it was worth telling Kelly-Marie that Nell Witchett had died, but couldn't think of any reason for doing so. If the girl didn't know already, all the news could do was potentially to upset her.

'But, apart from Ted Crisp shouting at him,' Jude went on, 'was there anything else that was upsetting Ray?'

Kelly-Marie was silent, processing her answer. Then she said, 'I think there was. He said he was worried about something, worried that people were trying to do harm.'

'Do harm to who?'

'I don't know, but he did say it wasn't anyone here at Copse-down Hall. Maybe it was something to do with his mother.'

'Or at work, at the Crown and Anchor?'

Kelly-Marie clearly hadn't considered this possibility before. 'Yes, I suppose it could have been.'

'But he didn't say who had told him about this threat, about the people who were trying to do harm?'

The girl shook her head very slowly. 'No, he didn't tell me that.'

'Well, had Ray had any unexpected visitors in the weeks before he died?'

Another slow shake of the head. 'I don't think so. But I'm not here when I'm at work.' The idea seemed to strike her as funny, and another huge infectious beam spread across her broad face. 'None of us have many visitors here, except for family people . . . well, the ones who've got family people.'

Jude gestured to the photographs. 'Are those yours?'

Kelly-Marie nodded eagerly. 'Mummy and Daddy and Rob and Daniel. My brothers.' She was clearly proud of them.

'And the dogs?'

'Marks and Spencer. That's a shop,' she explained.

'Yes, I have heard of it,' said Jude, with a smile.

'Do you have a dog?'

'No. My neighbour does.'

'What kind is it?' The sparkle in her eye showed they had

definitely got on to Kelly-Marie's favourite subject.

'A Labrador. But he's got a poorly foot at the moment.'

'Oh dear.' The girl seemed more upset by this news than she had when talking about Ray.

'It's getting better,' Jude reassured her.

'And what's the dog's name?'

'Gulliver.'

'That's a funny name.'

'Haven't you heard of Gulliver? He's a character from a book.'

The girl solemnly shook her head. Jude noticed there was something missing in the room. No books. She wondered how developed Kelly-Marie's reading skills were.

'Do you mind if we go back to what Ray said about thinking someone was going to do harm to someone?'

'Fine.'

'You said you didn't know who was under threat from whatever the harm was, but do you know what the actual threatened harm was?' The girl looked blank. 'What harm was going to be done . . . did Ray mention that?'

Another firm shake of the head. 'The police asked me that too, and I couldn't tell them either. I would tell if I knew. But I can't.'

The girl sounded so pathetically apologetic that Jude hastened to assure her there was no problem. 'You can't give me information you haven't got, can you?'

Kelly-Marie agreed that she couldn't, but still looked disappointed.

'So we know Ray was worried about some harm being done. We don't know what the harm was, who it was going to be done to, or who had told Ray about it. Is there anything else you can remember from the conversations you had with him?'

'Well,' the girl replied slowly, 'I think Ray thought it would be all right.'

'Sorry? What would be all right?'

'Whatever the harm was. He said there was a way of stopping it happening . . .'

'Yes?'

'. . . and he was worried about that.'

'Do you know why?'

'I think it was because it was something he had to do.'

'Ah.' The thought went through Jude's mind that that something might be changing round two trays of scallops . . . as he thought, the safe one for the unsafe one . . . though in the event it had been the other way round.

'And that was what worried him,' Kelly-Marie went on. 'Ray always worried when people wanted him to do things, when he had to take . . . what's that word?'

'Responsibility?'

'Yes. Responsibility.' She repeated the word slowly, savouring it. 'Ray was always worried he'd do things wrong, he'd let people down.'

'Can you remember when you had this conversation with him, Kelly-Marie?'

Her broad brow wrinkled with the effort of recollection. Then it cleared. 'Yes. Not last weekend, the weekend before. Because I was here on the Sunday. Usually I go to Mummy and Daddy's for Sunday lunch, but that weekend they'd had to go to Shropshire for a wedding. Ray told me about him having to take . . . responsibility . . .' she enunciated the word with great caution '. . . on that Sunday.'

The timing worked perfectly. They had had the conversation the day before the poisoning at the Crown and Anchor. But who on earth had set Ray up? Who had told him to take responsibility for the switching of the scallop trays? Who had convinced him that his actions would save the pub from an outburst of food poisoning?

179

Jude stayed with Kelly-Marie for a half-hour or so longer, but didn't get much more useful information. Soon she stopped trying and allowed the conversation to move on to Kelly-Marie's beloved family and dogs. She found herself making comparisons with Ray's situation. The girl clearly had loving parents and when they died, she would still have the support of her two brothers. Also her experience of sheltered housing at Copsedown Hall was much more successful than Ray's had been. She was managing very well.

'Have you got plans for the rest of the weekend?' asked Jude, as she rose to leave.

Kelly-Marie beamed. 'I'll see Mummy and Daddy tomorrow. And the boys. And the dogs.' It was the best prospect she could imagine.

Jude said she'd see herself out, but Kelly-Marie insisted on accompanying her to the main door. She knew her manners.

As she opened the front door, Kelly-Marie turned at a sound from the kitchen. In the doorway lounged a bulky figure with shaved head, combat trousers and a camouflage-patterned T-shirt. In his hand was a shiny new mobile phone. There was something familiar about the man, but Jude was astonished when Kelly-Marie said, 'Morning, Viggo.'

He had had a complete makeover. Gone were long hair and beard, gone the biker's leather kit. Jude could hardly prevent herself from gaping at the transformation.

He didn't respond to Kelly-Marie's greeting, but stared hard at Jude and said, 'On your way then, are you?'

She said she was, exchanged fond farewells with Kelly-Marie and, as she walked out into the stifling outside air, could sense Viggo's eyes boring into the back of her head. She didn't lose the feeling of being watched until she got back to Woodside Cottage.

CHAPTER TWENTY-FOUR

Jude felt sure she was missing something. It was like one of Carole's precious *Times* crosswords—all the information was there, it was just a matter of getting the details into the right order, of looking at the problem from that other perspective which would instantly provide the answer.

Jude thought back over the last week, from the time that she'd arrived at the Crown and Anchor to see Dan Poke the previous Sunday. There were a lot of loose ends, but some which, she was convinced, being joined up in the right way could form a revealing pattern of logic.

Thinking of missing links made her, rather uncharitably, think of Viggo. What could be the explanation for the dramatic change in his appearance? Well, there was only one person Jude knew who might have any information about Viggo. She rang Sally Monks.

'Sorry to trouble you at the weekend. Is it a bad time?'

'I'm cooking.'

'Oh well, if you're busy . . .'

'No, it's something that's going to take so long to cook, I can leave it for whole half-hours. It's for this evening.'

'A dinner party?'

'Rather low on personnel to qualify as a dinner party. There'll just be two of us.'

'Oh?'

'What I hope will be the original hot date, Jude.'

'Good luck.'

'I don't rely on luck. Just a visit to the hairdresser's first thing this morning, this rather spectacular fish dish, lots of Pinot Grigio and . . .' she giggled '. . . my natural charms.'

'Sounds an infallible combination.'

'I'm hoping so. Anyway, what can I do for you this steamy July morning?'

Jude was once again aware of the boundaries in her relationship with Sally. They would share a certain amount about their private lives, but always in general terms. No named individuals. It was a system that suited both of them very well.

'I was ringing about Viggo . . .'

'Up at Copsedown Hall?'

'Yes.' And briefly Jude told the social worker about the young man's sudden metamorphosis.

Sally Monks registered no surprise at the news. 'That's very much in character. Viggo was part of my caseload for a while, and he was always very suggestible. His sense of his own identity is very weak, so he identifies with other people. He feels safer if he's dressed like other people. Doesn't want to stick out in the crowd, and as a result really does stick out in the crowd. Because he's never part of that crowd. Always on the periphery. It's a stage most of us go through to some extent, usually in adolescence. You know, "The reason why my life is so terrible, why I'm so out of joint with the rest of the world, is that I haven't got the right clothes, the right hair style, the right make-up, I'm not listening to the right music . . ." You recognize what I'm talking about?'

'I certainly do.' Despite her exterior serenity, there were still memories of her teenage years which could make Jude cringe with agony.

'Anyway,' Sally went on, 'as I say, most of us grow out of it. Most of us at some level come to terms with what we are, and home in on a style of behaviour, a look, which we think suits us. Someone like Viggo, though, is still searching. And it's not just his appearance he changes. His name too. He hasn't been Viggo that long. He was Rambo when I first met him, then Conan for a while. I think he got Viggo from that actor in *The Lord of the Rings.*'

'And do the characters and names he takes on have anything in common?'

'Well, I suppose they all tend to be heroic at some level. Men of action. Secret agents. Heroes, even superheroes. "Aspirational role models" might be the technical jargon. Though, since most of them are famous for fighting and causing mayhem, I'm not sure that they are particularly good role models.'

'And where does he get the role models from? Are they people he meets?'

'Some are.'

'So he might meet someone, a man who impresses him with his masculinity, his toughness, and then Viggo will try to turn himself into a clone of that person?'

'I guess it could happen like that, but I don't think he meets that many people. Most of his heroes are people he sees on television, or in movies. Rambo—Viggo has always had an obsession with action movies. The more blood and violence, the more he likes them.'

'And do you think they'd have the effect of making him violent?'

Sally Monks hmmed at the other end of the line as she thought about her answer. 'I'm not absolutely sure about that. He's certainly suggestible, so I suppose he might fit the profile of the kind of young men who become suicide bombers. But I can't really see him going that far. I'd have to check out the psychiatrist's reports in the office, but my recollection is that he wouldn't be violent . . . unless under great provocation.

Certainly he has no police record and I can't remember him being reported for violence at any of the institutions where he's been over the years.'

'Has he been in some kind of care a long time?'

'Most of his life. Fractured family background, the usual story. Viggo's the kind of person who's always going to need special help. God knows what'll happen to him if Copsedown Hall is closed down, and he's thrown out to the tender mercies of "the community".'

'Has he got a job?'

'No.'

'Ever had a job?'

'He's been tried at various things, but it's never worked out. Even tried to join the army at one point, but he could never have hacked it. He's got very poor concentration. Starts things, but can't see them through.'

'So what does he live on?'

'That catch-all word "benefits".'

'Ah. I was just thinking . . .'

'Yes, Jude?'

'. . . that this habit—or obsession—he has for sudden make-overs . . . well, it can't come cheap, can it?'

'We're just talking about clothes, aren't we? Not too expensive.'

'Well, I don't know if it is just clothes. I mean, when he was a biker, would he have felt he needed to have a Harley Davidson too?'

'I'd be surprised if he got one. I'm fairly sure he doesn't have any kind of driving licence. He's—.' There was a sudden shriek down the line. 'Must go, Jude! My sauce is separating!'

'Well, bless you for talking. And good luck with the hot date!'

Carole arrived at her son's Fulham house promptly in time for lunch. Stephen seemed more relaxed than usual. Marriage and fatherhood had diluted the seriousness with which he took life, a characteristic which Carole knew he had inherited from her. Motherhood suited Gaby too. She hadn't lost all of the weight the pregnancy had put on, but was as effervescently cheerful as ever. And they both patently adored Lily.

Which was a feeling with which her grandmother could empathize. There was something so uncomplicated about the emotion engendered by that tiny little bundle of flesh. Her relationship to her son, Carole had always felt, had been made stressful by her own anxieties, but her reaction to Lily was much simpler. The little girl was easy to love.

Over lunch Gaby talked about the new laptop she was planning to buy that afternoon, and Stephen generously suggested that his mother might like to have the one it was replacing. 'Nothing wrong with it, just not as state-of-the-art as Gaby feels is necessary for a twenty-first-century woman like her.'

'You can talk, Steve. You change computers more often than I change my knickers.'

This badinage relaxed Carole even more. To be with a daughter-in-law who talked like that, and called her son 'Steve' . . . well, it must be almost like being in a normal family.

'That's because it's my work, Gabs darling. Anyway, Mum, it's a good offer.' Even better, Stephen had called her 'Mum'. 'If you want to have the old laptop, you can take it with you today.'

'Oh, I don't think so. You know me and computers . . .' Carole had always had a resistance to them. As usual with her, it was a fear of the unknown. She was not yet ready to take on a Faustian contract with Information Technology.

'Up to you,' said Gaby. 'But if you change your mind, it's all set up and switched on in the study.'

That afternoon, while Lily slept and her parents were off at PC World, to her surprise Carole did find herself drawn towards the study. And, rather tentatively, touching the keys of the laptop.

Jude sat that afternoon in the garden of Woodside Cottage under the shade of an apple tree. The clouds had rolled away, removing the pressure-cooker feeling of the day, but it was still unbearably hot.

Unusually for her, Jude was feeling restless. Though never quite as serene as she appeared to outsiders, she was a woman who normally had control of her emotions. Only love and compassion had the power to upset her inner calm, but neither of those was causing her current restlessness. It was still the feeling that she was missing something.

She wished Carole was there, so that they could toothcomb through the events of the last couple of weeks. Two memories might do better than one. But Carole, of course, was hopefully bonding in a one-to-one situation with her granddaughter. Jude would have to work it out on her own.

She felt sure that what she was missing was a detail from the previous Sunday, the night of Dan Poke's gig at the Crown and Anchor and its terrible aftermath. She focused her mind in video-camera mode, and tried to replay the sequence of events that she had witnessed. She made mental notes, ticking off the names of everyone who had been there and what they'd been doing.

Pretty soon she remembered a person neither Carole nor she had considered up to that point. Greville Tilbrook. He'd certainly been at the Crown and Anchor at the beginning of the evening, in the car park with his protesting acolytes. Jude remembered the almost unhinged fury with which he had reacted to the sight of the girl with 'Fancy a Poke?' across her bosom. Surely Greville Tilbrook's obsession hadn't been enough for him to kill Ray for wearing the same T-shirt? Still, it might be worth checking out the whereabouts of Fethering's Mr Civic Responsibility on the relevant evening.

But the thought was a new one, and a distraction. Not the missing detail which she was sure she had overlooked.

It took a while, but then she remembered, in a blinding flash. And flash was the operative word, because what she remembered was the fact that many of the audience at the gig had been using their mobile phones to take photographs. And one of the people her mind's eye could see distinctly doing just that was Zosia.

Jude's call found the Polish girl in her flat, between shifts at the Crown and Anchor. She was using her few hours of Saturday-afternoon freedom to work on her journalism course. Jude was constantly impressed by Zosia's unobtrusive industry. She was really making something of herself.

Jude's first question was about the Crown and Anchor. Had there been any more trouble?

'No. Not much business, but no trouble.'

'Were the bikers back yesterday evening?'

'Thank goodness, no. I think because the police got involved on Sunday that must have frightened them off.'

Then Jude moved on to the main purpose of her call. Zosia confirmed that she had indeed taken some photos at Dan Poke's gig. And that fortunately they were still in her phone.

'That's brilliant,' said Jude. 'Could I come round and have a look at them straight away?'

'Well, you could, but it might be simpler if I just sent them to your mobile.'

'Ah. Yes.' Jude felt slightly ashamed of her ignorance of the possibilities offered by new technology. 'Is it easy to do that?'

'Very easy,' replied Zosia, with that amused tolerance which the young reserve for their dealings with the old. 'I'll just check on my phone to see how many I took. It wasn't many, just I

187

think when Dan Poke was beginning his act. For most of it I was back behind the bar, serving drinks.' There was a brief silence. 'Just four. Four photos is all I took. I will send them to you as picture messages.'

'Do you have my mobile number?'

'Of course I have,' said Zosia patiently.

The pictures arrived with a speed that made Jude again feel guilty for not having explored her mobile's potential before. And though the screen on which they appeared was tiny, their quality and clarity was remarkable.

The first one showed Ted Crisp introducing his so-called friend Dan Poke. The landlord's expression of pained bafflement brought back to Jude the sympathy she had felt at the time for his humiliation. More interesting, though, than Ted were the other people who were in shot. Sylvia, near the 'stage' area, her arms draped round Matt.

The second picture was Dan Poke beginning his act.

Jude looked at the third photograph. This time Zosia had focused on the audience rather than the star. Amongst the busy crowd Jude saw herself and Carole, both caught at those mouth-opening, eyelid-drooping moments which are such a feature of most amateur photography. Standing just behind them, with his pre-makeover leather jacket, long hair and beard look, was Viggo. Nearest to the camera, poignantly, sat Ray, his eyes alight at the prospect of seeing 'someone from off the television'. Little more than an hour later his difficult bewildered life would have ended.

The fourth photograph was of the bikers. Jude didn't know why Zosia had taken it. Maybe for identification, a rogue's gallery, in case of further rowdiness at the Crown and Anchor. This idea immediately made her think of the police. Given Ted Crisp's resistance to the idea of having CCTV at the Crown and Anchor, surely the official investigation must have sought out any photographs taken on mobiles that Sunday night? She'd have to check that with Zosia.

In the crowd of bikers a figure stood out. Though clearly one of them—and in fact from his body language he looked to be one of their leaders—he wasn't in their livery of leather. He was the man with whom Jude had nearly had an altercation at the bar, the man with a scarred face and two and a half missing fingers. She remembered the rank body odour that came off him.

The photograph also provided the missing connection that had been troubling her all day. The man was wearing combat trousers and a sleeveless T-shirt with a camouflage design. As if to reinforce the point, on the edge of the frame Viggo was visible, looking at the scarred man with an expression that verged on the idolatrous.

Jude rang Zosia back straight away. First she asked if the police had seen the photographs.

'No. They didn't ask me for them. And, anyway, until you asked just now, I had completely forgotten about them. The police do not talk to me for very long. They just ask me what I am doing in the pub till the fight starts. I tell them that I am serving behind the bar all the time. I had forgotten I went to do the lights and took the photographs. Do you think I should ring the police and tell them?'

Jude was faced by a dilemma that had occurred more than once during her amateur investigations. The correct answer to Zosia's question was yes. If not necessarily a crime, it was certainly unethical to withhold evidence from the police. On the other hand, Jude desperately wanted to follow up the new information herself.

Without too much of a pang in her conscience, she replied airily, 'Oh, I don't think you have to, Zosia. I'm sure the police are busy with their investigation and have got lots of leads to follow up. I mean, if they get back to you and actually ask whether you took any photographs, then obviously you must tell the truth. Otherwise, if I were you, I wouldn't bother them.'

Zosia seemed quite content to accept this advice. 'Was there anything else, Jude? Because this project I'm working on has to be delivered by the end of next week and—'

'Yes, there is something else, actually. I know I sound like a complete Luddite, but could you explain to me how I can send the photographs you sent me on to someone else?'

With great forbearance—and not a little amusement—Zosia spelled out the procedure, which was second nature to her generation.

Jude followed the instructions to the letter and sent all four photographs to Kelly-Marie's mobile. The accompanying text read: 'DID ANY OF THESE PEOPLE COME TO SEE RAY IN THE LAST FEW WEEKS?' Jude was glad there was no one watching as she composed the message. She didn't do much texting, and it was a laborious process for her.

Then, because she was rather impressed by her new skill, she also sent the photographs to Carole's mobile.

Only ten minutes later Kelly-Marie rang back. 'I'm sorry. I'm clumsy with text.'

Join the club, thought Jude. 'But do you recognize any of the people? Have you see any of them at Copsedown Hall?'

'Yes, I have seen one,' Kelly-Marie replied carefully.

'Which one?'

'The one with the bad face.'

'You mean the scarred face?'

'Yes.'

'And are you saying he came to Copsedown Hall to see Ray?'

'No,' said Kelly-Marie. 'He came here to see Viggo.'

CHAPTER TWENTY-FIVE

When she went round to coffee at High Tor on the Sunday morning, Jude could see that her neighbour's time with her granddaughter had gone well. There exuded from Carole an air of satisfaction, the feeling of a job well done. And when asked about her babysitting, she couldn't restrain herself from enthusing about Lily's charms. 'She really responds to me, you know— she definitely knows who I am.'

Jude was always pleased to witness another step in what she had come to regard as the 'thawing' of Carole Seddon. But the proud grandmother's anecdotage would have to wait for another occasion; there were more urgent things for them to talk about. Quickly Jude brought Carole up to date with the progress she had made the previous day.

'Yes, I got the photographs you sent to my mobile.'

'Lucky Zosia had taken those, wasn't it, Carole?'

'A very useful record. And you think Viggo's modelled himself on that man with the scarred face, that that's his latest incarnation?'

'Yes. It fits with everything that Sally Monks said about his personality.'

'Does that mean you think he killed Ray?'

'I'm not sure. But I am sure that Viggo and the scarred man have information that'll help us get closer to a solution.'

Carole nodded. 'Now I come to think of it, I didn't see either of them that night at the Crown and Anchor after the fight had started.' Jude looked at her curiously. 'I remember looking out for them.'

'So either of them could be in the frame for stabbing Ray?'

'Perhaps. Mind you, in all that chaos it was fairly difficult to see anyone.' Carole shook her head in frustration, then said, 'So all we have to do is to find out who the man with the scarred face is.'

'Yes, that's all we have to do. And I've a feeling it may not be easy.'

'Well, come on, what do we know about him?'

'Beyond his physical description—the scarred face, the missing fingers—not a lot.'

'We also know that he's one of the bikers—or at least he knows the bikers. In fact, from the way he was behaving he seemed like the ringleader of the bikers.'

'Yes, OK, I'll go along with that. But where did he arrive from? Come to that, where did the rest of the bikers arrive from? Just suddenly they were in Fethering, at the Crown and Anchor, in something that almost felt like an orchestrated plan of sabotage, whose sole purpose was to destroy Ted Crisp's business. Where did they come from?'

Carole smiled triumphantly as she announced, 'Portsmouth.'

'What? How do you know that?'

'You were there at the same time. You should be able to work it out too.'

'Oh, stop being infuriating, Carole. Tell me what you're talking about.'

'I'm talking about Dan Poke's performance . . . routine . . . show . . . whatever the right word is.'

' "Act." '

'Act, all right. Dan Poke's act. Don't you remember, he went into a whole sequence about Portsmouth?'

'Yes, it's coming back to me.'

'And he started by saying he knew there were some people in from Portsmouth, and when he said that there was a big roar from the bikers.'

Jude's brown eyes sparkled as she caught up with her friend's train of thought. 'Yes, and he talked about some pub, didn't he? Some rough pub—what was it called?'

Carole's brow wrinkled. 'I can't remember. Don't worry, it'll come to me. Try to remember what else he said in the act about Portsmouth.'

'He said he lost his virginity there, and he said something about the hookers, and . . . ooh, he did the old "arsehole of the world" joke.'

'Oh yes.' Carole lips pursed into an expression of prim disapproval.

'But you're right,' said Jude excitedly. 'They did respond when Dan mentioned Portsmouth. So that narrows it down. The man with the scarred face comes from Portsmouth.'

Carole smiled beatifically as the memory came back to her. 'And he drinks in a pub called the "Middy".'

'Yes, that was it!'

'And a "Middy", of course,' Carole went on with authority, 'in a town with naval connections like Portsmouth is almost definitely an abbreviation for "Midshipman".'

'So all we have to do is find the address of the Midshipman pub in Portsmouth.'

'What's the best way to do that? Directory Enquiries?' asked Carole.

'Be quicker to do it on the Internet.'

'Oh,' said Carole, infusing the monosyllable with the instinctive note of disapproval that came to her whenever computers were mentioned. Then she remembered how much of the previous evening she'd spent on her inherited laptop.

But she didn't mention her new acquisition to Jude. When

193

Carole Seddon changed—which was something she strongly resisted throughout her life—she did so very gradually. She was embarrassed by revealing the workings of her mind to outsiders. Until she felt absolutely confident and competent in her computer skills, she was determined to maintain her stance of contempt for all such technology.

So the two women went next door to Woodside Cottage, where Jude switched on the laptop she had inherited from a former lover called Laurence Hawker. Carole peered over her shoulder with a mixture of censure and fascination as her friend connected to the Internet and Googled: 'Midshipman Portsmouth'. In seconds they had an address: Midshipman Inn, Hood Lane, Fratton, Portsmouth.

'See?' said Jude. 'Quick, isn't it?'

Grudgingly Carole agreed that it was indeed quick. Jude grinned. She was way ahead. Though she didn't know about the laptop already sitting in High Tor, she reckoned it would be a relatively short time before her friend finally succumbed to the magic of the computer. And, once Carole started, there'd be no stopping her.

'Well, Jude, what do we do now?'

'I would say we get to the Midshipman Inn as soon as possible.'

'When?'

'Right this minute.'

'What?'

'I've got to go and visit a healer friend this evening, so if we don't do it now we'll have to wait till tomorrow.'

Carole looked sceptical. 'So what do you propose we do? We drive to Portsmouth, we arrive in the pub on a Sunday afternoon, on the off chance that this scarred man is drinking there. We walk through the crowd of aggressive bikers surrounding him and—then what? Are we accusing him of something?

What? Starting last Sunday's riot at the Crown and Anchor? Having a hand in the killing of Ray Witchett? Being a role model for Viggo? I think we need a more definite agenda than that, you know, Jude.'

Her friend looked disappointed. 'It's the only lead we've got. There has to be some connection between him and Viggo.'

'Then maybe a better approach might be through Viggo. You've at least met him.'

'That's true. Maybe we'd do better to—' Jude was interrupted by her mobile ringing. 'Oh, hello. How nice to hear you. It was good to see you yesterday. Oh, is he? Well, thank you for the warning. Enjoy your Sunday lunch with your parents. Hope to see you soon. Bye.'

In response to Carole's interrogative eyebrows, Jude explained, 'Kelly-Marie. She rang to tell me that Viggo is coming to see me.'

'Why on earth would he do that?'

Jude grinned, knowing how much her answer would annoy Carole. 'Synchronicity.'

CHAPTER TWENTY-SIX

Viggo looked very big amidst the clutter of the Woodside Cottage sitting room. The loss of his beard and long hair did not seem to have diminished his bulk. His new uniform of camouflage T-shirt and combat trousers made Jude even more aware of his similarity to the scarred man whose photograph she had been looking at so recently. He held his new mobile phone like a badge of office.

Carole had stayed. After all, Jude was not supposed to be expecting her visitor. Besides, she did not particularly want to be alone with Viggo. Though Sally Monks had thought it unlikely that he would be violent, there was still something threatening in his demeanour.

He refused the offer of a drink, and there was a long silence after he sat down. It seemed as though he had only planned as far as getting to Woodside Cottage. What he did when he got there was still being processed in his slow brain.

Eventually he said to Jude, 'You came to Copsedown Hall. To see Kelly-Marie.' The accent he used was strange, with a slight American twang, as though it had been borrowed from one of his favourite action movies. It certainly wasn't the voice he had used when Jude had first met him with Ray in the Copsedown Hall kitchen.

'Yes, I did.'

'You shouldn't take advantage of her. She's not very bright.'

Jude was affronted. 'I have not taken advantage of her.'

'Then why did you come to see her?'

'Why shouldn't I come to see her?'

'Was it to talk about Ray?'

'It might have been,' said Jude with an unhelpful smile. She was unwilling to give out any information until she had worked out what had brought him to Woodside Cottage.

'You know Ray died?' said Viggo.

'I don't think anyone in Fethering could avoid knowing that, Viggo.'

He raised his hand in a gesture borrowed from some movie. 'Not Viggo. Call me "Chuck".'

Jude pretended she hadn't seen the look of exasperation on Carole's face, as she said, 'Very well, Chuck.' She reckoned the new name had probably been lifted from Chuck Norris, star of many martial arts movies.

'Ray had to die,' Viggo/Chuck announced portentously.

'What on earth do you mean by that?' asked Carole, who thought she'd been kept out of the conversation far too long.

'Don't ask questions. Accept reality. Ray's dead. That's all there is to it.' His delivery was staccato, but without spontaneity. The words sounded as if they had been practised in front of a mirror.

Carole spoke again. 'And do you have any idea who killed him?'

'Lady,' said Viggo, 'I told you not to ask questions.'

'Why have you come here?' asked Jude.

'I've come to tell you not to meddle in things that don't concern you.' The menace of what he said was again let down by his delivery. The learned quality of his words diminished the threat they embodied.

'And who's told you to tell us that?'

'Nobody. Nobody tells Chuck what to do.' He smiled a

strange smile which only seemed to work on one side of his face.

'So if you've come here on your own initiative, what's your reason for telling us not to meddle?'

This question patently confused him. Again he gave the impression that he hadn't prepared fully for this encounter. It was a moment or two before he said, 'Don't meddle. You don't need to know why.'

'And if we do meddle, as you call it,' asked Carole, 'what will happen to us?'

'Don't go there,' he replied, 'if you want to keep breathing.'

Jude was beginning to have a problem stopping herself from giggling. The young man's posturing was so inept, his American accent kept slipping and his B-movie dialogue made him almost pathetic. On the other hand, there still was something danger-ous about him. Who could say how far he would go in making his fantasies real? It would pay to proceed carefully.

Carole was not held back by any such inhibitions. 'Oh, for heaven's sake!' she said. 'You sound like a hitman from some second-rate thriller.'

The description seemed to flatter him rather than anything. 'Hitman? You could be right,' he responded. 'Second-rate—never.'

'Are you telling us you are a hitman then?'

He appraised Carole with narrowed eyes, then said, 'If I were, I wouldn't tell you. It's not a business you brag about. A good hitman doesn't stand out from the crowd. He takes his instruc-tions, does the job, gets the money and then sinks back into obscurity. All he does then is keep his gun clean and ready.'

'And do you have a gun to keep clean and ready?'

'I wouldn't tell you that either. Let's just say, when it becomes necessary, I'll be tooled up.'

'Where would you get a gun from?' asked Carole with

something approaching contempt. 'It isn't the kind of thing that you can just pick up at Fethering Market.'

Her tone annoyed him. 'You can get guns if you know the right people. A lot of military stuff got smuggled out of Iraq.'

Carole's 'Huh' showed how unlikely she thought that was.

'What kind of gun have you got?' asked Jude, more gently.

He smiled a strange half-smile, his mouth only curling up one side of his face. 'I favour revolvers. With them you can fill your spare time playing Russian roulette.' He laughed as if he'd just made a rather good joke, then looked serious again. 'Anyway, like I say, a hitman always sinks back into obscurity. Till the next job comes along.'

'Is that how you operate?' asked Jude.

He gave her a thin smile. 'Like I said, hitmen don't talk about their work. They just hit—hard, efficient, fast.'

'And is it your work as a hitman that makes you worried about my having visited Kelly-Marie yesterday?'

'Just lay off the kid. Ray's dead. Talking won't bring him back.'

'No, but it might help find who murdered him.'

He let out a little cynical laugh he'd heard from some film star. 'People who try to find murderers often get murdered themselves.'

'Well, I think that's a risk we might be prepared to take. Are you actually threatening us?'

'Not threatening. Warning.'

'And if we don't heed your warnings,' said Carole who was getting a bit sick of Viggo's play-acting, 'what are you going to do to us—go into hitman mode, get out your gun—which you have of course been keeping clean and ready—and blow us away?'

'Don't joke, lady. You could be playing with fire.'

This got the harrumph it deserved from Carole, but Jude

started on another line of questioning. 'The thing about hitmen is that they work to order . . .' Viggo nodded in acknowledgement of this self-evident rule of the profession. 'Contracts are taken out on people, and the hitmen fulfil the contracts. Is that how you work, Chuck?' She made the name sound as phoney as it was.

'I didn't say I was a hitman.'

'No, but you'd like to be one, wouldn't you?'

This question threw him. His facade of cool dropped just for a moment as he hissed, 'Yes. I could do it. I could do that kind of stuff. I have done that kind of stuff.'

'Have you?' asked Carole contemptuously.

'I . . . I . . .' He looked confused for a moment, then rescued himself with an old line. 'If I had, I wouldn't tell you. Like I said, hitmen keep quiet about their work.'

'You said earlier,' Carole went on, 'that nobody told you what to do.'

'That's right.'

'Which, if it's true, must mean that you're not a hitman. Hitmen, as we've established, do exactly what they're told.'

He was silent for a moment, trying to work out the logic of that. Jude, who had been fiddling with her mobile phone, joined the attack. 'So who would you take orders from? It'd have to be someone you respect, wouldn't it? You wouldn't take orders from someone you didn't respect, would you?'

'No,' he said cautiously, still not sure where this was all leading.

'So what kind of a man would you respect?'

'Someone who's tough. Someone who stands up to people. Someone who wouldn't give away any secrets even under torture.' As he itemized it, this wish-list, so far from Viggo's own character, sounded pitiful.

'Someone like *this*?' As she said the word, Jude thrust her mobile phone towards him. On the screen appeared Zosia's photograph of the scarred man with the bikers at the Crown and Anchor.

There was no doubt from Viggo's reaction that he knew who it was. However much he faffed around with subsequent denials, his first instinctive reaction had been the give-away. Eventually, he said, 'So what if I do know him? What's it to you, lady?'

'Some people think that that man started the fight at the Crown and Anchor last Sunday.' Jude wasn't too sure about the accuracy of what she was saying. She hadn't actually heard anyone express that opinion, but she thought it might elicit some response from Viggo.

'So what if he did? Fighters fight. That's what they do.'

'Do you know the name of the man in the photograph?' Carole asked suddenly.

'I don't do names.'

'Except to change your own from time to time, Viggo.'

That riled him. Carole's pale blue eyes took the full beam of his black ones. 'Chuck,' he said. 'I'm Chuck.'

'Then who was Viggo?'

'Someone else.'

Carole was getting sick of his gnomic responses. 'So who was the man in the photograph?'

'You won't get that out of me, even under torture.'

'Oh, for heaven's sake. You're talking to two middle-aged women in Fethering. We don't do torture.'

'Others do.'

'Yes, maybe.' Carole looked with exasperation towards Jude, who tried another approach.

'The man in the photograph went to Copsedown Hall to see you.'

Viggo didn't question her assertion. 'So?'

'Why did he come and see you?'

The man's face took on a pugnacious look. 'I can have friends, I can't I?'

'Friends? Heroes, maybe. Is he your hero?'

'Why shouldn't he be? He's a man of action. He's strong.'

'Does that mean you would take orders from him?'

'What do you mean?'

'You said you'd only take orders from someone you respected. The way you describe this man who came to see you, he's someone you'd respect.' Viggo nodded. 'So, what orders did he give you?'

The man's face closed down. 'Orders are secret. Information is only given out on a "need-to-know" basis. No operative should know what orders another operative has been given.'

Carole was beginning to wonder how much more of this nonsense they had to listen to, but Jude persevered. 'From the way you speak, you sound as if you are also an operative yourself.'

'You may make that observation, lady. I can neither confirm nor deny it.'

'Even under torture?'

He seemed unaware of the ribbing tone in her voice, as he solemnly confirmed, 'Even under torture.'

'So you wouldn't confirm whether you have also received orders from the man in the photograph?'

'You're right. I wouldn't.'

'Would you tell us whether the man in the photograph ever came to Copsedown Hall to talk to you?'

He smiled arrogantly. 'Some of us don't need face-to-face contact to get our orders.'

The way he looked at his mobile while he said this prompted Jude's next question. 'You mean you get your orders on the phone?'

That appealed to his self-importance. 'Text,' he said. 'Text received. Mobile discarded so there's no record of the message. Operative obeys order. Job done.'

'And what kind of job are you talking about?'

'Any job.'

'A hitman's job?'

'That, lady, I would never reveal.'

Carole and Jude looked at each other, raised their eyebrows and both mouthed, 'Even under torture.'

Viggo—or maybe Chuck—departed soon after. He left the two women feeling confused. Why had he come? He appeared to be threatening them, warning them off. But quite what he was warning them off was difficult to tell through all his posturing and secondhand dialogue.

'Why should he suddenly want to see you?' asked Carole. 'Why today?'

Jude spoke slowly as she pieced together a possible motivation. 'He saw me at Copsedown Hall yesterday. He saw that I had been talking to Kelly-Marie. Maybe he thinks I'm getting close to the truth of what happened to Ray, and he comes here to warn me off?'

'Do you think he'd work that out on his own initiative?'

There was a firm shake of Jude's head. 'I don't think he does much on his own initiative. Beneath all that swagger and bravado, Viggo's is a very weak personality. I reckon he reported my visit to Kelly-Marie to someone else, and that someone else gave him instructions to come and put the frighteners on me.'

'And who is that "someone else"? The scarred man?'

'We don't seem to have many other candidates for the role.'

In spite of the heat, a shiver ran through Jude. Inept though he had been, Viggo's visit had got her rattled. Both she and Carole were left with the uneasy sense that under certain circumstances the man could be dangerous.

CHAPTER TWENTY-SEVEN

The first surprise about the Midshipman Inn was how smart it was. The references in Dan Poke's act had suggested a very rough pub in a very rough area, but the exterior was neat and recently decorated. Decorated in exactly the same style as the Weldisham Hare and Hounds.

The same mulberry colour predominated, with the doors and window frames in pigeon-feather grey. The inn sign showed no representation of a young naval officer; instead the pub's name was written in neat grey calligraphy on a mulberry-coloured board. And the name on the sign had actually been shortened to 'the Middy'. The image was much more gastropub than old boozer.

The area where the building stood was also less rundown than Carole and Jude had expected from Dan Poke's jokes. Small Victorian cottages showed recent signs of renovation. Though a few they passed from where they parked the car were still shabby and sported the boards of bell-pushes that signified multiple occupancy, some had been turned into brightly coloured designer homes. Because it was a Sunday there were no workmen visible, but loaded skips in the road showed that local improvement was an ongoing process.

And in the middle of all this gentrification the Middy had a perfect location.

Stepping into the pub, Carole and Jude felt the welcome blast of air conditioning, icy after the July heat. The interior of the Middy maintained the mulberry-and-grey theme, though the floor, tables and chairs were solid chunky pine. So was the one long bar. Despite the pub's proximity to Fratton Park, home of Portsmouth Football Club, there were no big plasma screens for Sky Sports. On blackboards menu choices were displayed in italic chalk writing. Painted boards listed The Middy's theme nights, Monday, Curry Club. Tuesday, Quiz Night. Wednesday, Two-For-One Steak Special. Thursday, Comedy Club. Friday and Saturday, Live Music. Sunday nights appeared to have no theme. Nor from a quick look around the various bays separated by pine uprights, did they appear to have many customers.

As in the Hare and Hounds, the bar staff wore mulberry shirts with the grey logo of the pub's name across the breast pockets. At the bar Jude picked up a wine list, turned it over and pointed out to Carole a logo and a name.

'Look,' she said, 'Home Hostelries. We should have remembered. The Hare and Hounds at Weldisham was a Home Hostelries pub back when Will Maples used to run it.'

'Yes, of course.'

Jude turned the list the right way round and, from the surprisingly good selection of white wines, ordered two large Maipo Valley Chardonnays. Exactly what they'd had in Weldisham. In every detail, Home Hostelries pubs were clones of each other.

When Jude turned back to Carole with the drinks, her friend was making little nodding gestures over to a dark corner of the pub.

Where sat the man with a scarred face and missing fingers whom they had last seen fighting outside the front of the Crown and Anchor.

This was easier than they had dared hope, but the situation also presented difficulties. They were guilty of the same lack of planning as Viggo had demonstrated the day before. The logic of coming to the Middy had seemed obvious to both of them, but neither had given any thought to what they should do when they found their quarry. For Carole the scenario was particularly perplexing. She didn't think she was very good with new people even when she'd been introduced to them. And the thought of just walking up to a man of whose propensity to violence she had been a witness was very alien.

Characteristically, Jude did not suffer from such hang-ups. Nodding for Carole to follow her, she walked straight towards the alcove where the scarred man was sitting. He looked up at her with some puzzlement, but like most men approached by Jude, didn't object to what he was seeing.

'I think we've met before,' Jude announced, taking possession of a chair opposite him. Carole scuttled awkwardly to an adjacent one.

'Oh yeah?' The man looked fuddled. The pint whose remains he was spinning out was clearly not his first of the day.

Jude gestured towards it. 'Get you another of those?'

He nodded. 'Stella.'

Carole looked at her friend in desperation. Don't leave me alone with him, the pale blue eyes pleaded. But by then Jude was back at the bar.

Carole cleared her throat, trying to think of an appropriate pleasantry for the occasion, but couldn't come up with anything. The only sentence that came into her mind was: 'That was a very good fight you got involved in at the Crown and Anchor last week.' But she didn't think that would have been right.

Still, her silence didn't seem to bother the man. His eyes remained fixed somewhere in the middle distance. Perhaps he didn't care who approached him, so long as they bought him a pint of Stella.

Jude handed over what he required and the man thanked her, though without taking much notice of the supplier. His interest in her as an attractive woman had been eclipsed by the more urgent priority of a drink in his hand. He took a long swallow.

Jude continued her frontal approach. 'We saw you at the Crown and Anchor in Fethering, a week ago today, when that fight broke out.'

He wasn't as drunk as he had appeared to be. A light of caution came into his eye as he put his pint down on the table. 'So?'

'That was the night a man called Ray got stabbed.'

He nodded. 'I heard about it. That kind of thing happens when people get into fights.'

'Do you like getting into fights?' asked Jude with a directness that Carole wouldn't have been capable of.

He smiled. The scarring on his face meant that only one side of his face turned up. He had the original stiff upper lip. It was also spookily like the smile they had seen from Viggo when he came to Woodside Cottage. 'Fights?' the man echoed. 'Getting into fights outside a pub? That's not fighting, not if you've done the real thing.'

'By doing "the real thing", do you mean that you've been in the army?'

He nodded in appreciation of her logic. 'That's exactly what I mean.'

'And is that where you got the injuries?'

He nodded, his hand instinctively going up to the scarred side of his face. 'Patrol outside Basra. Roadside bomb. Killed the driver. I got this. Driver was my mucker.'

'I'm sorry.'

The hazel eyes he turned on Jude now didn't look drunk at all. 'Yes, everyone's sorry. Nobody can do anything about it, though. I was going to train as a chippy when I got out.' He waived the maimed hand from which two and a half fingers were missing. 'Not going to be much use with that, am I?'

207

'But presumably you had good hospital treatment for your injuries?' said Carole.

'Oh, yes. They patched me up all right. I even got some compensation. Not much, though. It doesn't go far.'

'And you still get benefits, don't you?'

'Yeah. They're not much, either. My dad was in the army. Signals.'

'During the Second World War?'

He nodded. 'Served out in Egypt. And he came back here and he was treated like a bloody hero. He'd done his bit to save us all from Adolf Shickelgruber. And I come back, and I've done my bit to save us all from Saddam Hussein . . . and does anyone give a shit? No, even here in Portsmouth, where you'd have thought they knew something about the armed forces, I'm treated like some kind of pariah. Oh yes, people say, sure you had a rough time, but the war you were fighting was one we shouldn't have got involved in in the first place. Illegal war. Turned Iraq into a bigger bloody mess than it was before we went in. Let me tell you, there's not a lot of sympathy for an Iraq veteran. They want to forget about us, bloody government does too. We're what's left, we're the mess. They want to sweep us under the carpet.'

'Do you live round here?' asked Carole.

He flicked his head back, gesturing in the direction of a shabby sixties tower block they'd noticed as they arrived. 'Flat up there.'

'Sorry, we don't know your name.' said Jude.

'No, you don't.' He seemed quite happy to let that status quo continue.

'I'm Jude, this is Carole.'

'Carole Seddon,' said her friend, who liked to have the niceties maintained.

He still didn't seem inclined to give them his name, so Jude persisted, 'I knew Ray, the man who died.'

'Oh yes?'

'And we've both met Viggo.'

A reaction flicked in his hazel eyes, then he seemed to make a decision and announced, 'My name's Derren Hart.'

'And you know Viggo, don't you?' For a moment he contemplated denying it. 'Or should I call him "Chuck"?' Jude went on.

'I've met him, yes,' Derren conceded.

'He seems to regard you as a hero,' said Carole tartly, 'even if nobody else does.'

'Viggo's got problems.'

'Apparently he once tried to join the army,' said Jude.

'He told me that. The army may be hard up for recruits, but they still aren't going to take on someone like him.' The man let out a bark of laughter. 'He's a few bricks short of a load.'

'So was Ray.'

'Yes. You know, I've met people who reckon anyone who goes into the forces must have mental problems. You join up with something where you're trained to obey orders without question. Some people reckon only a lame-brain would do that.'

'And what do you reckon?'

Derren Hart turned his hazel eyes on Carole, and there was a new, appraising look in them. Either he'd never been as drunk as he was pretending to be, or else he had sobered up very quickly. 'I reckon . . .' he said slowly, 'that in certain situations—crisis situations, battle situations—making people obey orders without question is the only way of getting things done. If someone stops to make a moral judgement, it's already too late. They'll have been blown away before they've made their decision.'

'And would you still believe in obeying orders without question?' asked Jude.

209

'It would depend who the orders came from.'

'Like Viggo said, the orders would have to come from someone you respected?'

'Maybe. There might be other reasons why you'd obey someone.'

'The amount of money they were paying you?' suggested Carole.

He didn't like that. The look of concentrated malevolence he turned on her made Carole certain that she'd touched a nerve. Derren Hart was in the pay of someone. Maybe he'd been paid to bring the bikers to the Crown and Anchor? And to start the fight there? If so, who was his paymaster?

'Look, why are you asking me these questions? What's your interest in all this?'

'Oh,' Jude replied with arch fluffiness, 'we're just two little old ladies from Fethering. There's been a murder on our doorstep and we're doing our amateur sleuthing best to find out whodunnit.'

In spite of himself, the half-smile again flickered across his face. 'Is that what you're doing? How sweet and charming. But has it possibly occurred to you that you're asking for trouble? A lot of murders happen because someone has been too curious and they present less of a risk dead.'

'Are you saying that that's why Ray was murdered?' asked Jude. 'He had information someone wanted kept quiet?'

'I'm not saying anything about Ray. I never met the bloke. I know nothing about him. I'm just saying that, though you present yourselves as a couple of harmless old biddies, you could be putting yourselves in serious danger.'

'From whom?'

'Like I said, less curiosity might give you longer lives.' It was clear where Viggo had got his B-movie lines from.

That thought prompted Jude to ask, 'You said you know

Viggo. How well do you know him?'

'I met him at a pub called the Cat and Fiddle.'

'Is that the one on the Littlehampton Road out of Fedborough?'

'Right. I used to go there with the bikers. Viggo kind of hung on to the group. He is a bit of a hanger-on by nature.'

'Yes. And when you first met him, was he dressed as a biker?'

'No, not the first evening. He'd got all the gear by the next night, though. The real bikers thought he was a joke. They didn't want him hanging around, but I said he wasn't doing any harm.'

'You took his side?'

'If you like. Though that makes it sound a bigger deal than it was.'

'You're not a biker yourself, are you?' Carole observed.

'I've got a bike,' Derren responded defensively.

'But you don't dress like a biker.'

'No, but I've got mates who're bikers. Guys I grew up with from round here.'

'Do they include Matt?' asked Jude suddenly.

'Matt?'

'Delivery driver who lives in Worthing.'

Derren Hart shook his head. 'Never heard of a biker called Matt.'

'But the ones you do know,' asked Carole, 'you can organize them to go anywhere you want to, can you?'

'What are you on about?'

He looked so angry that Jude thought she'd better leap in before Carole actually accused him of controlling a Rent-a-Mob operation. 'Sorry, could we get back to Viggo,' she said soothingly. 'Did he ask you about your time in the army?'

Derren Hart's anger vanished, and he seemed almost embarrassed as he replied. 'Yes, he was interested in that stuff. I told you, he tried to join up.'

'So you talked to him a lot about it?'

'A bit.'

A picture was beginning to emerge for Jude. Here was the ex-soldier, traumatized by his experiences in Iraq, desperate to talk about them, but finding nobody back home was interested. The only audience he could get was the half-crazed fantasist Viggo. Who no doubt lapped up everything he was told. And started to regard Derren Hart as an action hero to match those in his beloved movies.

'You know that Viggo's stopped dressing as a biker now, do you?' asked Carole.

The man didn't commit himself to an answer.

'He's now dressing exactly like you.'

'Is that so?' He couldn't keep a little tinge of satisfaction out of his words. He wasn't in a position to be choosy about his sources of hero worship.

'You know how impressionable he is?' said Jude. 'He'd do anything you tell him.'

'Really?' Again the small note of satisfaction.

Carole went into full interrogation mode. 'Have you told him to do anything?'

'What do you mean by that?'

'Viggo talked about hitmen getting instructions by text on mobile phones.'

Derren Hart's half-smile reappeared, and he chuckled. 'Listen, lady, we've agreed the guy's a fantasist. If he wants to believe in a world where assassination orders are issued by text message, we can't stop him, can we?'

'Did he talk about that kind of thing to you?'

'Look, he lived in a world of his own. A world full of violence and hitmen and Russian roulette and orders given by text message. He talked about lots of stuff, but it wasn't real, it was all in his head.'

'But you've never issued him an order by text-message?'

He held out his mutilated hand. 'One of the many things this is not good at is text messaging.'

'And you don't know of anyone else who might have issued text-message orders to Viggo?'

His shrug told them the unlikeliness of their getting an answer to that question.

'You went to see Viggo at Copsedown Hall . . .'

'How do you know that?'

'Another of the residents saw you arriving.'

'Who?'

'I don't think that really matters,' said Jude.

Her words had been designed to protect Kelly-Marie, but the curt nod Derren Hart made suggested that he had probably worked out the identity of the witness and filed away the information.

'But you didn't give him any orders then?'

The tautness of his 'No' suggested he was getting a little weary of their questioning, but Carole pressed on, 'And did you ever issue orders to Ray either?'

'I told you—I never met the guy.'

'Are you sure? Because we believe that someone told Ray to substitute a tray of scallops in—'

The scarred face closed down. Whether that was because the two women had got close to the truth, there was no means of knowing. Without speaking another word, Derren Hart downed the rest of his pint and left the pub.

CHAPTER TWENTY-EIGHT

Carole Seddon was normally very organized about her shopping. Regular trips to Sainsbury's, avoiding weekends, once a month to stock up on large essentials, once a week for food. Rarely was she in the position, like her less far-sighted neighbour Jude, of having to rush down to Allinstore, Fethering's only supermarket, for emergency rations. But that Sunday evening she was.

She'd only had a sandwich at lunchtime after Viggo's visit to Woodside Cottage, and was quite peckish by the time they left the Middy in Fratton. As she drove back to Fethering, she found herself visualizing the ham omelette she would cook when she got back. But on arrival, she found that the High Tor larder was devoid of ham.

Carole fed Gulliver, and checked out the dressing on his injured foot, but the image of what she wanted to eat wouldn't go away. From what she had in the fridge she could have made a cheese omelette, or a tomato omelette, but by now the image of ham in her head was so strong that she had no alternative but to make a beeline to Allinstore for the missing ingredient.

The supermarket, legendary for its lack of stock and the pillars customers had to negotiate in approaching the till, was not full at that time on a summer Sunday evening, and Carole found only one other customer ahead of her in the queue for the only till that was operating. Idly she thought that the Black Watch tartan suit was vaguely familiar, and when the woman turned

214

back with her purchases, Carole recognized the most avid of Greville Tilbrook's acolytes from his anti-Dan-Poke crusade.

'Oh, hello,' she said instinctively. 'I saw you last Sunday.'

'Did you?' asked the woman, a little alarmed.

'Yes. You were with Greville Tilbrook, in the Crown and Anchor car park.'

'Oh,' said the woman, now very alarmed, and she scuttled out of the supermarket.

Carole followed the woman's departure through Allinstore's front windows. And she saw the panic-stricken woman get into a silver Smart car.

Back at High Tor, her mind was seething with speculation. She was hardly aware of eating her omelette (which was just as well because Allinstore's ham was notoriously tasteless).

She had no proof that the Smart car owned by the woman in Black Watch tartan was the same one she and Jude had seen careering over the dunes on the night of Ray Witchett's death, but it was at the very least a coincidence. And if the car did belong to the woman, who appeared to be the acme of respectability, then why hadn't she wanted to face the police and made such a hasty getaway? Why, come to that, had she stayed in the car park until after Dan Poke's act had finished? Had Greville Tilbrook been with her? Were he and his acolytes planning to confront the departing crowd with their anti-blasphemy banners?

The other memory that kept recurring in Carole's mind was the one that had struck Jude—Greville Tilbrook's tirade against the wearers of 'Fancy a Poke?' T-shirts. Together with that came a vivid image of one such T-shirt, stained by Ray's lifeblood. Surely Greville Tilbrook's passionate views couldn't be so strong that he might have . . . ?

Her conjectures were interrupted by the ringing of her phone.

She answered it and felt a sudden chill when the speaker identified himself as Greville Tilbrook. 'I gather you spoke to Beryl.' Carole now had a name for the lady in Black Watch tartan. 'Are you in?' he asked urgently.

'Given the fact that I've just answered my phone, I must be, mustn't I?' She spoke with an uppity confidence she did not feel.

'Yes, but will you be there in a quarter of an hour?'

'Well, I was thinking of taking my dog out for a—'

'Don't leave till I arrive,' said Greville Tilbrook. He sounded very masterful. And even threatening.

Carole reached for the phone to ring Jude, but then remembered that her neighbour was going to see a healer friend that evening. For a moment there was a temptation to drive away somewhere, to let Greville Tilbrook find the house empty. But curiosity overcame Carole's fear, and she stayed put.

Her work at the Home Office had taught her that the most unlikely people turn out to be murderers. A few are monsters, but most are meek and ordinary. That evening in her sitting room at High Tor Greville Tilbrook looked very ordinary. But not meek. His face was again suffused with the kind of fury that Carole and Jude had witnessed in the Crown and Anchor car park.

'You have made me very angry, Mrs Seddon,' he announced through clenched teeth.

'I regret that, Mr Tilbrook,' she said, trying to sound cool, 'but since I don't know why I've made you angry, I'm not in a position to apologize.'

'You know things about me which I have worked very hard to keep secret.' Hardly surprising, thought Carole, if you did actually murder Ray. 'Mrs Seddon, you've been spying on me. And

you know what happens to spies when they're caught, don't
you?'

Carole couldn't fully understand her reactions. At one level,
she could observe the scene and see what a ridiculous pompous
little man Greville Tilbrook was. But another part of her was all
too aware of the manic light in his eye, and the danger that lay
within his anger.

'Are you threatening me, Mr Tilbrook?'

'It rather depends on what you do, Mrs Seddon. How you
plan to use the information you have about me.'

'You'll have to explain what you mean.'

'I mean—are you proposing to blackmail me?'

'Certainly not! I might consider passing on the information
that I have about you to the police.'

'The police?' He looked almost relieved at the idea. 'But this
is not a police matter. I meant—are you proposing to pass the
information on to my wife?'

'Your wife?' Carole hadn't the beginning of an idea of what
he was talking about.

'Perhaps I should explain . . . ?'

'I think perhaps you should, Mr Tilbrook.'

So he did. And, needless to say, given who was talking, the
explanation was not a short one. 'The fact is that, without wishing in any way to mislead or give a false impression, I do find
myself in a slightly delicate situation vis-à-vis the situation in
which I find myself . . . if you get my drift . . . ?'

Carole didn't get his drift at all, but somehow there was no
longer any menace in his manner, just acute embarrassment.
And she found that watching Greville Tilbrook squirm was a
most enjoyable spectator sport.

'Not to put too fine a point on it, Mrs Seddon, and without
wishing to cause any hurt to any individual—most particularly
not to my lady wife, a very fine woman who has been more than

a helpmeet to me in the many and varied guises—or, if you will, hats—under which I conduct my life, the main inspiration of which, I may say without fear of contradiction, has always been a sense of civic responsibility, I would be very unwilling to have jeopardized a more than satisfactory status quo by any negative or counter-productive dissemination of information into the wrong ears. Fethering, by its nature, being, as it is, a village—a fact wherein, for many people, lies much of its charm—can at times, however, suffer from that natural propensity within village communities—and indeed many other small, tight-knit communities—for the business of any one individual to be regarded as the business of everyone. I refer, of course, to the proclivity amongst the mature citizens of an environment—'

'Mr Tilbrook,' said Carole patiently, 'what on earth are you talking about?'

He looked aggrieved to be interrupted. 'I am talking about, as it were, what happened at the Crown and Anchor a week ago today.'

'Yes, it was very regrettable.'

'It certainly was. And I really do feel, without putting too fine a point on it, that the best solution, from the point of view of all concerned, would be that the whole incident should be forgotten.'

'You've rather changed your tune.'

'I beg your pardon?'

'On Sunday you were carrying placards saying Dan Poke shouldn't be allowed to perform. Now you're saying the whole thing should be forgotten.'

'It was not the, for want of a better word, performance by Dan Poke, to which I was, by the same token, referring.'

'Then, to what were you, "by the same token, referring"?'

Carole couldn't resist quoting Greville Tilbrook back at himself, but he didn't seem to notice her mockery as he replied,

'I am referring to something which, by any stretch of the imagination, and when all's said and done, is undoubtedly more important than that.'

'Ah, you mean the murder?'

'No, Mrs Seddon! Are you being deliberately obtuse?'

'I have never been deliberately obtuse in my life!'

'I am referring, Mrs Seddon, to what you told Beryl you had seen!' Carole could only look bewildered. She wasn't aware of having told Beryl she'd seen anything. Greville Tilbrook went on, 'Listen, none of us is, as it were, perfect. And, for my sins, I am not excluding myself, to be quite honest, from that category. The fact is that Margaret, my wife, whom I do not believe you have, up until this moment in time, had the pleasure of meeting . . . ?'

Carole confirmed that she hadn't.

'Well, Margaret is a very fine woman. Had we had any children, though we were not blessed in that way, she would undoubtedly have been an excellent mother to them. She is universally acknowledged to be, and this is something I can vouch for myself, a very fine housekeeper—or even, as I believe the popular phrase is these days, "homemaker". She also has a commendable sense of civic responsibility. Margaret and I have, hitherto, lived a life of few arguments and, one cannot avoid the phrase, considerable domestic happiness. But, if I were to venture a criticism of my lovely wife—which I am only doing now, because of the gravity of the current situation—it might be that she is less affectionate than others of her sex—or should one say "gender" nowadays—might, in the final analysis, be.'

Carole didn't supply any further prompts. She just listened in amazement as Greville Tilbrook continued, 'But when I met Beryl, I discovered that I had found a woman of, not to put too fine a point on it, a woman of considerably greater *warmth*, if you get my drift, than I had hitherto encountered in the marital

219

home. And, though I have used the not inconsiderable powers of prayer and conscience to divert myself from the track on which I had, in a manner of speaking, embarked, I eventually came to the conclusion that I owed it to myself, for a moment not considering anyone else, to take advantage of the little extra happiness that was being offered to me, in the guise of—or, if you prefer, the form of—Beryl.'

Carole gaped. 'Are you saying that you and Beryl are having an affair?'

'Of course that's what I'm saying! And don't pretend you don't know, Mrs Seddon! After all, you're the one who told Beryl that you'd seen us together last Sunday in the Crown and Anchor car park.'

Her knee-jerk reaction was immediately to explain that that hadn't been what she meant, but she managed to curb the instinct. Having an embarrassed, apologetic Greville Tilbrook on the back foot would be infinitely more useful than facing his normal self-righteous persona. So, in a voice which she thought rather neatly combined pity and disapprobation, she said, 'Well, you must understand, Mr Tilbrook, that the situation does put me in something of a quandary . . .'

'Yes, I can see that, Mrs Seddon.'

'Because, although I obviously have no wish to do harm to any other human being, one cannot forget that there is a moral dimension.'

'Oh, I do so agree.'

'So what would your advice to me be on what to do next?'

'Nothing! Don't tell anyone!' The verbal simplicity of his answer was a measure of his panic.

Carole let him sweat for a moment before responding. 'And that would be my instinctive reaction, Mr Tilbrook. I'm not a busybody. I have no wish to destroy a marriage . . .'

'Oh, thank you so much, Mrs Seddon.'

'. . . but, on the other hand, there is more than just a marriage to be considered here.'

He gaped at her. 'How do you mean?'

'Like you, I also have a sense of civic responsibility. And unfortunately, the evening which you chose to canoodle with your girlfriend in the Crown and Anchor car park . . . in your car, was it?'

'Her car.'

The image of the highly respectable Greville Tilbrook and Black Watch Beryl grappling in the confined space of a Smart car was irresistibly funny. Carole had difficulty restraining her laughter, as she asked, 'And your canoodling took place, I assume, after the two other lady protesters had gone home?' He nodded. 'Well, unfortunately, on that very evening there was a fight at the Crown and Anchor, which led to someone being stabbed to death.'

'I know that, Mrs Seddon! That is why I am so concerned that my, as it were, peccadillo should be kept quiet.'

Carole nodded sagely, enjoying her complete control of the situation. 'I can see that, yes.' She let him agonize through another silence. 'So was it the outbreak of the fight that caused you to leave Beryl's car?'

'No. I took the view, as it were, that during the fighting, it might be a better plan of action for me to, not to put too fine a point on it, lie low.'

'In Beryl's car?'

'Yes.'

'With Beryl?'

'Yes.'

'So what did you do when the police arrived?'

'As soon as I heard what can only be described as the sirens, and saw the, as it were, blue lights, I took the decision that discretion was, not for the first time in my life, the better part of

221

valour and, not wishing to beat about the bush, I made my escape.'

'With Beryl? I saw a Smart car driving like crazy across the dunes with all the bikers.'

'No, I thought it might be exacerbating the, as it were, risk, if I were to stay in the car. Beryl drove off on her own.'

Carole was suddenly alert. 'So which way did you escape? You didn't go back along the road into the village?'

'No, I thought that, since that was the direction from which the police were arriving, it might perhaps not be the wisest of courses—and might indeed prompt questioning of a kind that I was anxious to avoid, should I have taken that route . . .'

Carole couldn't resist turning the knife in the wound of his embarrassment. 'I'm very surprised, Mr Tilbrook, that you, such a stern advocate of civic responsibility, did not stay to offer the police any assistance they might want from you as a witness to what had happened at the Crown and Anchor that night.'

His mouth opened and closed like that of a goldfish. Greville Tilbrook couldn't come up with a single word, let alone a subordinate clause.

Carole had played with him long enough. 'So which way did you escape?' she asked urgently.

'I thought if I went past the pub down to the beach, I could walk along to the Fether estuary and go back into the village that way.'

'So you went past the back door of the Crown and Anchor, the one that leads into the kitchen?'

'I suppose I must have done.'

Now finally she had an explanation for the sound of retreating footsteps on the shingle that she and Jude had heard that night.

'And did you see anything?' He hesitated. 'Mr Tilbrook, I am prepared to keep quiet about what I know of your shabby escapade with Beryl . . .' (or rather what you were generous enough to tell me of your shabby escapade with Beryl) '. . . on the condition that you tell me everything you witnessed at the back of the pub last Sunday evening.'

He weighed his options. The process didn't take long. 'Very well,' he capitulated, 'if you swear you'll never breathe a word about me and Beryl . . . ?'

'I swear it.'

'I saw two figures outside the back door of the Crown and Anchor. I was hurrying past, I couldn't see much detail. But first there was just one, a small man who seemed to be waiting for something . . .'

Ray Witchett waiting for his autograph from Dan Poke.

'. . . and then another man went round the side of the pub towards him.'

'What did this other man look like?'

'One of the bikers. Dressed in leather. He was tall with long hair and a dark beard.'

Her breath was tight as Carole asked, 'Did they seem to know each other?'

'Oh yes,' Greville Tilbrook replied. 'They greeted each other like friends.'

Ray hadn't known any of the bikers. Only someone who looked like a biker.

Viggo.

CHAPTER TWENTY-NINE

It was nearly midnight when the phone at Woodside Cottage rang. Jude was in bed, but not yet asleep. Her mind was still full of the news she had received from Carole, of Greville Tilbrook nearly witnessing Ray's murder.

The caller was Kelly-Marie. 'It's something bad,' she said.

Carole hadn't been asleep either—in fact, she had been sitting in her nightdress, finding her way with increasing fascination around the laptop she had inherited from her daughter-in-law. When she got Jude's call, she immediately said that they should both go to Copsedown Hall. Apart from anything else, it would be quicker in the Renault. Not all the roads in Fethering had street lights, and they didn't want to be stumbling around in the dark.

So they both threw some clothes back on and set off together.

Kelly-Marie was standing just inside the door, waiting for them. She was wearing a flowered cotton dress, which made her look even more like a child. It was presumably the Sunday best she had put on in the morning to go and have lunch with her parents.

'Viggo? Is it something to do with Viggo?' asked Jude, as the girl let them in.

Kelly-Marie nodded. 'I wasn't sure who to call. I thought I'd call you first.'

'Very sensible.' Quickly she introduced Carole. 'Where is he?'

'In his room.'

She limped ahead of them up the stairs. 'Are the other residents around?' asked Jude in a whisper.

'Asleep. They have to work in the morning. I don't think they heard it. Only me. His room's next door to mine.'

There was only a safety light on on the landing, but Jude could see that the door to Kelly-Marie's room was closed, and the one to Viggo's was ajar. The girl lingered outside, unwilling to enter, while Jude and Carole went in.

Given what lay in the armchair, it was surprising that Carole and Jude could take in any other detail of the room, but they were both aware of shelves upon shelves of DVDs and videos, arranged in a surprisingly organized way. On the table in front of the armchair stood a laptop computer, its screen opened but blank. The floor was littered with empty Stella Artois cans.

The entry wound on Viggo's right temple was neat and had only dribbled a little. Blood from the exit wound, though, splattered over the armchair, sofa, walls and shelves of DVDs.

His right arm had dropped down over the side of the armchair. Just below it on the floor lay the revolver.

As the two women moved forward, pressure on an uneven floorboard was sufficient to jog the laptop screen out of hibernation. The image on the screen had been frozen, the DVD paused. Carole saw the haggard faces of men under pressure in a sweaty bamboo cage.

'*The Deer Hunter,*' Jude murmured. 'The Russian roulette scene.'

Carole looked down. She knew nothing of guns, but she could see the number of bullets, the backs of which showed in the revolver's cylinder. Every chamber appeared to be full.

'Not very good odds for Russian roulette,' she observed.

CHAPTER THIRTY

Neither of them got much sleep that night. By the time the police had been called, and by the time the police had arrived and conducted some basic questioning, it was well into the small hours. And the image of Viggo, still so vivid in their minds, was not conducive to peaceful slumber.

They reassembled blearily next morning over very strong coffee in the sitting room of Woodside Cottage.

'Typical, isn't it?' said Carole. 'Just when we think we've identified our murderer, someone blows him away.'

'So you think Viggo was murdered too?'

'Don't you?'

'I'm not so sure. I mean, he could have been, but then again playing a macho game of Russian roulette . . . well, it would have been in character. He was so obsessed with all that hard-man stuff. Did you see the titles of all those DVDs and videos? And he did mention Russian roulette when he came here.'

'Yes, but nobody plays Russian roulette with six bullets loaded into the gun.'

'They might if they wanted to be sure of the outcome.'

'How do you mean?'

'Look, let's say Viggo did murder Ray . . .'

'Which seems very likely from what Greville Tilbrook saw.'

'I agree. Well, say he did do it. And he thought he was being brave and macho, living up to the image of all his hard-man heroes, but then slowly he realized what he'd done, that he had actually killed a man. Not just a man, but someone he knew. For a man like Viggo, who spent so much of his time in fantasy, that reality could be pretty shocking.'

'And he might have killed himself from remorse?'

'It's possible.'

Carole's sniff made clear how much she thought of that idea. 'I think it was a set-up. Somebody else shot him. The Russian roulette business was just set-dressing.'

'Maybe. But why would someone want to kill him?'

'Well, for the purposes of argument, let's make two assumptions . . . First, that Viggo did stab Ray and, second, that he didn't do it off his own bat. That someone set him up to do it.'

'Gave him the order by text on his mobile phone?'

'Quite possibly.'

'Pity we haven't got Viggo's mobile phone to check his messages, isn't it?' said Jude ruefully.

'Yes, very selfish of the police always to keep that kind of evidence to themselves,' Carole agreed. 'But, moving on . . . Let's say we're talking about one villain, who, while possibly not actually committing either of the crimes, set them up, in both cases taking advantage of particularly susceptible and pathetic men . . .'

'All right. I'm with you so far.'

'So this person takes advantage of Ray's good nature and desire to make everyone happy, and persuades him unknowingly to introduce the dodgy scallops into the Crown and Anchor kitchen. But then our villain hears, probably from Viggo, that you've been snooping around Copsedown Hall, asking Ray questions. Suddenly poor Ray becomes a security risk, there's a danger he might tell you everything. So the same person—our villain—takes advantage of Viggo's love of cloak-and-dagger stuff, underground operations and all that, and issues the order for him to kill Ray.'

'I agree that all of this is possible, but I still don't see—'

'I haven't finished,' said Carole severely. 'This person arranged to have Ray killed before he could spill the beans about what had been going on. And he arranged to have Viggo killed for just the same reason.'

'So what's the common factor?'

'Jude, you are being particularly dense this morning. The common factor is you. Or us, if you like. Ray was murdered just after he'd nearly told you who'd set him up to swap the scallops. Viggo was murdered just after you and I revealed our suspicions of Viggo—or at least showed an unhealthy interest in him—to Derren Hart in Fratton. I think we should be very careful from now on, Jude. We're up against someone ruthless enough to kill two men with mental-health problems. I don't think he—or she—would be too bothered about adding a couple of middle-aged women to the list.'

Jude was silent. She took a long sip of coffee. It didn't dispel the woolliness in her head as much as she had hoped. Then she asked, 'How much do you think Ted is involved?'

'I don't think he's involved in the murders.'

'Not in actually committing them, no. But he's holding out on us. He's definitely got more information than he's letting on about. He complicated things at the start by trying to protect Ray—and look how that ended up. I think he could tell us a lot more.'

'I'm sure he could, but since he currently won't talk to us at all, I don't see how we're going to get it out of him.'

'Maybe not, but I think it's worth another call.'

Jude dialled the number of Ted's flat, then the Crown and Anchor main line. Answering machines on both. Maybe the landlord wasn't there. She thought it was more likely that he just wasn't taking calls. For a moment she contemplated leaving a message informing him of Viggo's death, but she decided against it. If Ted Crisp was as involved, as he was in her worst imaginings, he'd already know what had happened.

Jude, uncharacteristically gloomy—she needed her sleep—looked at Carole and shook her head. 'I just don't know where we go next.'

'Well, I do,' said her friend. 'We follow up the only other lead we have.'

'I didn't know we'd got another lead.'

'Something we got from Derren Hart.' Jude still looked bemused, but the confidence in Carole's pale blue eyes was growing. 'Do you fancy a pub lunch, Jude?'

'I don't think Ted's any more likely to talk to us face to face than he is on the phone.'

'I wasn't thinking of the Crown and Anchor. I was thinking of another pub.'

'Oh?'

'The other one where Derren Hart said Viggo used to go drinking with the bikers.'

'Ah, yes.' There was now a matching sparkle in Jude's brown eyes. 'Of course, I'd forgotten about that.'

'So I think lunch at the Cat and Fiddle, don't you?'

'Excellent idea.'

'It's not as if we don't know where it is.'

Carole and Jude had been to the Cat and Fiddle before, because Zosia's brother Tadeusz Jankowski had worked there before his premature death. They remembered how little they'd liked the place. Though it had a perfect position, right on the banks of the Fether, and did very good business, particularly in the summer, they had recoiled from its phoney, country-and-western-influenced style. They winced inwardly as they remembered the bar staff, dressed in red-gingham shirts and dungarees.

Carole and Jude also remembered the pub's over-the-top

landlady, Shona Nuttall. She'd had no inhibitions about talking to them before, even though the thing she had most wanted to talk about was herself. But maybe she'd have some useful recollections of Viggo's and Derren Hart's biker crowd.

The interview they were anticipating was, however, not to be. As Carole slowed the Renault down to enter the Cat and Fiddle car park, she found her way barred by a high gate of solid wood. The frontage of the pub itself was also fenced off and its windows boarded up.

But the site looked very neat and under control. What was happening was a makeover rather than a close-down. This was confirmed by a printed board on the fencing, which read: THE CAT AND FIDDLE WILL BE RE-OPENING ON 1 OCTOBER AS ANOTHER WELCOMING AND LUXURIOUS HOME HOSTELRIES TAVERN.

CHAPTER THIRTY-ONE

So they did end up having lunch in the Crown and Anchor, exactly two weeks after the food-poisoning incident that had started them on their current investigation. There were a few more customers—mostly holidaymakers—than there had been on their previous visit, but the pub wasn't doing anything like the volume of business it should have been in the middle of a hot July.

Ted Crisp was there, but without being overtly rude, he made it clear that he didn't want to engage in conversation with them. After a friendly enough wave on their arrival, he suddenly had urgent things to do in the kitchen.

Zosia served them. She looked tired, her customary brightness dimmed. The stress surrounding the Crown and Anchor was getting to everyone. They got their large Chilean Chardonnays, and both went for salads, chicken for Carole, salmon for Jude.

'I see we're not Ted's favourite people today,' Jude observed to Zosia.

'Not just you. No people are his favourite people. He is in a bad state.'

'Is he still on the whisky?' asked Carole.

The Polish girl nodded glumly. 'I think so. He is very unhappy, but he will not talk about what is making him unhappy. He . . . what is that idiom you have? He puts it in a bottle?'

'He bottles it up,' said Jude.

'Yes, that is what he does. Which does not help. This "bottling-up", I think, makes things worse for people.'

Carole, for whom life had been one long process of bottling-up, nodded.

'We'll get it out of him eventually,' said Jude.

Zosia grinned, without much optimism.

'Has Ted heard about the latest death?' asked Carole. 'Up at Copsedown Hall.'

'Oh yes. News of tragedy travels fast in a place like Fethering, that I have learned since I have been here. There is more gossip, I think, even than in a Polish country village.'

'Did Ted say anything when he heard the news?'

'I don't know. I was not here when he was told. But he certainly does know.'

Just as they were about to find a table, Jude noticed a book propped up behind the bar. *A Poke in the Eye,* by Dan Poke. When she pointed it out, Zosia said, 'This was left the evening he did his act here. It was for sale, I think, but nobody wanted to buy it because the cover was torn or something.'

'Could I have a look at it?'

Jude took the book over to the empty alcove Carole had found for them. When she opened it, she realized that not only the torn dust jacket made it unsaleable. The spine had broken in more than one place, leaving the contents like an unevenly sliced loaf of yellowing pages.

'Must've been published quite a time ago,' Jude observed. She checked on the copyright page. Yes, the book was nearly ten years old. 'So that was when Dan Poke was presumably at his peak of popularity.' Carole looked at her quizzically. 'Publishers tend only to go for showbiz autobiographies from the really hot names. People who're currently big on telly. I suppose you don't know how well his television career's going at the moment, do you?'

Jude had supposed correctly. Carole left her in no doubt that the sort of programmes people like Dan Poke might be involved in were not her favoured viewing.

'No, but you can't miss them, when someone's really hot. You see them on trailers between other programmes. Television celebrities are all over the newspapers.'

'Yes, even *The Times*,' said Carole with an aggrieved sniff, 'quite often has colour photographs of showbiz nonentities on the front page. It's sometimes terrifying how downmarket that paper's gone, you know.'

Jude wasn't really listening; she was following a train of thought of her own. 'No, I don't think I have seen much about Dan Poke recently . . .'

'So in what way is that relevant?'

'Just thinking. I mean, OK, he's been on telly, so he's still a big name in a little place like Fethering, but I think it's a while since he was really in the big time . . .'

'I repeat my question: in what way is that relevant?'

'I don't know. He just seems to indulge in all the behaviour of a big star, when probably he isn't that big a star.'

'Isn't that how *show business* works?' asked Carole acidly.

'Yes, maybe . . .' Jude's eyes strayed back to the book's copyright page. 'Huh, and he didn't even write it himself, anyway.'

'What?'

Jude pointed out to her friend the words: 'Copyright © 2001 Richard Farrelly'.

'So? Lots of show-business autobiographies have ghost writers.'

'Not so often for comedians. Particularly the stand-ups. They pride themselves on producing their own material.'

Carole couldn't see that that was particularly relevant either, and their conversation moved on to other topics. But later, when Ted Crisp himself delivered their salads, Jude asked him, 'Who's Richard Farrelly?'

His face was still set in an expression which said he wasn't going to engage in conversation with them, but he couldn't see the harm in responding to that.

'Why do you ask?'

Jude indicated *A Poke in the Eye* on the table. 'Because Dan Poke got him to ghost his autobiography.'

Something that was almost a grin appeared through the thatch of Ted Crisp's beard. 'Richard Farrelly didn't ghost it.'

'What?'

'Richard Farrelly is Dan Poke. Oh, come on, what are the chances of a comedian's parents christening him with a gift of a name like "Dan Poke"?'

'You mean "Dan Poke" is a pseudonym? Dan Poke is really Richard Farrelly?'

'That's exactly what I mean.'

'Oh, Ted, while you're here, could we just have a word about—?'

But Carole was cut short. 'Sorry, a lot to get on with.' And the landlord vanished back into the kitchen.

Jude sighed and looked across at her friend with sympathy. She'd detected that Carole was taking Ted's brusqueness more personally than she was. But then Carole Seddon took everything personally. 'Don't worry. We'll soon all be friends again.'

'I'm not worried,' Carole lied. 'If he wants to play games, well, it doesn't bother me. What I'm much more concerned about is where we go next in our investigation, having drawn a blank at the Cat and Fiddle.'

'Yes.' Jude took a mouthful of her excellent salmon salad and looked thoughtful. Then she said, 'I wonder if we have drawn a complete blank at the Cat and Fiddle . . .'

'Hm?'

'OK, the pub appears to be under new ownership, but that doesn't necessarily mean that the old owner's vanished off the face of the earth.'

'Shona Nuttall,' said Carole.

'Exactly. I mean, she may have sold up the pub and taken off to spend the proceeds in well-heeled retirement in Tenerife or somewhere.' The recollection of the woman with her deep perma-tan encouraged this image. 'On the other hand, she might still be living locally.'

'Who'd know that? Ted?'

'Possibly. Though in his current mood he wouldn't tell us.' The skin around Jude's brown eyes crinkled as she tried to nail down an elusive memory. Suddenly it came to her. 'Zosia might have a contact number for Shona Nuttall. They certainly met when she was trying to find out what had happened to her brother.'

Given the slackness of custom in the Crown and Anchor, it wasn't difficult to attract the bar manager's attention. And yes, she did still have a home number for Shona Nuttall stored in her mobile. Though whether the ex-landlady was still living there, Zosia couldn't say.

Jude rang the number straight away. It was answered by Shona Nuttall. When told that her caller wanted to know the circumstances of her selling the Cat and Fiddle, she said yes, she was more than happy for them to come and talk to her about it.

CHAPTER THIRTY-TWO

'What's your recollection of Shona Nuttall?' asked Jude, as the Renault purred sedately towards Southwick.

'Pushy. Full of herself.'

'You didn't take to her?'

'Certainly not. She's far from being my kind of person.'

Jude smiled inwardly. What Carole was saying was that she didn't normally mix with pub landladies. And this from a woman who'd had a brief affair with a pub landlord. But Jude knew better than to make any comment on the anomaly.

'Anyway, you didn't take to her either, Jude.'

'No, I agree.'

'Well, since we both feel the same on the subject, why did you raise it?' asked Carole, almost petulantly. The effects of the lunchtime Chardonnay had dissipated. Their lack of sleep the night before was catching up with both of them.

'It was just, talking to her on the phone . . .'

'Yes?'

'. . . she sounded different.'

The address Jude had been given was probably not far from the sea, but you wouldn't have known it. Southwick was another of the interlocking sprawl of villages which make the area between Brighton and Worthing a virtually continuous suburb. And the house which Shona Nuttall owned was, like so many in that part of the world, a bungalow. Its dimensions were adequate for one person, but not lavish.

Carole and Jude were both shocked by the appearance of the woman who opened the door to them. She was undoubtedly Shona Nuttall, but totally transformed from the Shona Nuttall they had met not so long ago as the queen of the Cat and Fiddle. She was still of ample proportions, but whereas her body had previously been restricted by corsetry, everything had now been allowed to hang loose, and gravity had exacted its revenge.

Her large cleavage was still on display, but, without the engineering which had formerly thrust it upwards, had the texture of muslin and slumped like an old ridge tent. Her style of dress had changed too. Carole and Jude remembered her in a spangly top and tight trousers. Now she shuffled around in a sweatshirt and jogging bottoms. And she was wearing none of her bulky gold jewellery.

But it was in her face and hair that the change was greatest. Without any make-up, the skin was sallow and sagging. The flash of a gold tooth in her unlipsticked mouth looked somehow grotesque. And, unmonitored by regular visits to the salon, the colouring had grown out of her hair. Some had been carelessly swept back into a scrunchie, the rest hung, lank and grey, around her face.

When Carole and Jude introduced themselves, Shona Nuttall claimed to remember their previous encounter, but seemed to have little detailed recollection of the occasion. Still, that was perhaps to be expected, given the number of customers who pass through a pub, particularly a well-situated one like the Cat and Fiddle.

She ushered them through into her sitting room and seemed relieved when they refused her half-hearted offer of tea or coffee. On a small table beside her seat on the sofa was a large glass of colourless fluid. The way Shona Nuttall subsequently drank from it suggested the contents were stronger than water. Probably vodka, the almost odourless favourite of alcoholics everywhere.

The impression that Carole and Jude received from the room was of universal velvet. The heavy bottle-green curtains were velvet. The pinkish chairs they sat in, though actually covered in Dralon, had the feeling of velvet. Even the olive-coloured carpet looked like velvet. And on various surfaces stood photographs in frames of burgundy velvet. All of them featured Shona hugging glazed-eyed customers at the Cat and Fiddle. There seemed to be no family photographs.

The room was not exactly untidy, but it gave off a feeling of dusty disuse. Despite the July heat, all of the windows were shut, and it took Carole and Jude a little while to realize that there was air conditioning—an unusual feature in a bungalow on the South Coast. But the air conditioning couldn't completely flush out the smell of old cigarette smoke.

Once various inconsequential pleasantries had been exchanged, Carole announced, 'What we are really interested in, Mrs Nuttall—'

'It's Shona, please, love. Everyone calls me Shona. And, actually, I never was "Mrs". Only "Miss". Ploughed my own furrow,' she added, with an attempt at her old heartiness.

'Very well, Shona, Jude and I were interested in why you sold the Cat and Fiddle. When we were last there, it all seemed very well set up and thriving.' This was a slight exaggeration. On the winter evening when they had visited business had been slack. But the pub was well known for doing a brisk trade in the summer. That was ensured, if by nothing else, by its location, perched on the river outside Fedborough. In one direction was a view of the rolling South Downs; in the other the tidal waters of the Fether swelled down towards the English Channel.

'Yes, yes, I was doing very well,' Shona agreed. 'And I'd

always planned to sell up and retire at some point. The Cat and Fiddle was my nest egg, going to fund my retirement. It was just . . . well, I hadn't planned to do it quite so early.'

'So why did you—?'

But the ex-landlady wasn't ready to answer that kind of question so soon. 'I mean,' she went on, 'without false modesty, I think I made a bloody good publican. I brought a bit of atmosphere to that place, everyone said so. And I also think publicans can do some good. You know, people come in weighed down with their problems . . . trouble at home, trouble at work, all their little worries about health and that . . . and after a drink or two they realize that life's not all bad.' She took a breath. Carole tried to get in, but wasn't quick enough. 'You know, the job of running a pub involves a lot of different skills, but I think one of the most important is acting as a kind of therapist. God, the stuff you have to listen to behind the jump . . .'

' "Behind the jump"?' Carole echoed curiously.

'Means "behind the bar". Expression publicans use.'

'Where does it come from?'

'No idea. Anyway, as I was saying, I reckon we publicans take a lot of burden off the NHS, you know, and the social services. The amount of listening we do, it's got to help people, hasn't it?'

'Yes, I'm sure lots of people have cause to be very grateful to you,' said Jude.

'But you still haven't told us why you sold the pub earlier than you intended,' insisted Carole.

'Had a good offer.' Shona Nuttall shrugged. 'Recession supposed to be coming. Smoking ban had hit business a bit. Pubs closing down all over the country. So I got out at the right time, as it turned out.'

Despite the positive nature of her words, there was a wistful-

239

ness in the woman's delivery which made Carole press harder. 'Was that all there was to it?'

'I don't know what you mean.'

'I think Carole's asking whether you found yourself under any pressure to sell.'

The blowsy ex-landlady looked at both of her interrogators in turn, as though assessing how much she should tell them. Then she conceded, 'Yes, there was a bit of pressure, yes.'

'What kind of pressure?'

She sighed, took a sip of her drink and reached forward to a packet on the table in front of her. 'Sorry, I need a cigarette. Better have it quickly before the bloody government bans people from smoking in their own homes.'

She lit up, took a long drag, sighed again and began. 'Look, pub business is a funny old world. You can be taking it in hand over fist one day, next nobody wants to know. It's all to do with reputation and goodwill. Keep the image of your premises right and you can be sitting on a goldmine. And I think I done well with the Cat and Fiddle over the years. 'Course I started off with a lot going for me. For a start, I came into some family money, so I didn't have to mortgage myself up to the hilt. And then again the location's hard to beat, this is an area where there's always going to be a lot of tourists. Anyone who managed to lose money at the Cat and Fiddle during the summer must be an idiot.

'But I built the business up slowly. Built up my staff, built up the reputation of the place, got it into the right pub guides, on the right websites. Though I say so myself, I done a good job.

'And yes, I always planned to retire some time, but obviously I wanted to do it when the time was right, when I'd get the maximum payback on my investment. And I did have offers. Location like the Cat and Fiddle, the big chains are bound to be interested. But I didn't like the idea of my pub just going the way of all the others, being branded, looking exactly the same. I wanted the Cat and Fiddle to keep its individuality.'

Which was rather ironic, because, to Carole and Jude's minds, she had created an environment that had made the Cat and Fiddle look exactly like a cloned pub owned by a big chain. But of course neither of them said anything as she went on, 'I had a lot of the big boys look at the place over the years. I mean, it was never going to go to a Wetherspoon's or an All Bar One, they always concentrate on urban locations, but there are quite a lot of chains that deal with country pubs and, as I say, the offers were there. The most persistent came from a set-up called Home Hostelries . . . you heard of them?'

Carole and Jude nodded. The name was all too familiar to them.

'Well, they started off small and then got bigger by taking over other smaller chains. Took over Snug Pubs a few years back.'

'I've heard of them,' said Carole, immediately making the connection with the KWS warehouse in Worthing that had handled their deliveries. And with Sylvia's fiancé, Matt.

'And quite recently Home Hostelries swallowed up the Foaming Flagon Group. They are becoming very big players indeed. And they kept making offers to me, but I always thought the offers were too low. I was hanging on for more, and I was sure I could get it, though as time went by all the other interests seemed to fall away, and it was only Home Hostelries who wanted to buy.

'Then, what, about nine months ago . . . running up to Christmas it was, I started to get trouble at the pub.'

'What do you mean by trouble?' asked Carole.

'Rowdiness. Youngsters drinking too much. Fights. Had to call the police more than once. And it was a bad time of year for that to happen. Got lots of tables booked for staff Christmas dos, that kind of stuff and yes, they're all drinking more than they should, but it wasn't the business clientele who was starting the fights. Though some of them did get involved.'

'So who was starting the fights?' asked Jude.

'A whole new crowd started coming into the pub. Bikers.' Carole and Jude exchanged looks and almost imperceptible nods. 'And once that kind of thing starts, it's difficult to stop. You know, the whole point of a pub is that it's open to anyone, and, yes, you can bar individuals, but it's difficult to shut out a whole group. And you might end up just antagonizing them, which would only make things worse. So I was trying to keep control of the place, but there were a lot of scuffles breaking out in the car park at closing time. And, somehow, every one of them, however minor, ended up getting reported in the *Fedborough Gazette*.'

Again Carole and Jude exchanged brief eye contact. A pattern was starting to emerge.

'You didn't have any incidences of food poisoning at the pub during this period, did you?'

'Funny you should mention that, because yes, a couple of weeks before Christmas, like when we're at our absolute busiest . . . a whole practice of solicitors got sick after their Christmas party.' Potentially entertaining though this image was, neither Carole nor Jude laughed. 'They blamed the Coquille St Jacques starter that they'd had, but I'm sure it couldn't have been that. I always maintained the highest standards of hygiene in my kitchen—I was almost obsessive about it, and the Health and Safety inspectors have never found anything to complain of—so I've no idea how it happened. I think those solicitors all got one of those vomiting bugs which seem to be around in the winter so much these days. But that was not the way they saw it. And, needless to say, the incident didn't do anything to help the image of the Cat and Fiddle.'

'Presumably,' said Carole, 'the food poisoning also got coverage in the local paper?'

'Oh yes. Front page of the *Gazette*. I was even asked to be interviewed for the local television news. But of course I said no. I'm a very private person.'

Carole and Jude both recalled that on their last encounter with Shona Nuttall she had demonstrated a very different attitude to the media, crowing about her recent appearance on the television news, but neither of them commented on the inconsistency.

'Anyway,' Shona went on, 'all this was having a disastrous effect on the business. Lots of firms ringing in to cancel their Christmas parties. Families with small children—who used to be quite a staple of the lunchtime trade—well, they kept away from a place that was getting a reputation for violence. And the pensioners, who'd always come in for their special-rate meals, they stopped coming.

'Within a couple of months, the Cat and Fiddle, from being one of the most popular, must-visit pubs in the area, had virtually emptied. And I was so stressed, I thought I was going to have a breakdown.'

At this recollection an involuntary tear trickled down her wrinkled cheek. She dashed it away, took a large swallow from her drink and busied herself lighting another cigarette.

'And it was because you were so stressed,' Jude suggested gently, 'that you agreed to accept Home Hostelries' offer for the Cat and Fiddle?'

Shona Nuttall nodded, then filled her lungs and blew the cigarette smoke out in a grey line which wavered with the tension in her body. 'Yes,' she agreed. 'though by then they were offering less than they had been before. Less than I'd previously thought was not enough. But by then I was so . . . I don't know . . . Tired? Battered? All I wanted to do was to get away from the place.'

'And who did you deal with at Home Hostelries?' asked Carole. 'Was it always the same person?'

A note of caution came into Shona Nuttall's eyes. 'I didn't deal with anyone in particular. The sale of the Cat and Fiddle was all done through my solicitors.'

'But you mentioned there had been offers for the pub from Home Hostelries before. Were none of those direct to you?'

She shook her head and reiterated, 'All through the solicitors.'

Carole and Jude both had the instinct that she was lying, but they couldn't see any way of making her reveal information she was determined to withhold. In both their minds the same thought arose: that whoever Shona Nuttall had dealt with at Home Hostelries, he or she had really put the frighteners on her. The ex-landlady wasn't going to risk further trouble by giving them a name.

But there was one other detail that could be checked. Jude got out her mobile and found the photograph Zosia had taken on the comedy night at the Crown and Anchor. 'About these bikers who came . . .' she held out the picture of Derren Hunt '. . . was this man with them?'

Shona Nuttall looked at the image with distaste. 'Yes, he used to come. Was one of the ringleaders, I think.'

'Did you ever find out his name?'

'Good heavens, no!' The very idea shocked her.

'Or speak to him?'

'I may have served him a drink. I certainly never had a conversation with him.'

Jude clicked on to another photo, the one which featured Viggo, and proffered it to Shona. 'Do you recognize him?'

The ex-landlady shrugged. 'Looks vaguely familiar. But I couldn't be sure. That lot in their leather gear . . .' she shuddered at the recollection '. . . they all looked alike to me.'

'And what about the small man beside him?'

No, she had never seen Ray Witchett before. She hadn't seen photos of him on television or in the papers either. Carole and Jude got the impression that not much news filtered through into the velvet fastness of that Southwick bungalow.

There was a silence. Shona puffed away at her cigarette as though her life depended on it. She looked pathetic, broken and alone. Neither Carole nor Jude had warmed to her in her former brassy mode, but it was sad to see any human being so reduced. The Cat and Fiddle had not just been her business; it had been her family, her whole existence.

There was one more question Carole wanted to ask, though. 'Did you ever do comedy nights at the pub?'

'No,' came the reply. 'Our country and western evenings were very popular. And our quiz nights. But I never liked the idea of comedy nights. Comedians these days are so vulgar, aren't they? Scattering four-letter words about like nobody's business. That wasn't the sort of thing that would have appealed to the kind of clientele I wanted to frequent the Cat and Fiddle.'

'But did anyone ever suggest to you that you might do a comedy night?'

'Well, it's funny you should ask that, actually. I did have a call . . . oh, last autumn I suppose it was . . . from quite a well-known comedian, offering to start a series of comedy nights for me. I said no, because I'd seen him on television and he was rather vulgar there, so what he might have been like in a pub I really didn't like to imagine. But I was surprised by the call, because he really was quite a big name.'

Carole and Jude both felt pretty sure they knew the answer, but they still had to ask the question.

'His name,' Shona Nuttall replied, 'was Dan Poke.'

CHAPTER THIRTY-THREE

Surprisingly, it was Carole's idea to Google Home Hostelries. When they got back to Woodside Cottage from Southwick, their tiredness had gone and they were both keen to get on with their investigation.

'I mean, we do now have a direct connection,' said Jude excitedly. 'The campaign against Shona Nuttall at the Cat and Fiddle started in exactly the same way as what's happened to Ted at the Crown and Anchor.'

'But it didn't lead to murder there.'

'That might just be because Shona Nuttall cracked earlier and accepted the reduced offer.'

'I'd put any money on the fact that Ted's also had approaches from Home Hostelries. If only he'd talk to us . . .'

'We need to find out more about the company.'

And it was then that Carole had suggested using Google. Jude was amazed that Carole Seddon, who had at times almost made a religion of her technophobia, was actually suggesting using a computer as a resource. What's more, she appeared familiar with both the language and the use of computers. Jude grinned inwardly. She had known the moment would come; it had only been a matter of time. But she made no comment, as she booted up her laptop and found the Google screen. 'Would you like to take over?' she offered.

'Oh, very well,' said Carole, as though it were the most natural thing in the world.

She keyed in Home Hostelries and looked at the options thrown up. There were plenty of links to individual pubs, pub guides, restaurant and tourism sites. 'What we really need is their home page. See if we can get any relevant names.'

'What, Carole? Are you planning to confront their managing director with accusations of planning a wrecking campaign against Shona Nuttall and Ted Crisp?'

Carole took no notice of the irony in her neighbour's voice as she replied, 'If necessary.'

Their search took quite a while, and they went up many blind alleys into promising websites which all recommended—'The Home Hostelries hospitality experience—graceful drinking and gourmet dining—both available in our personally selected character pubs. Special occasion, family celebration or just a friendly drink to unwind at the end of the day—whatever it is you're looking for, you'll find it in a Home Hostelries pub.'

But eventually they got to a home page for the company. Carole clicked on the 'About Us' tab and found a potted history of Home Hostelries. It was a tale of continuing growth over a relatively short period. Founded in Horsham by two young entrepreneurs who had bought up three West Sussex pubs in the early 1990s, they had continued to add to their portfolio at an accelerating rate. Soon it was not just individual premises they were buying up, but other small chains and breweries. Shona Nuttall had mentioned Snug Pubs and the Foaming Flagon Group, but they were only two of many. Though its headquarters remained in Horsham, the Home Hostelries brand had spread from West Sussex to adjacent counties, and was now expanding into the West Country and East Anglia. New purchases were even taking its reach north of London and into the Midlands. They were also moving away from their base of country pubs and into urban premises (of which presumably the Middy in Fratton was an example). The website left no doubt that Home Hostelries was rapidly becoming one of the country's largest hospitality chains.

The names of the two successful entrepreneurs from Horsham who had set the whole thing in motion were unfamiliar to the two women crouched over the laptop. 'Let's see if we can find a list of directors somewhere,' said Carole.

It didn't take long. Again, most of the names meant nothing. One did, though.

Richard Farrelly.

The real name of the comedian Dan Poke.

'Of course, the name under which he wrote his autobiography.' Carole sounded disappointed, illogically feeling that she should have made the connection before. 'But how're we going to contact him? Through his agent?'

'I've got his number,' said Jude.

'How on earth have you got that?'

'When I first met him in the Crown and Anchor, he gave cards to me and Zosia.'

'Why?'

'I think the implication was that if either of us fancied him, we should give him a call and he would be generous enough not to kick us out of bed.'

'What?' Carole looked appalled. 'Surely no men actually behave like that, do they?'

'Some do. The thick-skinned type who don't care what people think of them. It's partly a joke, partly trying it on. A persona they're trying to project. Particularly in showbiz. There are a lot of women out there who're . . . turned on by celebrity.' Jude had been going to use a less decorous phrase, but avoided it out of consideration for Carole's sensibilities. 'And men like that do get their offers taken up just often enough to make it worth their while. Happens a lot in the music world too . . . Encourages the bad-boy image. You know, there are still groupies out there looking to add a famous name to their list.'

'Are there?' Carole pondered this. 'Erm . . . you've never been a groupie, have you?'

'Not exactly,' replied Jude, simply for the devilment of watching her neighbour's reaction. And maybe adding one more to the manifold mysteries of her past.

Awkwardly, Carole moved the subject on. 'Well, I find it most odd. I thought celebrities were meant to guard their privacy, not give out their home phone numbers to all and sundry.'

'The number I've got won't be his landline. It's probably a mobile he keeps just for the purpose of women ringing him. His totty hotline.'

That drew a predictable wince from Carole.

'Anyway,' Jude announced, 'I'm going to ring him. See if he does want to meet.'

'Isn't that rather dangerous . . . I mean, if he's involved in the kind of thing we think he may be involved in?'

'I won't agree to meet him anywhere except a public place of my choosing. Treat it like it was a blind date, you know, meeting someone through online dating.'

'Have you ever actually done that, Jude?' asked Carole, her eyes owlishly large behind the rimless glasses.

'Not very often,' came the mischievous reply.

'Oh. Well, I think you'll be taking a big risk meeting Dan Poke—or Richard Farrelly or whatever he's called. And if it's sex he's after, as you suggest, though he may agree to meet you in a pub, he's not going to want to stay in the pub, is he? He's going to want to take you back to his place.'

'Carole, I am quite capable of saying "No" to men. It's something in which I have had a lot of experience.'

'Have you?' said Carole rather wistfully. She had always felt that with most men her looks had said 'No' long before any verbal response had become necessary.

'Anyway, come on, Carole, we both want to get to the bottom of what's been going on. We want to find out if there really has been an organized campaign of harassment against the Cat and Fiddle and the Crown and Anchor. We also want to know who killed Ray and Viggo. And do we have any other leads at the moment apart from talking to Dan Poke?'

Carole was forced to concede that they didn't.

'Then I'll call him.'

'Yes. Erm . . . Jude, you don't think you should suggest that I should come and meet him as well, do you?'

'For the kind of encounter he's envisaging, I don't think he'd want a gooseberry there, no.'

Carole Seddon blushed.

Dan Poke didn't answer the phone, but he rang back later in response to the message. Yes, he remembered Jude. If she wanted to meet up with him—'That could be quite enjoyable.' He was starting 'a little mini-tour of gigs' on the Wednesday, but he would be free the next evening. He'd got a flat at Notting Hill. If she got out of the tube station and went along Pembridge Road—

Jude interrupted him and suggested they meet in a bar she knew just near the tube station. He came up with predictable lines about how difficult he found being in public places, how ordinary people regarded celebrities as common property. Jude insisted; they would meet in the bar or not at all. Dan Poke seemed eventually to be amused by what he took as a show of coyness on her part, but he did agree to meet her there at six-thirty the following evening.

As soon as she had finished that call, she rang through to the bar which was to be their rendezvous. It was a place she had often frequented in the company of an actor with whom she'd lived in Notting Hill for a couple of years. She was relieved when the phone was answered by a voice she recognized. Yes, it was Garcia, and he was still running the place. And of course he remembered Jude. Was she still with . . . ? Silly man, said Garcia, always was rather immature, didn't realize what he was giving up.

It would be wonderful to see her the following evening. Jude was always welcome at Garcia's place. And yes, though they weren't the same individuals, his bouncers were as tough as they had ever been.

Jude put the phone down, confident that her security was in place for the following evening's meeting.

CHAPTER THIRTY-FOUR

Jude was going to catch the first cheap train up to Victoria the next morning. When she heard this plan, Carole had objected, 'But you're not meeting him till the evening.'

'No, but there's some shopping I want to do,'

'What? Clothes?' In Carole's view, it wouldn't hurt if her neighbour bought some different clothes, to make herself look a bit less of a hippy. Though, mind you, she didn't have to go up to London to do that. The Marks & Spencer's in Worthing would, in Carole's view, have been perfectly adequate.

But no, Jude said it wasn't clothes. What then? It was with an impish grin that Jude revealed that there were some shops round Covent Garden she wanted to look at. They specialized in crystals.

'Oh,' said Carole dismissively. 'Well, I suppose if you want to spend a steaming hot day traipsing round Covent Garden looking at crystals . . .'

In her neighbour's absence, Carole felt restless. As a result, Gulliver got an extra walk, which he was almost too hot to appreciate. And he had the dressing changed on his leg, which had nearly healed. But Carole still felt ill at ease. Even though she had found a rather good free online computer course, her attention kept straying from the screen. She was keen to learn more about the mysteries of the laptop, which she no longer even pretended to resist, but she just couldn't sustain her concentration.

Partly, she knew that she was a little jealous of Jude. Carole Seddon had amazingly sensitive antennae for slights, particularly in the area of criminal investigation. Although she fully accepted the logic of Jude's meeting Dan Poke on her own, she didn't like feeling excluded from any part of their enquiry.

There was also an unease in her mind, similar to that which Jude had felt over the weekend, a sense that there was something obvious she wasn't seeing. There was another connection to be made somewhere in relation to the deaths of Ray and Viggo, but she couldn't for the life of her work out what it was.

It was in the early evening, after a long, hot and frustrating day, that the lightbulb finally came on in Carole Seddon's brain. She had once again Googled Home Hostelries and was ploughing through the endless links offered when she came to a reference to another local pub.

The Hare and Hounds in Weldisham. Of course! That had been made over in exactly the same way as the Middy in Portsmouth. And in fact it had been in the Hare and Hounds that she'd first heard the words Home Hostelries some years before. It must have been one of the first pubs bought by the chain.

Carole decided that she would take Gulliver for yet another walk, this time on the Downs near Weldisham. And then she would have a drink in the Hare and Hounds. She didn't know what she was expecting to find there, but it was the nearest place with a Home Hostelries connection. And going there would give her the illusion of contributing as much as Jude to their investigation.

The bar run by Garcia had been exclusive before Notting Hill attained maximum trendiness, and it had become more exclusive as the area became richer. The decor hadn't changed in all that time; it was still predominantly black, the contours broken up by darkly tinted mirrors and the gleaming steel of the bar.

A famous television actress was sharing a bottle of wine—and by the appearance of their intimacy would soon be sharing more—with a very recognizable *Newsnight* anchor. They were relaxed; they knew no publicity stories ever made their way out of the club. Jude congratulated herself on her choice of venue.

Garcia greeted her like a long-lost sister and, once she had caught up with news of his very extended family, Jude took her drink to a shadowy corner table and sat down to wait for Dan Poke.

While she was walking an ecstatic Gulliver on the Downs near Weldisham, Carole asked herself why she had come there. And the only answer she could come up with was the feeble one of 'instinct'. Oh dear, she was beginning to think like Jude. Next thing she'd be talking about the 'auras' and 'atmospheres' of places, about 'synchronicity' and other mumbo-jumbo.

But something still told her she was right to have come to the village. Going to another Home Hostelries pub might provide some clue, some connection to ease the confusion of her speculations. The trip was a form of research.

There were already quite a few customers at the pub, but because of the heat most of them were sitting at tables outside. The wine list was, of course, identical to that they had consulted in the Middy, so Carole once again ordered Maipo Valley Chardonnay. She went for a small one this time, righteous because she was driving.

The girl who served her, purple-haired, nose-studded and wearing a mulberry shirt with grey logo across the breast, was perfectly friendly, but not much use as a research source. She handed over the change and Carole had just started on, 'I used to come to this pub a long time ago . . .' when the girl said,

'Sorry, I must serve that customer over there.' Carole took her drink to a table near the bar.

'Hello, darling.' Dan Poke arrived in the bar and, as he kissed Jude full on the lips, he squeezed the flesh of her waist. He confirmed she was all right for a drink—she had hardly touched hers—and moved towards the bar.

'One of the girls will take your order,' said Jude.

'Oh. Right.' He came to sit opposite her. Jude felt she had scored a small victory. Dan Poke clearly hadn't been to the club before, and he did look slightly ill at ease in the unfamiliar environment. Jude had a minimal territorial advantage.

He was dressed in grubby jeans and T-shirt. The grey ponytail hung lankly, greasy with sweat, and there was thick stubble round the square of his beard. He'd certainly not made any effort to smarten himself up for her. Once again, Jude was struck by what an unattractive man he was.

As promised, one of the waitresses appeared and he ordered a Belgian beer. 'Don't bother with a glass, love. And, to save you asking, yes, I am Dan Poke.'

'Oh,' said the girl without interest, and returned to the bar.

'I'm surprised you don't offer her one of your cards,' said Jude.

'Oh, come on, darling, I do have standards.'

'She looks very pretty to me.'

'I don't mean standards about that. I mean I have standards about not handing out my cards when I'm actually on a date with another woman.'

'How very gracious of you.'

'Yeah, one of the last old-fashioned gentlemen.' He smiled what some woman must once have told him was a seductive smile. 'I'm very glad you rang me.'

'Well, you interest me.'

255

'Yeah, a lot of women find that,' he said complacently. 'And they tend to get even more interested after I've shagged them.'

An experiment I am not going to put to the test, thought Jude. But she said, 'I found your act very interesting when I heard it in Fethering.'

'Probably a bit naughty for a sleepy little shithole like that. But I was only doing it to help out an old mate.'

'Ted Crisp.'

'Right.'

'You heard about the murder that happened that night, didn't you?'

' 'Course I did. All over the bloody media, wasn't it?'

'What did you feel about it?'

'Feel about it? Why should I feel anything?'

'Well, it did happen straight after your gig.'

'So what? Doesn't make me responsible for it, does it? Hot night, people had drunk a lot, a fight broke out. At least, that's how I heard it happened. Anyway, you start fighting, people are going to get hurt. Reflection of the society we live in. Binge-drinking and all that. I'm not saying it's a good thing, but it's nothing to do with me. That night I just done me act and pissed off before the trouble started.'

'Off to a woman in Brighton, I heard.'

'Yeah.' He smiled at her lecherously. 'I'm afraid I do suffer from an overactive libido.'

'Bad luck,' Jude commiserated as though she were sharing his joke.

'Fortunately, though, I know how to get treatment for the condition.' As he said this, he placed a hand unambiguously on her thigh and moved it upwards.

Jude shuddered inwardly. He really was such a repellent little creature. She could never understand men who, in the teeth of the evidence, regard themselves as irresistible to women. Dan

Poke, she felt sure, was the sort who, when she did finally express her deep lack of interest in going to bed with him, would mark her down as a lesbian. No woman of normal tendencies could resist his charms.

On the other hand, she had to admit that she had played up to his self-image. Ringing him had been tantamount to presenting herself as a piece of meat for his enjoyment. And she would probably need to maintain that front until she could get the information she wanted out of him.

Jude didn't remove his hand, but he took it away when she asked, 'Did you hear that there was another violent death in Fethering?'

'The Russian roulette bloke? Yes, I heard about it. Now you're not going to blame me for that one too, are you? I was nowhere near the place when it happened.'

'No. I just wondered if you knew the man.'

Dan Poke shook his head vigorously; the lank ponytail flipped to one side. Was Jude imagining it, or was there a new caution in his manner? She went on, 'He was in the audience at the Crown and Anchor the night you appeared.'

'So? Darling, I do a lot of gigs. They're attended by a lot of punters. They all know what I look like. I haven't a clue what any of them look like. People in the street often think they know me because they've seen me on the telly. Think they bloody own you, and all. It's just one of the things that happens when you're a celeb.'

'So you were never introduced to Viggo?'

'Look, what is this? Some kind of third degree? I thought you were here because you wanted a shag. Quick, uncomplicated sex. I get my rocks off, you get the thrill of shagging a celeb. Or have I misunderstood the reason why we're meeting here?'

Jude's cover wasn't quite blown, but she didn't think she could sustain the pretence much longer. So she opted for the truth. 'The reason we are meeting here is that I want to talk to you about your role as a director of Home Hostelries.'

CHAPTER THIRTY-FIVE

While she drank her Maipo Valley Chardonnay, Carole was kicking herself for not bringing *The Times* with her. She felt exposed sitting alone drinking in the Hare and Hounds. She never had thought of herself as a 'pub person', and doing the crossword would make her look much less awkward. Besides, that day's was a rather difficult one. She hadn't filled in many clues over her lunch of soup and bread and she wanted to re-engage with its intellectual challenge. But her copy of *The Times* was sitting on the kitchen table at High Tor.

So she sat and sipped, trying to give the impression of the kind of person whose rich and busy mental life stopped her from looking like a woman in a pub drinking on her own. And meanwhile, she observed the behaviour of the bar staff. Apart from the purple-haired one who had served her, there was another girl and two young men. The older of the two, from the way he ordered the others around, was clearly the manager. And in fact there was a sharpness, a shifty alertness about him, which reminded Carole of the previous incumbent of the job, Will Maples.

Carole decided that he was the one she should talk to. Achieving that goal meant careful management of her Chardonnay. She had noticed that the manager only served at the bar as a last resort. His juniors had first call on the customers and, only when they were all fully occupied, would he actually dispense drinks.

She watched and waited until he was free. In the meantime she took out her mobile, to give the illusion of busyness. Idly she summoned up the photographs which Zosia had taken and Jude had forwarded on.

She found the shot of the bikers watching Dan Poke's act, the one with Derren Hart in the middle of the group. And for the first time, because she was trying to look as though she had something to do, she scrutinized all of the people in the photograph. She saw the tall man called William who had spoken to Dan Poke after the gig. The man who had been sitting drinking Belgian beer with a group of other smartly dressed young men.

And suddenly she realized where she had seen him before. Shadowed by the effects of the flash, his face had lost its chubbiness. And Carole Seddon recognized the man she had last seen some years before behind the bar of the very pub she was sitting in. It was Will Maples. The Home Hostelries manager who had disappeared after being unmasked as a drug dealer.

A new thought burgeoned in Carole's mind, a thought that needed confirmation. And she might be able to get that confirmation from the current manager of the Hare and Hounds. Fortunately, on a hot summer evening, a lot of people relished the idea of a drink on the fringes of the South Downs, so the pub was filling up. Carole waited till all four bar staff were busy serving customers, then slurped down the remains of her drink and positioned herself behind the man who'd just been served his round by the manager.

The young man looked up at her with a professional grin. 'What can I get for you, madam?'

'Another Maipo Valley Chardonnay, please. It's very good.'

'All our Home Hostelries wines are carefully selected, madam. Will that be a large one or a small?'

'Small, thank you.'

Fortunately for Carole, there wasn't an open bottle of the Maipo Valley Chardonnay, so the manager had to take a corkscrew to one. This gave her a little window of opportunity to say, 'I met someone recently from Home Hostelries . . .'

'Oh, really?'

'Yes, we were introduced, but I'm afraid I've forgotten his name. I wonder if you might know him?'

'Without a name it's going to be pretty difficult for me to—'

'I do have a photograph.' Carole proffered her mobile to the manager and pointed to the man she thought was Will Maples.

'Oh yes, I know him all right. Well, you have been moving in the upper echelons of the company. That's one of Home Hostelries' very big cheeses.'

'A director?'

'No, he's not actually a director yet, but I should think it's on the cards that he will be soon.'

'What's his name?' asked Carole, trying to hide the tension she was feeling.

'Will Maples. In charge of Acquisitions.'

Carole could have kicked herself. Now she'd had it confirmed, the likeness was so obvious. But men's looks change, particularly in their early forties. Suddenly bodies you could never imagine with an ounce of fat on them spread sideways. Entire contours are re-formed. Add to that Will Maples's dyed hair and the thick-framed glasses and he had become unrecognizable. Carole wondered whether he'd recognized her as one of the busybodies who had caused his abrupt departure from his previous job at the Hare and Hounds.

Though she thought she knew the answer to her question, she asked the current manager to spell out what that meant by 'in charge of Acquisitions'.

'Will Maples is in charge of selecting and purchasing new pubs to add to the Home Hostelries family.'

'Ah,' said Carole Seddon. 'Thank you.'

'What is this?' asked Dan Poke. 'What the hell are you up to?'

Jude looked straight into his eyes. 'Are you denying that, under your real name of Richard Farrelly, you are a director of Home Hostelries, the pub group?'

He let his anger dissipate and took a deep breath. When he replied, he was cautious. He wanted to know how much she knew. 'Very well,' he said calmly. 'I don't deny it. But since when has it been illegal for people to have more than one job?'

'Never. How long have you been a director?'

'Seven or eight years. When I was doing all that telly, I made a lot of bread. I wanted to invest it somewhere, somebody mentioned Home Hostelries, and I was interested to find out more about them. I am a bit of an expert in pubs, you know.'

'Oh?'

'Come on, darling. Doing stand-up, you spend half your life in pubs. You get to know the good ones from the bad, you get an idea of what kind of business they're doing.'

'So Home Hostelries took you on as a kind of consultant?'

'You could say that. An investor too. Television's a very fickle medium. I was flavour of the month for a while, but I knew it could end at any minute, so I wanted to make myself financially secure. Doing that through a business that really interested me . . . what's the harm in that?'

'I don't think there's any harm in that.'

'Good.' He looked at his watch. 'Well, I think I'm about to go back to mine. Are you coming or not?'

'No.'

'Right. Well, thank you, Jude, for a totally fucking wasted evening.'

He rose to leave, but her next words changed his mind. 'I want to talk about the involvement of Home Hostelries in the murder of Ray Witchett.'

Dan Poke froze, then sank back into his chair and said in what was little more than a whisper, 'What?'

'It's my belief,' said Jude evenly, 'that Home Hostelries had been trying for some time to add the Crown and Anchor in Fethering to their chain of pubs.'

'So?'

'In spite of the fact that Ted Crisp had no desire to sell. I think he became the victim of a campaign of harassment which was organized by Home Hostelries.'

'Come off it, Jude. You're talking about a pukka company here. Home Hostelries doesn't need to organize campaigns of harassment. There are pubs closing every week all over the country. If we want to buy places, we're spoiled for choice.'

'Except that you are very picky in your choice of where you buy. You only want places with the best possible locations. Like the Crown and Anchor. Like the Cat and Fiddle on the Fedborough road out of Littlehampton.'

Dan Poke looked puzzled.

'You're not denying that the Cat and Fiddle has been bought by Home Hostelries?'

'Certainly not. It's undergoing major refurbishment. Reopening as a Home Hostelries pub in October, if my memory serves me right.'

'It does. And before she gave in and agreed to sell to Home Hostelries, the landlady had suffered almost exactly the same kind of harassment as Ted Crisp's been getting at the Crown and Anchor.'

'Where've you got this from?'

'Shona Nuttall herself,' Jude replied implacably. 'The ex-landlady of the Cat and Fiddle.'

'Have you worked all this out off your own bat?'

'I have been working on it with a friend.'

'Male friend?'

'Female friend.'

'Nobody else involved?'

Jude thought quickly before answering that. If she was sitting opposite a man capable of murder, then she and Carole might well be at risk. Time perhaps for a tactical lie. 'We have kept the police up to date with our investigations.'

Dan Poke laughed and Jude realized it had been a silly thing to say. He didn't believe her, and as a consequence any threat she might have represented to him had been diluted. 'Oh yes, I'm sure the police have been really grateful for the input of two old biddies from Fethering.'

Ten minutes before Dan Poke had been keen to get her into bed; now suddenly she was an old biddy from Fethering.

'Tell you what,' he went on, 'even though you're talking rubbish, it's potentially dangerous rubbish.'

'Dangerous to whom?'

'To the reputation of Home Hostelries. Who've you talked about this to—apart from your friend?'

'And the police,' Jude offered feebly.

'Oh yes, of course. *And* the police.' His tone ridiculed the idea. He drummed his fingernails on the arm of his chair. 'We need a meeting.'

'What? Who?'

'You, your friend, me . . .'

'Down some dark alley?'

'Don't be fucking stupid! I'm talking in the Home Hostelries boardroom. You have to realize just how serious the allegations you're making are. I've got your number. I'll give you a call.'

And with that Dan Poke left the bar. And left Jude with the feeling that she hadn't managed the encounter very well.

She asked Garcia to lend one of his bouncers to see her to Notting Hill tube station, which he did without demur. But on the short walk there, she didn't see any homicidal stand-up comedians lurking in the bushes. And all the way back on the tube and train to Fethering, Jude felt rather stupid.

CHAPTER THIRTY-SIX

The summons came in a phone call the following morning at nine-thirty sharp. Dan Poke, sounding very businesslike and making no mention of their encounter the previous evening, invited Jude and her friend to a meeting at the Home Hostelries headquarters in Horsham. He said he would like to make the meeting as soon as possible, 'because of the nature of the situation'. They agreed to meet that very morning at eleven-thirty.

Carole had told her the previous evening what she had discovered about Will Maples's role in the Home Hostelries company, and on the way up to Horsham in the Renault they discussed the likelihood of his also being at the meeting.

Dan Poke had given very precise instructions and also told Jude that parking would be reserved for them. This was a considerable relief to Carole, who knew of old that Horsham was one of those towns in which it was impossible to find a parking space. The slot allocated for them was right next to Will Maples's distinctive pale-blue BMW.

The Home Hostelries building breathed success from every shiny glass storey. The air-conditioned atrium where they approached Reception was high and daunting, a temple to corporate achievement. They were expected and, moments after their arrival, a girl in a mulberry business suit with feather grey trim escorted them to the lift, in which they were whisked up to boardroom level.

Their question in the car was answered immediately. Will Maples was there, as well as Dan Poke, who looked incongruous in a dark suit and tie. He had shaved since the night before. The little square of beard on his chin looked like some form of scouring pad.

The third member of the greeting party Carole and Jude had not met before. A woman in her thirties with square-cut blonde hair and a pinstriped trouser suit was introduced to them as 'Melissa Keats, a member of the company legal team'.

They sat at one end of a long boardroom table, Carole and Jude on one side, the other three opposite them. The atmosphere was that of a rather daunting job interview, and the two women felt certain that that was the intention. They were being subjected to a course of corporate intimidation. The girl who'd brought them up in the lift poured coffee for those who required it, and then left the room, closing the door behind her.

His colleagues seemed to expect Will Maples to take charge, which he duly did. Dan Poke was uncharacteristically quiet in this business environment; he seemed to be waiting for his colleague to give him permission to speak.

Carole and Jude had seen plenty of Will Maples's smarmy smiles in his days at the Hare and Hounds, but there was none on his face that morning. 'We've called this meeting because you two ladies have been spreading rumours about the business activities of Home Hostelries which we believe to have no basis in truth. So it seemed sensible to meet to find out where you got these ideas from and maybe to clear the air. Now I believe, Mrs Seddon and, er . . .' he looked down at some notes in front of him '. . . Jude, that the allegations you have made concern recent events at the Crown and Anchor pub in Fethering . . . ?'

'Which Home Hostelries wishes to buy,' said Carole.

'I don't deny that we have expressed an interest in the property,' Will Maples purred smoothly. 'It is the sort of public house that would fit well into our portfolio. But we have no immediate plans to buy it, because the owner does not wish to sell.'

'Ah, but this is the point,' said Jude.

'What is the point?'

'You've been putting pressure on Ted Crisp so that he will sell to you, and at a lower price than the pub is worth.'

'Really?' asked Will Maples.

Melissa Keats chipped in, 'I think I should point out that it is against the law to make allegations against people—'

But the solicitor was silenced by an upraised hand from her superior. 'If you don't mind, Melissa, let's hear everything the ladies have to say first. Then I think we will be in a better position to judge whether there is any truth at all in their allegations.'

'Very well, Will,' she said, duly submissive.

'So, Mrs Seddon and Jude, could you define this "pressure" which you claim Home Hostelries has put on the landlord of the Crown and Anchor?'

'It started with the food-poisoning,' Carole replied. 'Some scallops that weren't fresh were introduced into the Crown and Anchor kitchen.'

'But not by anyone from Home Hostelries.'

'We believe,' Carole went on, 'that the scallops came in a delivery from KWS warehouse, which, as you know, holds stock for Snug Pubs, which are now a part of the Home Hostelries group. The delivery man's name is Matt.'

While her friend talked, Jude was studying Dan Poke's face intently. She was sure she saw a reaction when the name of Sylvia Crisp's fiancé was mentioned. But he quickly covered it up.

'If what you say was correct,' said Will Maples, 'then there should be some record of it in the KWS office. Nothing gets delivered without an order form.'

'The paperwork has disappeared.'

'Has it, Mrs Seddon? Well, well, well. How unfortunate.' Now there was a smile on Will Maples's face. An infuriatingly complacent one. He made a note on a pad in front of him. 'So . . . this food-poisoning from . . . scallops was it you said? You believe it to have been deliberately engineered, but you have no proof of that. Isn't it more likely that the outbreak arose because of some carelessness, some lapse of hygiene in the Crown and Anchor kitchen? The weather has been exceptionally hot.'

Jude couldn't help herself from bursting out, 'Ted Crisp's standards of hygiene cannot be faulted. He sees to it that that kitchen is kept spotless.'

Will Maples gave her a patronizing smile. 'I've heard exactly the same thing from every landlord I've ever encountered . . . often in the teeth of the evidence. On occasions even when I have heard the cockroaches being crunched underfoot. Publicans, Jude, are not, generally speaking, the most truthful of individuals.'

'All right,' said Carole. 'Let's put the food-poisoning on one side and move on to the bikers.'

'Bikers?' Will Maples echoed.

'Yes, you know what bikers are?'

'I certainly do.'

'Well, don't you think it's rather strange that, just after the Crown and Anchor's reopened after the food-poisoning business, it suddenly gets invaded by a horde of bikers.'

'I gather,' said Will Maples with a little self-congratulatory smile, 'that bikers go where they choose. The life of the open road is what they seek, and which particular drinking hole they favour . . . well, I'd have thought that was up to them.'

'These particular bikers were an organized rent-a-mob.'

'Organized? By using that word, Mrs Seddon, you imply that there must have been someone doing the organizing.'

'There was.'

'And I don't suppose by any chance you've got a name for that person, have you?' His patronizing tone was now on the verge of being downright rude.

'As a matter of fact, I do. He is an ex-soldier invalided out of Iraq, who lives in Fratton. His name is Derren Hart.'

This time Jude saw an unmistakable twitch of recognition from Dan Poke. And Will Maples too seemed momentarily taken aback by the mention of the name. But he was quickly back into his smooth insolence. 'And are you telling me, Mrs Seddon, that this Mr . . . Hart, was it . . . has admitted to his involvement in organizing wrecking crews of bikers?'

Carole was forced to admit that he hadn't.

'So, as with the food poisoning, what you have is a supposition, but no proof to back it up?' He smiled across at the solicitor. 'Not the kind of case that would stand up in court, would it, Melissa?'

She agreed, with a pitying look at the two women, that it wouldn't.

Will Maples's smile grew broader. 'I must congratulate you on the power of your imaginations, ladies. Were there any other allegations against Home Hostelries that you wished to make?'

'I am certain,' said Jude, 'that the fight at the Crown and Anchor after Dan Poke's gig was started deliberately.'

The Acquisitions manager's neatly suited shoulders shrugged. 'Aren't all fights started deliberately? Someone takes offence at something another person has said or done, they throw a punch. The punch is returned, a fight ensues. I'd say that was deliberate.'

'I mean that Derren Hart and his bikers deliberately started the fight to give the Crown and Anchor a reputation for rowdiness.'

'And, once again, the small matter of proof . . . ? Did your

Mr, er, Hart come to you on penitent bended knee to confess his anti-social behaviour?'

Again, Carole could not pretend that he had.

'We seem to be shooting down your allegations at a rate of knots, don't we, Mrs Seddon? Is there anything else you wish to raise?'

'Just the fact that what's happening at the Crown and Anchor is a carbon copy of what had happened at the Cat and Fiddle a few months previously.' There was momentary eye contact between the two men at this, but they quickly covered it up. 'Shona Nuttall definitely believes that she was bullied into selling her pub at a reduced price.'

'Does she?' said Will Maples.

'And would she he prepared to stand up in court to make that allegation?' asked Melissa Keats.

'No. I think she's too demoralized by the whole business.'

'Ah,' said the solicitor with something that wasn't far from satisfaction. She then looked sternly at the two women. 'I think, if you have nothing further to add, I should clarify the legal position to—'

'We do have something further to add,' protested Jude. 'We haven't yet mentioned the biggest allegation of all—the murder of Ray Witchett.'

Will Maples raised a languid eyebrow. 'Are you suggesting that one of us stabbed him?'

'No. The murder was done by a friend of his called Viggo.'

'Well, maybe you should be looking for a confession for this Viggo, rather than from us.'

'Viggo is dead.'

'Oh, how unfortunate.'

'As you well know.'

Will Maples gave another shrug, neither confirming nor rebutting her assertion.

'But we believe,' Jude went on, 'that Viggo was put up to the stabbing by Derren Hart, who was acting on orders from you!'

That did it. The floor was handed to Melissa Keats, who gave Carole and Jude a very thorough dressing-down. She quoted at them from the laws of slander and defamation. She spelled out to them the dire consequences of their repeating any of their allegations in any forum, public or private. And she left them in no doubt that, if the situation were ever to come to a court of law, the not inconsiderable resources of the Home Hostelries group would be deployed against them.

Carole and Jude left the building feeling like schoolgirls who'd just had many strips torn off them by their headmistress.

Silence reigned in the Renault for the first twenty minutes of the journey back to Fethering. Then Jude announced, 'I'm more certain than ever that they did it.'

'I agree,' said Carole. 'But how on earth are we going to prove it?'

CHAPTER THIRTY-SEVEN

In the rush to Horsham that morning Jude had omitted to pick up her mobile, which had been on its charger in her bedroom. Presumably Zosia had tried that first, before leaving a message on the Woodside Cottage landline.

It was short and to the point. 'Please call me. Ted has decided he's going to sell the Crown and Anchor.'

Jude summoned Carole, and the two women went down to the pub straight away. No further tidying had been done to the frontage. The place looked boarded-up and condemned. Most lunchtime customers had kept their distance too, like animals steering clear of a dying member of their pack. The only ones who had visited the plague spot were sitting at the tables outside.

Which at least meant Carole and Jude could talk to Zosia in the bar without fear of eavesdroppers. The Polish girl looked exhausted; she had the expression of someone who had tried everything, and none of it had worked. Ed Pollack, who had dealt with the very few lunch orders, lolled against the bar, looking equally dispirited.

Carole's first question was: 'Where is Ted?'

Zosia shrugged. 'I don't know. He was here when we both arrived at ten thirty. That's when he told us he was selling up.'

'Did he give you any details as to why?' asked Jude.

'He said he'd been fighting a losing battle for too long, and he was sick to death of the whole business. He said there had been an offer on the table for a while, and it was time for him to cut his losses and accept.'

Carole and Jude both felt certain that they knew where the offer had come from, but neither said anything.

'So that's it,' said Zosia, and a tear glinted in her hazel eye.

Carole tried to reassure her. 'Both you and Ed are highly qualified. I'm sure you won't have any difficulty finding other jobs.'

'That's not the point,' said the chef gloomily. 'I came back down here because my mother was ill. But now she's on the mend I'm going to stay. Zosia and I like working here. We like working for Ted.'

'Yes,' Zosia agreed. 'He's a . . . what's that word you taught me, Jude? Curmudgeon? Yes, Ted's a curmudgeon and he's sexist and he's a bit racist too, but his . . . what do you say? "His heart is in the right place"?' Jude nodded. 'I do not like to see him being destroyed like this.'

'And, Zosia, you've no idea where he is now?'

'No.'

'He just told us the news,' said the chef, 'and then said he had to go out. For a business meeting, I think he said.'

Carole and Jude exchanged looks, knowing that in both of their minds was the same image. Ted Crisp in the gleaming Horsham office of Will Maples, signing over the ownership of the Crown and Anchor to Home Hostelries.

'And you don't know why suddenly he made the decision?' asked Carole. 'Had anything changed? There hadn't been any new trouble in the pub?'

Zosia shook her head. She couldn't think of anything.

'It wasn't anything new,' said Ed Pollack. 'At least I don't think it was. Just an accumulation of all the old stuff. I think mostly he was under pressure from his ex-wife about the divorce. That's what he implied to me.'

Zosia looked at him curiously as he explained, 'He said it this morning while you were putting the chairs out. He said, "She wants her pound of flesh, and the only way I can give it to her is by selling the Crown and Anchor." I assumed he was talking about his ex-wife.'

'Sounds like it,' said Carole glumly. Then she sighed in exasperation. 'All the effort we've put in, and we've got nothing to show for it. Ted's going to sell the Crown and Anchor. Oh, I wish there was something we could do!'

'I think the best thing we can do,' said Jude, 'is to take advantage of the fact that we're standing in a pub, and order two large Chilean Chardonnays.'

While they were at it, they decided that they might as well order lunch too. Ed Pollack recommended the Dover sole, 'nice and light in this hot weather'. They both agreed and went despairingly to sit in one of the shady alcoves. They were silent. Neither of them could think of anything useful to say.

They ate their Dover sole in silence too. It was excellent, but they were both too preoccupied to notice the taste. Another large Chilean Chardonnay each might have lifted their mood, but they both felt too listless to go up to the bar.

Eventually, Carole announced, 'So Sylvia has won. She'll get her divorce settlement—half the proceeds of the sale of the Crown and Anchor or whatever it is—and she'll be able to marry the odiously boorish Matt, and live happily ever after.'

'Whereas poor old Ted . . .' Jude didn't need to finish the sentence.

'Hm. I wonder if Sylvia knows yet about her good fortune . . .' Carole was thoughtful for a moment, then said, 'Maybe I should tell her. Could I borrow your mobile, Jude?'

Her neighbour looked on in astonishment as Carole focused her memory to recall the relevant number and keyed it in.

'Ah, hello, Sylvia. This is Carole Seddon speaking.'

'Carole Seddon?' asked the puzzled, nasal voice.

'The Carole Seddon whom you believe to be the current girlfriend of your ex-husband.'

'Oh yes.' Sylvia contrived to get a lot of contempt into the two syllables.

'I just wondered whether you had heard from Ted.'

'About what?'

'About the fact that he's decided to sell the Crown and Anchor.'

'Yess!' came the ecstatic hiss from the other end. 'A result— hooray! I must tell my solicitor. She'll be as chuffed as I am.'

'About your solicitor . . .' Carole began.

'Yes?'

'How did you find her? Personal recommendation? Just going through the Yellow Pages?'

'No. It was a bit of luck, actually. I just had a flyer through my letterbox, saying that there was this solicitor who specialized in divorce where the participants in the marriage have been apart for a long time and, basically, screwing money out of ex-husbands. It came at a time when things were a bit tight financially . . .'

'When you'd just been kicked out by your double-glazing salesman,' Carole suggested tartly.

'Look, if you've only rung up to bitch at me—'

Carole realized that she should have restrained herself from making the dig, and quickly said, 'No, no, no. All I was ringing to say was . . . well, I suppose to congratulate you . . . You've got what you wanted.'

'I certainly have.'

'Your solicitor sounds quite a powerful person.'

'She certainly is. Really tough. I didn't reckon I would ever get much out of Ted, but she amazed me with the sort of sums she was talking about. And she's pretty sure she can run circles round the kind of solicitor Ted's going to find. She's very high-powered.'

'She sounds it. A useful contact to have. By the way, for future reference, what's her name?'

Sylvia Crisp replied, 'Melissa Keats.'

CHAPTER THIRTY-EIGHT

'God, is there no end to their dirty tricks?' asked Carole. 'They deliberately targeted Sylvia to put even more pressure on Ted. A flyer through the letterbox—I bet hers was the only house in the street that received that delivery. Why would a hot-shot lawyer like Melissa Keats, who's probably exclusively retained by Home Hostelries, bother with a sordid little divorce case?'

'In the cause of feminist solidarity?' Jude suggested.

'I'm sure that's how she presented it to Sylvia, but come on, you don't believe that's true, do you?'

Jude admitted that she didn't really, no.

'Ooh, this is so frustrating!' Carole pressed her knuckles hard against her forehead. 'We've now got yet another definite link between Home Hostelries and the harassment of Ted Crisp, and yet we still don't have a shred of proof! I just can't think of anything else we can do. I suppose we could try to find Derren Hart again, see if we can get anything more out of him, though I very much doubt if he'll talk to us. He certainly won't if he's had a warning call from Will Maples or Dan Poke. But what else can we do?'

'One thing I could do,' said Jude, 'is to have a word with Kelly-Marie. I haven't talked to her since the day Viggo died. She might have some news from Copsedown Hall. I mean, the police must've been there investigating Viggo's death, apart from anything else. It's worth trying.'

She rang through. Kelly-Marie had done a morning shift at

the retirement home that day. She was back at home. And she'd love to see Jude.

'The policemen talked to me a lot about Viggo,' said the girl. They were once again in her neat flat with all its dog pictures and figurines.

Jude had noticed on the landing that the young man's room was still sealed off with scene-of-crime tape. 'Did the police let you stay here while they were investigating?'

'They said it'd be better if I went to my parents. Then they called this morning to say I could come back if I wanted to. And I did want to. I like it here. I like it at Mummy and Daddy's too, but here I'm more independent.'

Jude was amazed by the girl's calm. Here she was in a flat right next door to the scene of a particularly messy death, and yet she seemed to have a method of processing shock that would be the envy of other, more traditionally 'normal' people.

'Did you get any impression of what the police thought about Viggo's death?'

'They thought he was playing a game of Russian roulette.' She spoke the words carefully, as if she had only recently learned them.

'But they didn't say whether they thought he'd been playing it on his own?'

'I didn't know more than one person could play Russian roulette.' The girl's broad earnest face looked puzzled. Clearly the idea hadn't entered her head that anyone else might have been involved in Viggo's death.

'Did you tell the police about the man with the scarred face coming to see Viggo?'

'Oh yes. I told them about both times he came.'

'Both times? You told me he came here before Ray died, but when was the other time?'

'He came that evening, the evening Viggo died.'

Jude's brown eyes sparkled with amazement. 'Really? And was he still here when you heard the shot?'

Kelly-Marie shook her head. 'No, he had left about half an hour earlier. I was in the kitchen when he went. He talked to me.'

Jude's mind was racing as she pieced the scenario together. Derren Hart had come to see Viggo, primed him with beer and put the suggestion of Russian roulette into that most suggestible of minds. He had also perhaps loaded the revolver, telling the poor deluded victim that Russian roulette should be played with all the chambers full, or maybe only one empty. The ex-soldier hadn't actually done the killing, but he had set it up.

But surely he hadn't done it off his own bat? Derren Hart must have been obeying orders, just as surely as Viggo had obeyed orders to kill Ray. A trail of orders which had to lead back—though probably not in a way that could be traced—to Will Maples at Home Hostelries.

Suddenly Jude remembered details of Viggo's rambling fantasies, tough-guy talk about orders arriving by text on a mobile phone, the mobile phone being jettisoned and the job done. Was that how he had received the order to kill Ray? And maybe, after Derren Hart's visit, it had been another text message that had finally persuaded him to pull the trigger of the revolver pointing at his temple?

Hard on the heels of that came another recollection, of something Kelly-Marie had said, about how Viggo had always been throwing away perfectly good stuff, clothes and things, as he underwent his latest makeover. And how the girl had salvaged some of his cast-offs and taken them to the Oxfam shop.

Scarcely daring to hope that her intuition was right, and yet at the same time robustly confident, Jude asked, 'Kelly-Marie, did you ever see Viggo throw away a mobile phone?'

'Yes, I did,' came the most welcome of replies.

'When?'

'It was a Sunday. I remember. Because I'd been to have lunch with Mummy and Daddy and they'd just dropped me back here.'

'Do you remember which Sunday it was, Kelly-Marie?'

'Not last Sunday . . .' She looked confused as she tried to work it out. Then her face cleared. 'It was the Sunday that Ray was going to see Dan Poke from off the television.'

Ray Witchett's last day on earth.

'I remember,' Kelly-Marie went on, 'as I came into the hall that Sunday from saying goodbye to Mummy and Daddy, I saw Viggo coming downstairs. And he looked, I don't know, like he was doing something wrong . . . there's a word . . . ?'

'Furtive?'

'Perhaps. I don't know that word. Anyway, when I got back up here, I looked out of the window and I saw Viggo walking along the street, down that way. And there was one of those big boxes for rubbish . . .'

'A skip?'

'Yes. A skip. Like in skipping.' Kelly-Marie smiled, pleased at the notion.

'And you saw Viggo drop something in it?'

'Yes. And I thought it was probably something that was still valuable, because Viggo was always throwing away good stuff. So later in the evening, I went down to the . . . skip . . . and I found what he'd dropped. It had gone quite deep down the side, but I managed to pull it out.'

'It was a mobile phone?' asked Jude, hardly daring to hope.

She was rewarded with a huge beam and a nod.

'I don't suppose, Kelly-Marie . . . that you've still got it?'

The beam grew broader as the girl crossed to a drawer and produced from it a brand-new-looking mobile phone. She handed it across to Jude. 'I wasn't sure what to do with it. I know Oxfam take clothes, but I don't know whether they take mobile phones. I was going to ask Mummy and Daddy, but I forgot.'

Jude looked with disbelief at the phone in her hand. Could it be that she finally held in her hand the evidence she had despaired of ever finding?

She was initially frustrated, because, of course, the phone, sitting in a drawer for over a fortnight, had no power. But fortunately it fitted the same charger as Kelly-Marie's mobile, so they soon had the handset plugged in and active.

Jude went into the 'Short Messages' menu and selected 'Inbox'. There were two messages. Jude opened the more recent one first, the last communication Viggo had received before he threw the mobile away. It was timed at 15.17 on the Sunday of Dan Poke's gig at the Crown and Anchor, and couched in the sort of espionage-movie language which held such a fatal attraction for Viggo.

AGENT 217 IS BECOMING A DANGER TO THE PROJECT. LIQUIDATE HIM. KNIFE, NOT GUN. THE MONEY WILL GO INTO THE USUAL ACCOUNT. JETTISON THIS MOBILE. K.

Now perhaps they had some proof.

CHAPTER THIRTY-NINE

Then Jude checked the first text message. It had been sent the day before the poisoning in the Crown and Anchor that had started their investigation. It read:

TIME TO ACTIVATE AGENT 217. SCALLOPS PLAN AS DISCUSSED — DELIVERY AT TEN-THIRTY TOMORROW MORNING. RELYING ON YOU TO PERSUADE HIM TO DO IT. K.

So who the hell was 'K'?

As she walked back to Woodside Cottage, Jude was aware of a huge temptation. The enquiries she and Carole had made so far in this case had been deeply frustrating. They had been reacting to events, to new information. Rarely had they been proactive.

And now Jude had a chance to be just that. She switched on the precious mobile and checked its power. Yes, it had just enough juice from its time on Kelly-Marie's charger. She summoned up one of K's text messages and, before she had time to change her mind, keyed in a reply.

THE NET IS CLOSING IN. I AM ON TO YOU.

That should flush him out.

In previous investigations Carole and Jude had had a somewhat unsatisfactory relationship with the police. They had either been warned off or patronized. The impression had certainly been given that the police were quite capable of doing their job on their own, and the last thing they wanted was offers of help from enthusiastic amateurs, particularly from women of a certain age.

But the detective Jude was put on to when she rang the Hollingbury Major Crime Unit was polite and, even more gratifying, interested in what she had to tell him. His name was Detective Inspector Wilson, and he was absolutely up to speed on the investigations into the deaths of Ray Witchett and Viggo. He knew about Copsedown Hall and Kelly-Marie, and he responded instantly to the mention of Derren Hart. 'Yes, he's someone we very definitely want to speak to. He's gone to ground for the moment, but don't worry, we'll track him down.'

Jude felt a little silly. The detective's knowledgeable manner reminded her that, all the time she and Carole had been stumbling in the dark, the official enquiries had been proceeding, using the full resources of manpower and forensic expertise. Though Detective Inspector Wilson remained polite, she didn't get the feeling she was telling him anything that he didn't know.

Until she came to Viggo's mobile phone. That was a surprise, and it interested him very much. He wanted her to spell out exactly how it had come into her possession. Then he asked where she lived, and said he would be with her in as long as it took. As soon as she ended that call, Jude rang Carole. It was their joint investigation, they should both be present to hand over their findings to the police.

When he arrived, Detective Inspector Wilson was courteous, but didn't want to hear too much about their theories of the crimes. It was only the mobile that interested him. He asked again how Jude had discovered it. By now feeling rather childish about the text reply she'd sent, she didn't mention that. But they'd surely find a record of it when they examined the mobile. She was only putting off the inevitable rapping of her knuckles.

Detective Inspector Wilson took the mobile away, with assurances that he'd keep Carole and Jude updated on any new developments on the case. This they did not really believe. They reckoned, if they did hear more, it would be from the news media along with everyone else, rather than in a personalized call from Detective Inspector Wilson.

As a result, after his departure, both Carole and Jude felt extremely flat. They had ridden the roller coaster of the investigation and, now they were so close to the end of the ride, someone else was going to enjoy the fun of the denouement. Rotten life sometimes, being an amateur detective.

They went back to their separate houses. At a loose end, unable to decide what to do next, Jude put a call through to Kelly-Marie. Just to assure the girl how much the police had appreciated her discovery of the mobile phone. And to warn her that they were quite likely to come to question her again.

'Oh, that's all right,' said the girl. 'The policemen were very friendly when they talked to me before.'

'Well, you definitely did the right thing keeping that mobile of Viggo's.'

'Thank you.' Kelly-Marie sounded disproportionately grateful for the commendation.

'Incidentally, you said you'd forgotten to tell your parents about the mobile. Did you mention to anyone else that you'd got it?'

'No, I don't think so.' Then she remembered. 'Oh, just one person.'

'Who was that?'

'The scarred man.'

'The one who came to see Viggo?'

'Yes. That night, before Viggo died, I told you I was in the kitchen, and he talked to me. He asked if I'd ever seen a mobile of Viggo's and I told him.'

So Derren Hart knew of the mobile's existence. Which almost definitely meant that his paymasters did too. An icy chill spread over Jude's shoulders as she asked, 'Did he ask to see it?'

'He did, but then a couple of the other men from the house came into the hall, and he went away.'

'Kelly-Marie, just stay where you are.' Jude tried to keep the panic out of her voice. God, she'd been so stupid. Her impulsive text reply had alerted 'K'. If Derren Hart was K, then he'd reckon the text had come from Kelly-Marie, who so far as he knew still had Viggo's mobile. If Derren wasn't K himself, then he'd pretty soon pass on the information to the person who was.

'My friend and I are coming to see you straight away,' said Jude, as calmly as she could. 'And I'm sure the police will be there soon too.'

'There's someone arriving now,' said Kelly-Marie casually. 'There's a car parking outside.'

'A police car?'

'No,' the girl replied. 'It's pale blue.'

CHAPTER FORTY

There was no mistaking Will Maples's BMW, conspicuously outgleaming the other shabby vehicles parked on the Downside Road. Its presence at least meant that he hadn't abducted Kelly-Marie. But that small bonus was wiped out by the deduction that he was still inside the building with her.

The main door to Copsedown Hall was on the latch, which, while convenient for Carole and Jude, was also potentially worrying. Maybe Will Maples had left it like that for reinforcements to arrive. He had a habit of delegating his dirty work. Was Derren Hart about to arrive? Or was the ex-squaddie thug already in the building?

Carole and Jude sped up the stairs. There were voices coming from Kelly-Marie's flat. Jude flung the door open.

The scene revealed looked surprisingly unthreatening. Kelly-Marie was sitting in her usual chair. On the sofa sat Will Maples, still dressed in the suit they had seen that morning. Beside him, to the women's surprise, was Dan Poke. Though none of the three actually had drinks, Carole and Jude got the incongruous feeling that they had interrupted a polite tea party.

Will Maples made no attempt to pretend that he was pleased to see them. 'My God, you two busy-bodies get everywhere, don't you?'

But Kelly-Marie beamed welcome. 'It's good that you've come, Jude. These gentlemen want Viggo's mobile. And you've got it, haven't you?'

'Not any more. I've handed it over to the police.'

Will Maples let out a dry laugh. 'Yes, I'm sure you have. Jude, I suggest you just give it to me. Then this whole affair can be ended without anyone getting hurt.'

'Without anyone else getting hurt, you mean,' said Carole combatively.

'Oh, more allegations do we have here?' asked Will Maples sardonically. 'I thought you'd exhausted all of those this morning. I also thought you had taken on board what Melissa Keats told you. If you persist in this kind of slanderous behaviour, you could both be looking at a very long custodial sentence.'

'Not as long as the one you could be looking at,' snapped Carole.

He spread his hands wide in an insufferable gesture of calming. 'As we established this morning, you have not a shred of evidence against me, no proof of my involvement in any wrongdoing.'

'I would say the fact that you're here,' asserted Jude, 'the fact that you're trying to get Viggo's mobile, is proof of your involvement.'

'And we also,' said Carole, 'now know about Melissa Keats's involvement. Very altruistic of her, wasn't it, to offer to help poor Sylvia Crisp with her divorce?'

That prompted a reaction. The two men on the sofa exchanged looks, and Dan Poke murmured, 'I always said that was going too far. We—'

'Shut it!' hissed Will Maples. For the first time he did look discomfited by what was being said. But as he turned back to the two women, his expression became threatening. 'Look, I've had it up to here with you two. And if I were capable of even a quarter of the crimes you accuse me of, I'd have thought you would realize how very stupid you're being by constantly hounding me. If I was actually responsible for the death of Ray Witchett, or this character called Viggo, do you think I would have any compunction about adding a couple of middle-aged snoopers to my list of killings?'

A thin smile played about Carole's lips, as she said, 'You're getting into a rather dubious area of logic here, Will. For your threats to have any validity, we must believe that you did have something to do with the two deaths. If, as you insist, you're innocent, then we have no cause to be frightened, do we?'

There was a silence. Kelly-Marie looked around her rather full flat in bewilderment. 'I'm not sure what's happening. Would anyone like some tea?'

But her instinct as a hostess was ignored. Will Maples dropped his threatening manner and came in on another tack. He sounded very reasonable as he said, 'Look, I can to some extent see where you're coming from. The recent sequence of events at the Crown and Anchor could look suspicious, as though there actually were a campaign to get Ted Crisp out. The food poisoning, the bad newspaper headlines, the bikers, the fight . . . yes, it does look a bit too organized to be coincidental. But if you imagine that a company of the public profile of Home Hostelries would get involved in dirty tricks of that kind, you have very little knowledge of the business world. On the other hand, it is possible that someone inside the company might have acted off their own bat, might have hoped to advance his career by helping to acquire new properties for Home Hostelries . . .'

'Who're you talking about?' asked Carole.

Will Maples looked pityingly at the man next to him on the sofa. 'I always said it was a bad idea, Dan.'

'What?' The comedian's eyebrows shot up in amazement.

'But you insisted. You said you could do it undercover, and nobody would ever find out what you were up to.' The Acquisitions manager turned to the two women. 'Yes, I'm afraid you were right about some of the dirty tricks—and there you see the man responsible for them.'

'You mean he's "K"?' asked Jude coolly.

That did stop Will Maples in his tracks. 'What?'

'The "K" who gave instructions to Viggo to set up Ray—and to kill him.'

He tried to recapture his former insouciance, but the shot had hit home. 'I've no idea what you're talking about.'

'She is talking about the fact,' said Carole, 'that she found Viggo's mobile, which still had K's texted instructions on it. Instructions sent by "K".'

'If you're looking for "K", then there he is!' Will Maples swung round and pointed at the comedian.

'You bastard! I had nothing to do with it!' Dan Poke's words came out like a hiss of steam. Suddenly his hands were around his colleague's throat. The two of them struggled awkwardly to their feet. Then there was a quick movement from Will Maples's hand, and Dan Poke recoiled, clutching at his face. Blood spurted through his fingers from a slashed cheekbone.

'You bastard!' he repeated. 'I told you you were going too far. Yes, Home Hostelries has always been in a competitive market, but we didn't have to go to the lengths you took us to. We didn't have to get involved in murder.'

'I was never involved in murder. Viggo may have been. Derren Hart may have been. None of it can ever be traced back to me.'

Blood was pouring down the comedian's hand, soaking into the fabric of his shirt and suit sleeve, but he wasn't about to back off. 'No? I think if I stand up in court and give evidence, something might be traced back to you. And if Derren Hart does the same, your position could look decidedly precarious.'

'And,' said Carole, 'since the police have Viggo's mobile in their possession, I shouldn't think it'd be long before they come looking for you.'

'Shut it!' shouted Will Maples. Carole and Jude had been watching Dan Poke, so it was only then that they noticed the Stanley knife in the other man's hand. They also saw him move swiftly across the room, lift Kelly-Marie out of her chair and hold the bloody blade against her neck.

He had given up on denials. He'd made a quick assessment of his position, and, with the police having been alerted, decided his only option was escape. He edged the girl towards the door. Kelly-Marie, not quite sure what was happening, smiled hopefully, but with an edge of anxiety.

'You three stand by the window,' ordered Will Maples. 'If I can't see you there when I get into the car, I'll kill the girl.'

They moved to the window. He'd devised as good a method as any other of giving himself time to make his getaway.

He backed towards the door, Kelly-Marie still held in front of him. There was a trickle of blood on her throat, but that was Dan Poke's, dripping off the Stanley knife. It wasn't hers. Yet.

She still looked confused rather than upset. And Jude felt deeply wretched. It was her reckless stupidity that had caused this. If she hadn't succumbed to the temptation to reply to K's text . . .

What happened next was very sudden. The open door behind Will Maples was slammed into his back. He swirled in surprise to find himself facing Detective Inspector Wilson, who quickly disarmed him. Another detective appeared from the landing and the two overpowered the Home Hostelries Acquisitions manager and snapped the cuffs on him.

It wasn't the moment for long explanations, but Carole and Jude did gather that Detective Inspector Wilson and his colleague, aware of the potential danger to Kelly-Marie, had hidden themselves in the adjacent room that used to belong to Viggo. They had used listening devices in there and monitored all the conversation from inside Kelly-Marie's flat.

The Detective Inspector said he'd be in touch, and the two policemen left with their prisoner and his potential chief accuser. They were going to take Dan Poke to hospital to get the gash in his cheek stitched up. Then there would be a lot of questioning for both men at the Hollingbury Major Crime Unit.

Once again, Kelly-Marie seemed remarkably unfazed by an incidence of violence. After they had watched the departing police car through the window, she turned back to her visitors with a huge beam on her face. 'Now,' she said, 'would anyone like a cup of tea?'

CHAPTER FORTY-ONE

Will Maples was arrested and charged with a variety of offences, including murder. Viggo's mobile provided a strong evidential link to him, a chain of command through Derren Hart and Viggo to Ray. Though he had committed no acts of violence himself, Will Maples had definitely been the one who gave the orders.

With a deeply resentful Dan Poke as a prosecution witness, there was never much doubt about the verdict. Will might have done better with the power of the Home Hostelries legal team behind him, but he didn't have it. The company had ignored the allegations of drug-peddling and continued to employ him after his ignominious departure from the Hare and Hounds at Weldisham. He was very good at his job of 'persuading' landlords out of pubs on prime sites, and Home Hostelries had been happy to turn a blind eye to the morality of the methods he used. But a murder charge was a different matter entirely. They washed their hands of him.

The one person who might have provided the final proof of his guilt wasn't around to give evidence. Derren Hart, aware that the police were on his trail, had gone to ground. Probably using techniques from his army training, he had simply disappeared.

Only for a few weeks, though. Then his body was found floating in the sea off Portsmouth. He might have been helped on his way, but that could never be proved. Will Maples might have arranged from remand prison to help him on his way, but that could never be proved either. Anyway, there were enough drugs and alcohol in Derren Hart's system for him to have fallen into the sea by accident. Or indeed on purpose. Either way, he wouldn't be around to testify against Will Maples. Derren Hart became just another statistic among the thousands of lives destroyed by the illegal war in Iraq.

And Will Maples became another statistic among prisoners serving life for murder. Meanwhile, at Home Hostelries the job of 'winkling' publicans out of properties that the company had its eyes on was handed over to younger, equally shark-like men built in the Will Maples mould.

Needless to say, there were no charges against anyone else in the company hierarchy. Certainly not against Melissa Keats. She had done nothing wrong. If she wanted to use her spare time to help an ill-used woman get a decent divorce settlement, well, that was up to her . . . The Home Hostelries PR team moved in and the whole affair was glossed over. Will Maples had been a dangerous maverick, working on his own without company approval, a bad apple who would soon be very properly paying for his misdeeds.

In the event, though, Melissa Keats did cut all ties with Sylvia Crisp, who ended up using a much less aggressive solicitor. And, since Carole Seddon had meanwhile organized a rather good one to represent Ted Crisp, the eventual divorce settlement did not do Sylvia many favours. The view of the court was that, since she had done nothing to help her husband build up the business of the Crown and Anchor, she had little claim on its profits. And Ted was able to pay her off without selling the pub.

During the divorce proceedings, Matt decided that he didn't like being Sylvia Crisp's fiancé any more, and dumped her. A very embittered woman, she moved out of the area.

Dan Poke couldn't be proved to have done anything illegal either. He kept his directorship at Home Hostelries and continued to advise them on suitable properties to target as he trailed from pub to pub his increasingly tired stand-up material. He still maintained his Jack-the-Lad exterior, proffering cards to all the women he met. But he got very few take-ups. In some ways it was no surprise when, on the eve of his fiftieth birthday, he was found hanging in his dressing room after a gig in a shabby club in Telford.

There was a happier outcome for Sally Monks. The 'hot date' she'd been preparing for when Jude rang her turned out to be more than a 'hot date'. He was Mr Right, and by the end of the year Sally Monks was married to him.

Kelly-Marie continued to see her adored family and dogs every Sunday. The rest of the week she managed very well on her own at Copsedown Hall. Which she would continue to do until some misguided government cost-saving exercise closed the place down.

Meanwhile the people of Fethering went about their daily routine as they always had. There was a bit of a scandal when Greville Tilbrook left his wife and set up house with Beryl. Local feeling did not allow them to stay long near the footpath which they had fouled, and they moved soon afterwards to a village in Somerset, where Greville Tilbrook took no civic responsibilities at all.

Another casualty of Will Maples's campaign of harassment survived surprisingly well. Carole and Jude had reckoned Shona Nuttall would probably drink herself to death in her dusty velvet bungalow in Southwick, but to their surprise, they heard that she had sold up there. She had had her hair redyed and moved out to open a bar in Benalmàdena on the Costa del Sol. There she became a great favourite with British ex-pats, round whom she frequently threw her flabby arms and with whom she was frequently photographed. And out there, quite cheerfully, she did drink herself to death.

Her old domain, the made-over Cat and Fiddle, reopened, serving exactly the same 'hospitality experience' that customers would get from the Hare and Hounds in Weldisham, the Middy in Fratton or any other of the ever-increasing number of pubs in the 'Home Hostelries family'.

But the Crown and Anchor in Fethering did not succumb to such uniformity. It remained defiantly unconventional, reflecting the character of its landlord, Ted Crisp. Zosia ran the bar with exemplary efficiency, but still managed to get her journalism degree. And the fame of Ed Pollack's cooking went so wide that booking a table on Fridays and weekends became quite difficult. Though Ted Crisp loathed the word, more than one newspaper review described the Crown and Anchor as a 'gastropub'.

For Carole and Jude life in Fethering continued much as before. Jude felt increasingly restless, sensing that she was in desperate need of new stimulus, but she did not share these thoughts with her neighbour, knowing they would only upset her. And Carole's life was softened and enlivened by the existence of her granddaughter, who grew more beautiful with every passing day. Carole felt quite soppy about Lily, and would send the little girl frequent emailed pictures from the laptop which was now such a central feature of High Tor.

Oh, and Gulliver's leg healed completely.

ABOUT THE AUTHOR

Simon Brett worked as a producer in radio and television before taking up writing full-time. As well as the much-loved Fethering series, the Mrs Pargeter novels and the Charles Paris detective series, he is the author of the radio and television series *After Henry,* the radio series *No Commitments* and *Smelling of Roses* and the bestselling *How to Be a Little Sod.* His novel *A Shock to the System* was filmed, starring Michael Caine.

Married with three grown-up children, he lives in an Agatha Christie-style village on the South Downs.